"You're beautiful,"
Arren Barkley Whispered.

Ti froze as his words echoed in her head. Her heart beat wildly, and a band of iron pressed around her chest. She stared at him speechlessly. Before she could move, his arms were around her and his mouth covered hers.

His lips were gently on hers, yet molten in their heat. Without her realizing it, her hands were on his back, pressing him to her, caressing the powerful muscles beneath his shirt. Then a voice in the back of her mind called to her, and she heard it.

She drew her lips away, anger flashing in her eyes, and forced the unexpected passion to flee.

"Don't ever do that again!" she said in a low voice. Her eyes locked with his, and she stepped back from him.

"I won't apologize," he said. "I won't promise what you ask, either. Ti, from the minute I saw you, I wanted you, and I won't stop wanting you."

Dear Reader,

We, the editors of Tapestry Romances, are committed to bringing you two outstanding original romantic historical novels each and every month.

From Kentucky in the 1850s to the court of Louis XIII, from the deck of a pirate ship within sight of Gibraltar to a mining camp high in the Sierra Nevadas, our heroines experience life and love, romance and adventure.

Our aim is to give you the kind of historical romances that you want to read. We would enjoy hearing your thoughts about this book and all future Tapestry Romances. Please write to us at the address below.

The Editors
Tapestry Romances
POCKET BOOKS
1230 Avenue of the Americas
Box TAP
New York, N.Y. 10020

Gentle Fury

Monica Barrie

A TAPESTRY BOOK
PUBLISHED BY POCKET BOOKS NEW YORK

An *Original* publication of TAPESTRY BOOKS

 A Tapestry Book published by
POCKET BOOKS, a division of Simon & Schuster, Inc.
1230 Avenue of the Americas, New York, N.Y. 10020

ISBN: 0-671-49426-0

First Tapestry Books printing September, 1983

10 9 8 7 6 5 4 3 2 1

POCKET and colophon are registered trademarks of Simon & Schuster, Inc.

TAPESTRY is a trademark of Simon & Schuster, Inc.

Printed in the U.S.A.

*I would like to dedicate this,
my ninth novel,
to my lifelong friend and advisor,
Allan Suchman.*

—M.B.
POMONA, N.Y.
APRIL, 1983

Gentle
Fury

Prologue

West Texas, 1860

UNDER THE HEAT OF THE LATE-SPRING TEXAS SUN, A small army drilled. Three recruits stood stiffly at attention, their clothing proclaiming them as anything but soldiers: buckskin pants, sweat-stained cotton shirts, high, well-polished riding boots and, topping off the nondescript uniforms, three identical wide-brimmed hats.

In contrast, the officer before them was a picture of military perfection. He stood ramrod straight in his blue-and-gold uniform; his shoulders and hat were decorated with the bright golden braid of his rank. Beneath the officer's hat, green-flecked hazel eyes surveyed the troops.

"At ease," he called in a deep and resonant voice. The three soldiers let their rifle butts slide to the ground in immediate obedience of the command. A collective, relieved sigh accompanied the movement.

The officer nodded his head and took a deep

breath before he spoke. "Today we begin your training. By my estimate, war will be declared within the year. I want you to not only be prepared, but acceptant of the fates that bring our country to war. It will not be a pleasant time." He paused to look into each of their faces. When he finished gazing at the third, he spoke again.

"Each of you has been issued weapons. You have a Springfield musket, the new Henry rifle, a knife, and the Colt officer's revolver, caliber forty-four. Today you will have your first practice with the Henry rifle. I want your total concentration. Is that clear?" he asked in a loud voice.

The three soldiers-in-training nodded their heads.

"Ti, Jenna, Kay, from this moment on you will answer loudly! There will be no more silent nodding of your heads."

"Yes sir!" replied the three teenage women who gazed openly at their father. Three sets of identical hazel eyes locked with the officer's as they waited for his next command.

"That's better. Ladies, we've already discussed the reason for what we're doing, but I want to be sure you understand completely. Most of the *good* men of our nation will be fighting. I don't know how long the war will last, but contrary to everyone's opinion, I believe it will be many long and nasty years before it ends. I will not have you defenseless in my absence. When you've finished this training, each of you will be the equal, in *all* the aspects of fighting and self-defense, of any soldier in the army."

Major Sam Bennett's features softened and he smiled in spite of himself as he looked lovingly at his daughters. The three young women returned his warm smile, but behind the six eyes that gazed up at him flickered a spark of amusement.

In the hours, weeks and months following Sam Bennett's words, that spark of amusement in the three sisters' eyes faded, replaced with the knowledge, understanding and ability to use proficiently each of the weapons their father had given them.

Chapter One

West Texas, 1864

CRESTING THE LOW RISE, TI BENNETT REINED IN HER horse and stared into the distance.

A dust cloud proclaimed riders on the road. After several moments Ti was able to make out two figures through the dust. Another long second of scrutiny showed one rider to be wearing the uniform of the Federal Army. They were between the rise and the ranch, on the ranch's main road.

Ti Bennett whirled the horse and spurred him forward as she bent low against the gelding's powerful neck. The two men would reach the ranch before her, but by only a few moments. The uniform bothered Ti. Why would a Union soldier be riding openly through a state whose loyalties lay with the South?

Ti knew she would have the answer soon, but she couldn't help her thoughts. As she rode, she straightened in the saddle and drew the Colt from its

4

holster to check it. Then, without pausing in her gallop, she checked the blue-tinted Henry rifle.

The two riders dismounted, and after tying their horses to the rail, turned to see two women walking toward them; one held a rifle, the other a Colt.

"You told me, but I couldn't believe it," Arren Barkley said as he watched the women approach.

"Never doubt me," replied Captain Steven Markham, personal adjutant to General Sam Bennett.

Arren stared at the women with a mixture of delight and humor. The two were dressed like men, with buckskin pants, checked cotton shirts and high boots. But Arren saw, in the serious set of their faces, they meant business.

Both were good-looking, and of about the same medium height. Arren couldn't tell too much about their figures, but what he saw, he approved of. Their tightly pulled-back hair reflected a yellow haze from the sunlight. When the women were about twenty feet away, one stopped and put a restraining arm on the other. She squinted against the glare of the sun at the men's backs, until a slow smile spread across her face.

She holstered her pistol and began running forward. "Steven . . ." she yelled, her arms opening wide.

She jumped the last five feet as Steven Markham reached out to her. He caught her in midair and whirled her around before gently setting her back on her feet.

"You're a captain!" she said as her eyes swept across his sun-faded, but golden braid.

"What else? And you're still a tomboy," he responded with a mischievous smile.

"Father? Is he all right?"

"Fine," Steven replied, releasing Kay Bennett a second before her sister Jenna reached them.

"Hello, Steven," Jenna said in a husky voice.

"Hello, Jenna, it's been a long time."

As Steven spoke, Arren watched the interplay between Jenna Bennett and the man he'd spent the last two hectic, wearying weeks with. He smiled, remembering the description the captain had given him of the three Bennett sisters, and especially the way he'd spoken about the middle one, Jenna. He hadn't been sure before, but he was now. Steven Markham was definitely taken with her.

"Ladies," Steven finally said, although his eyes stayed locked on Jenna's, "this is Arren Barkley. Arren, the lady on the left is Kay Bennett, and this is her sister Jenna."

Again, Arren did not miss the way Steven spoke Jenna's name. "Ladies," Arren said as he tipped his hat.

"Mr. Barkley," they replied with a nod.

"Steven, is something wrong with Father?" Jenna asked, concern suddenly evident in her eyes.

"No, ma'am. Is Ti home?"

"She's checking on some strays by Eagle Creek. She should be back soon," Jenna said.

"We've been sent here by your father. I must give Ti a letter," Steven said formally. The two sisters looked at each other for a brief moment before nodding to Steven.

"There's no need to wait for her out here in the sun, let's go inside," Jenna said, accepting for the moment that her father had written only to Ti. It would involve ranch business, she reasoned, as her father had left Ti in charge of the ranch.

"I'd like to clean up if I may," Arren said, following the others toward the house; his words were accented by his hands slapping dust from his pants. Before they reached the house, the sound of hooves echoed in the air. The four turned as one to see a rider coming toward them.

Ti slowed the horse as she reached the ranch house. She saw her sisters and the two men walking toward the house and relaxed. If there had been something wrong, she would have known it by now. The sisters had prearranged signals for every manner of emergency. You had to, there were too many bad things happening around the area; too many women disappearing.

Ti stopped her horse next to the ones already tied to the rail and dismounted gracefully. She didn't bother tying Samson's reins; he was trained to stay in one spot if his reins were dropped over his head. She started toward the small group, and when she was close enough to see each of them, she smiled.

She recognized Steven immediately and waved. Then, when her eyes swept across the stranger's face, her breath caught in her throat. Even though the dust and grime of the road had caked his face and covered his clothing, Ti saw he was incredibly handsome.

Light blue eyes, the color of a clear mountain lake, gazed at her from under his hat. His full mouth, straight nose and squared chin all fit perfectly with his high cheekbones. He was taller than Steven, and his shoulders were broad. Ti sensed that beneath the dusty shirt was a massive and well-muscled chest. His pants fit closely, outlining powerful thighs before tapering into tall boots. Her concentration on the stranger was so total that she missed the slight movement of Kay's arm as Kay nudged Jenna and they glanced quickly at each other.

Stop it! she told herself in an effort to free the smile that was frozen on her mouth. The tip of her tongue darted out to moisten her lips, and she was finally able to speak.

"My God, Steven, don't you know better than to be parading in a Federal uniform?" she scolded. Her voice carried her concern and worry plainly to everyone's ears.

"We came in through New Mexico, no problems," he said confidently.

"You were lucky. Why are you here?" she asked, unable to stop herself from being curt, yet wondering why she was at the same time.

"Ti!" Jenna admonished. "Father sent him. At least have the courtesy of letting them clean up and have something to drink."

"Ti, may I introduce Arren Barkley?" Steven said with a smile. He'd known Ti for seven years, since she was sixteen, and was used to her every mood.

"Mr. Barkley," Ti said as she offered her hand to him. She was pleasantly surprised at the lack of hesitation on his part when he took her hand and grasped it firmly.

"A pleasure, Miss Bennett," Arren said, holding her green-flecked eyes with his.

Ti's heart beat loudly as she gazed at him, and she tried not to acknowledge the little tremors that ran along her arm the moment his hand touched hers.

"Thank you, Mr. Barkley," Ti replied.

"Arren."

Ti nodded as Arren released her hand. Ti's fingers felt as if they'd been burned; she could still feel the strength of Arren's grip on her skin.

"Ti, Steven has a letter for you," Kay said; curiosity and eagerness filled the youngest sister's words.

"Shall we go in?" Ti asked, ignoring Kay, but unable to take her eyes from Arren's face.

Without realizing what she was doing, Ti raised her hand to Arren's face. Her index finger flicked at something on his chin, and a small piece of road dirt fell free. A shallow cleft, neatly dividing the halves of his chin, was now visible.

"That's better," Ti said in a low voice.

"I don't know whether I should thank you, or be embarrassed," Arren conceded.

"Neither," Ti replied.

With that, everyone turned and went into the coolness of the house.

After Kay had taken both men's hats and placed them on the rack next to Ti's, Steven turned to the oldest sister.

"This is for you. Your father asked me to deliver it personally," he said. Drawing an envelope from the inside pocket of his uniform, he handed it to Ti. Then, with a smile, he drew Arren with him and disappeared down the hallway.

"I'll bring the shaving gear to the bath," Kay called.

"I'd better get them towels while you heat up the water. They need a bath desperately," Jenna said, wrinkling her nose.

While this was going on, Ti stared at the envelope addressed to her. Her father's bold handwriting was on its face, and she wondered why Steven had come all this way to deliver it. Something in his voice hadn't sounded right when he'd spoken, she realized.

Slowly, with her intuition warning her she would not like the contents, she opened the envelope, withdrew several sheets of paper and began to read.

Because Sam Bennett was going to raise three daughters in a part of the country that was almost barren of women, he'd built his house in a vastly different way than most.

He wanted his daughters to have the same degree of privacy that he and his sisters had had when they lived in Philadelphia. So, as the large main house was constructed, a special room, which he called the "bathroom," was built. It was much more than a necessary room as most houses had. Perhaps because he was a soldier, and used to the ways of men, he overcompensated for his daughters.

In this combination necessary room, which he called the "bathroom," were private commodes, three bathtubs, and three vanities for the girls. A wall divided the room from another, smaller "bathroom" that was his own.

Now, in the girls' "bathroom," each in a tub of warm water, were Steven and Arren. "Have you ever seen anything like this before?" Steven asked.

"Not quite," Arren admitted as he looked around again. The room was comfortable, and he luxuriated in the rarity of the bath. But as Steven spoke, Arren tuned out his words. His mind was filled with thoughts and visions of Ti Bennett. From the moment he'd first seen her, something had happened inside him. When he'd gazed into her large almond-shaped eyes, he'd thought he was drowning within them. Gleaming white teeth had peeked out from behind peach lips which were shaped like the two halves of a perfectly formed bow. Her small nose and the deep tan of her skin fascinated him as nothing had before.

When she'd offered him her hand, it had been such a natural motion that he'd taken it quickly. Although there were calluses on her palm, her skin had still felt like the softest of velvet. Long after he'd released her, he could feel her hand in his.

He'd been able to make out the full womanly figure her pants and loose-fitting shirt had been unable to hide. He'd seen the swell of high breasts pushing against the cotton, and had enjoyed the way her belt drew in the buckskin pants and showed off her slim waist.

"What the hell is wrong with me?" he asked himself.

"She is!" he answered.

"What?" Steven asked.

"Nothing," Arren replied quickly. "Thinking out loud," he explained. He'd never met a woman who held herself as confidently as Ti Bennett. He'd also never met a woman who sparked his desire so instantaneously.

"Here are your towels," Kay said, stepping into the "bathroom" without knocking and going to a vanity, where she placed the towels next to the bowl of hot water and her father's spare razor and strop.

"Thank you," both men replied.

"How's Ti?" Steven asked.

"She hasn't said anything yet, but she's read the letter three times. She doesn't look happy," Kay added.

"I didn't think she would be," Steven said as he exchanged a glance with Arren.

"Jenna's fixing lunch. She keeps mumbling something about Steven and smoked ham. Would you like a stronger drink than coffee?" Kay directed the sudden question to Arren as her eyes darted over the part of his chest that rose above the soapy water.

"Coffee's fine," Arren said. Steven nodded silently in agreement and Kay left the room. Arren hid his smile as he looked at the young captain's face.

"Smoked ham?" he said.

"The way the Bennetts do it is not to be believed," Steven said.

"I do think Jenna has some feelings for you," Arren commented in a low voice, thinking about the way the middle sister had looked at the captain when they arrived.

"Do you think so?"

"Count on it," Arren said in a light voice, but his tone changed suddenly when he spoke again. "Now, tell me about Ti. . . ."

"Dammit, Ti, they'll be finished in a few minutes," Jenna whispered.

Ti looked up at her sister, and then returned her gaze to the letter. The devastation filling her mind held her tongue prisoner. She could not believe what she'd just read, but the proof was in her father's distinctive handwriting.

In a low voice tinged with sadness, Ti Bennett spoke. "Father says that we're to leave the ranch. That Mr. Barkley is going to drive the herd to California, to the ranch Father bought a few years ago. We're to go with Steven to New Orleans. From there we take a clipper to New York, where Father will meet us and bring us to the family house in Philadelphia."

"No!" Kay cried, reaching quickly for the letter. Ti released it as she fought back her tears.

"Why?" Jenna asked, her voice soft and low.

"The war is going against the South. Father thinks it will be over soon. He's very much afraid of what will happen then. He thinks the soldiers who will be homeless will end up as scavengers, destroying everything in their paths. He feels Texas, and this ranch, will be in that path and wants us protected."

"But he taught us how to protect ourselves!" Kay stated proudly without lifting her eyes from the paper.

"How can he be so sure?" Jenna asked.

"He says he was wounded in Georgia, not seriously," she added quickly, "and after he recovered, they posted him to Washington. He was promoted also. He's a general now," Ti said, forcing herself to smile as she looked at her sisters. "He's in the War Office, and they've made him a presidential adviser too."

"He should have been one before the war," Kay cut in. "If they had listened to him then, the war would already be over."

"I don't think so," Ti said with a shake of her head. "But," she continued, looking at Jenna again, "it was when he was in Georgia, he writes, that he saw the ransacking begin. He knows it will reach us by the end of the war."

"I don't think we should leave," Jenna said.

"I agree," Kay added when she handed the letter to Jenna, and stood with her hands on her hips, her legs spread slightly apart. "We can take care of the ranch!"

"Do you remember the promise we made Daddy?" Ti asked in a whisper. Three pairs of eyes met and locked. Slowly Kay and Jenna nodded their heads. "We promised we would obey any commands he sent us. We promised, and we'll have to keep our word."

"I don't want to leave our home," Kay whispered, her eyes filling with moisture she could not stop.

"We'll be back," Jenna vowed solemnly.

"You will," Steven Markham said as he entered the room and stared boldly at Jenna. Ti looked up, and when she did, she froze. Arren Barkley stood next to him. Dressed in clean clothes, with his face neatly shaved and his longish dark hair slicked back, he was startlingly handsome. Ti's sharply drawn breath exploded in her chest.

"Lunch is on the table," Jenna announced.

As everyone moved toward the dining room, Ti stood quickly. In three strides she was at Arren's side. She touched his arm lightly and motioned for him to wait until the others were gone. Then, when they stood facing each other, Ti took a deep breath.

"Who are you?" Ti asked. Her eyes were firmly fixed on Arren's as she spoke.

"Your servant," he replied in a husky voice.

"I don't think so," Ti whispered under her breath.

It was very late; Ti knew she should be in bed, but she couldn't sleep. In the wake of the day's disastrous events, the afternoon had fled too quickly, and before they'd realized it, the large clock in the living room was chiming eight. Jenna and Kay prepared a light supper while Ti bathed and changed into a dress, just as both Jenna and Kay had done earlier in the afternoon. They sat down to eat at nine, but the air over the table was heavy as each of the sisters thought about the future.

Earlier, after eating their lunch in a tension-filled silence, the five people had discussed what would be happening. Ti, for some reason, sensed something wrong with her father's letter and his instructions that this stranger, Arren Barkley, be allowed to drive the herd west. It wasn't in the letter itself, but some underlying sense warned her all was not right. Not only that, but her father stated, strictly, several times, that *she* was not to interfere in any decisions Arren made.

For the first time in her twenty-three years, Ti Bennett felt out of control. For over three years she'd been running the ranch. In all that time, it had been she who made the decisions, took action and did whatever had been necessary, from facing down rebellious cowhands to standing her ground before the Indians and stopping them from taking more cattle than agreed. Now that responsibility was being taken from her by a few strokes of her father's pen. Ti didn't like that at all.

Also, she thought, it just wasn't like her father.

But she knew he'd written the letter. Through the painful mists that shrouded her mind, Ti admitted there was yet something else bothering her—Arren Barkley. She'd never experienced the emotions which had threatened to overwhelm her today. She'd never felt her heart race with just one sidelong glance at a man. And she'd never met a man she'd not been able to shrug aside. She could not shrug Arren aside. She'd tried, and all she got for her efforts had been a smiling face floating tantalizingly before her eyes.

"Damn!" she whispered to the horses inside the corral. It was then that Ti made up her mind. She would obey her father's instructions to the very letter, but she would also see to it that as long as Arren Barkley was at the ranch, he would not change anything her father had already set up.

She knew he was capable of doing that; she'd seen his strong will in his crystal eyes. "Dangerous eyes," she said to Samson, the spotted gelding who had been her horse since he'd been broken.

The horse lifted his head and snorted disdainfully before pushing against the fence in his effort to reach Ti's hand.

Arren stood alone on the wooden planked porch of the ranch house, and, shrouded in darkness, watched Ti's silhouette outlined against the corral. He'd spent the entire afternoon watching her, and with every passing minute the certainty of his thoughts grew.

He'd never met a woman like her before. It wasn't her beauty, which she had in overabundance; nor was it the full, womanly figure he'd finally seen when she'd appeared for dinner in her formal dress. No, it was the way she held her head, and in the way she'd met his eyes boldly whenever they'd spoken.

From the moment she'd reached out and touched his chin, he'd found himself wanting her. But overshadowing this newfound desire was the reason for his being here. Yet, having met Ti Bennett, something within him came back to life. Something he'd hidden in the dark recesses of his mind.

The low Texas sky stretched endlessly above, and a myriad of stars winked down. He exhaled suddenly, his mind made up, and left the porch, heading toward the corral.

Ti's concentration was broken when she heard footsteps behind her. Turning just as Arren reached her side, she drew in her breath.

"Do you always come out to say good night to your horse?" he asked.

"I do a lot of strange things," Ti replied, fighting to keep her voice level under his roaming gaze.

"Not so strange," he said.

"For a woman?"

"For anyone. Ti, don't hate me because of what I have to do," he said, and saw her stiffen for a brief second.

"It's not you. Arren, it will be hard not to wake up here in the mornings. It will be even harder not to be able to get on Samson and ride the ranges," she admitted, but even as she did, she wondered why she was telling him this.

"The war will end soon, you'll be back," he declared.

"But it won't be the same."

"You're beautiful," he whispered.

Ti froze as his words echoed in her head. Her

heart beat wildly, and a band of iron pressed around her chest. She stared at him speechlessly. Before she could move, his arms were around her and his mouth covered hers.

Tremors raced along her back, and the iron band grew tighter, making it impossible for her to breathe. His lips were gentle on hers, yet molten in their heat. Without her realizing it, her hands were on his back, pressing him to her, caressing the powerful muscles beneath his shirt. Then a voice in the back of her mind called to her, and she heard it.

She drew her lips away, anger flashing in her eyes, and forced the unexpected passion to flee. "Don't ever do that again!" she said in a low voice. Her eyes locked with his, and she stepped back from him.

"I won't apologize," he whispered. "I won't promise what you ask, either. Ti, from the minute I saw you, I wanted you, and I won't stop wanting you."

"How dare you," she hissed, her anger growing beyond any bounds she'd ever known. Her heart still beat furiously, and her breath was harsh and drawn as she stared at him. "The next time you touch me, you'll regret it," she promised. Turning, she walked away, conscious of Arren Barkley's eyes on her back, and trying, uselessly, to rid herself of the taste of his lips on hers, and the feel of his hands on her back.

Ti was lost in the magical land surrounding her. The wild country around her was not, to her eyes, wild. The flat plains of Texas did not reach this far, and the fifty thousand acres of the Bennett ranch marked the changing land that would, in the hazy distance ahead, turn into the mountain ranges of New Mexico.

The ranges were more like foothills, but it was for that reason Sam Bennett had chosen this site. Water was plentiful, with several creeks on the property, and two mountain-fed streams that ran full until the scorching heat of midsummer dried them up, as it did everything around them.

But even while Ti rode, losing herself in the land she lived on, she was constantly aware of two things: Indians and the man who rode next to her. The Indians had not been a problem for several years, except for the occasional theft of a few head, but she knew the same did not hold true for Arren Barkley.

Glancing sideways for an instant, Ti felt her chest constrict. From the moment she'd read her father's letter, she'd felt an unbearable loss. That, and her underlying intuition that something was wrong. *There was something about Arren Barkley that was wrong.*

Or was she just reacting to the knowledge that in a few weeks she would become just another woman and lose the freedom she'd become accustomed to? *No,* she tried to tell herself. Arren Barkley did not fit into any mold she could think of. She knew instinctively he was not just another cowboy, not a wrangler taking a herd of cattle to California. The way he walked, the way he carried himself, the tone of his voice and the arrogance he wore around himself like a cloak, all told Ti he was anything but what he'd claimed.

Another flashing thought skipped through her

mind. What had he claimed himself to be? *Nothing*. All he'd said was that he was taking the cattle west.

Ti stopped her wandering thoughts and concentrated on what was happening. They'd spent the morning riding, with Ti showing Arren the ranch and answering all his questions. It had been a strange morning, with tension hanging heavy between them. At noon they'd stopped at the edge of the stream cutting across the east range to eat the lunch Jenna had prepared for them. The water of the stream was only at half its spring height, and Ti had known that within a month it would be dry; however, the stream of the west range would stay for at least two more months. In fact, most of the cattle had been herded there already. These thoughts had paraded through her mind as she had studied Arren carefully. But she'd had to take her eyes from his when the awareness of his physical power had struck her again, although he'd done nothing but smile at her and eat the smoked meat.

Ti shook her head, forcing herself to concentrate on the here and now. She slowed Samson, and saw Arren do the same with his large bay gelding. Again her mind played tricks with her as she took in the sight he presented.

The horse he rode suited him well. The large bay, at least sixteen hands, was a powerful, surefooted mount which she knew had been trained to perfection. Sitting astride him, Arren looked even larger than he did on the ground. Ti shivered, thinking about how large and powerful he had looked last night when they'd stood near the corral.

He sat straight in the saddle, his hips moving gracefully with the rhythm of the horse's lope. Stop!

she ordered herself. Finally she halted Samson and breathed deeply.

"We'll have to start back now," she said.

"How far are we from the house?" Arren asked as he took off his hat and wiped his brow. His blue eyes narrowed when he searched the landscape.

"A little over an hour," Ti replied.

"Why aren't there more men on these ranges?"

"As I told you, we've been moving the herds to the other side of the ranch. The grazing here is about used up, and the water is running low."

"That's not what I meant," he said, fixing her with a steady stare.

"Then explain yourself."

"Why are you leaving the ranch unprotected here?"

Ti stared at him. A flash of anger gripped her. He was doubting her abilities to run this ranch! In a voice dripping with ice, she spoke slowly and clearly. "Unprotected against what?"

"Anything. Indians, Rebs, you name it."

"Mr. Barkley. We have nothing to fear from the Indians around here. We've made our own peace with them, and any strange Indians who come into the territory answer to them. As far as Rebs are concerned, we're Northerners in a state whose sympathies lie with the South. We've learned to live with that, and we can defend ourselves quite well."

"Against a small army?" he asked with upraised eyebrows.

Ti saw humor fill his eyes, and her anger deepened. "Against anyone!" she spat. Another thought hit her, and she stared coldly at him. "Or is it that you can't accept the fact that a mere woman can take care of a ranch properly!" A shadowy smile etched his lips in response to her words, and she lost her temper.

Moving fast, Ti whirled Samson around, and even as the horse was turning, Ti had drawn the Henry rifle from its sheath, cocked it and raised it to her shoulder. She squeezed the trigger and the blast echoed across the range. Before she had finished the mounted turn, she'd fired four times, and the rock skittered in four different directions.

"Very good," Arren said, "but a rock isn't a man."

"No," Ti replied over her shoulder, her eyes fiery in challenge, "I've learned a man is easier to hit than a rock." Arren's smile froze. Sheathing the Henry, and without a backward glance, she started off in the direction of the ranch house.

They rode in silence, and just as the sun reached the horizon, the ranch house came into view. When Ti slowed Samson to a walk, she breathed a sigh of relief. The anger she'd felt had slowly diminished as the miles passed beneath Samson's hooves.

"Ti," Arren called, motioning her to stop. She did, but stared straight ahead.

"Are we going to duel with each other until we leave?" he asked. His eyes probed her face, and Ti sensed again the powerful aura that was so much a part of him.

"We're not in a duel," she said stiffly.

"Then what would you call it?" he asked in a low voice.

"I don't know what to call it. The only thing I know for certain is that I don't trust you at all!" she spat. "Now, are you quite finished with me for the day?"

"For the day, Ti, just for the day."

Ti stared at him, unable to tear her eyes away. His words echoed loudly in her ears, and she knew that he meant exactly what he'd said.

Chapter Two

Ti was on the west range, riding hard. Samson's powerful stride moved her across the valley floor in effortless bounds. She didn't know where she was going, and didn't care. The sun hurled down its hot rays, but they mattered not to her.

Reining Samson to a halt near a lone tree, she gazed around and dismounted. When her feet touched the ground, she turned and gasped.

Arren Barkley stood three feet from her. He hadn't been there before, but he was there now. "I want you," he whispered. Ti drew away, but he followed her. Before she could get away, his steel fingers grabbed her and pulled her to him. His mouth covered hers, and her breath caught even as she tried to fight him. Her blood turned to liquid fire, racing madly along her veins, scorching her until she could no longer move.

Only then did the ruggedly handsome man loosen

his hold and draw his lips away. "You can't fight me now," he whispered.

"No," she breathed in response, realizing the truth of his words and closing her eyes in surrender. They came together again, and his hands roamed along all the soft contours of her body, until she could no longer think.

"No!" Ti screamed as she sat up in bed. Her breathing was forced, and she willed herself to open her eyes and look around. She saw all the familiar things of her room, and as she took security from them, her breathing returned to normal.

The dream had shaken her badly, and when she lay down again, she tried to understand what it meant. Glancing toward the window, Ti saw the first gray tentacles of dawn in the sky, and knew there would be no further sleep for her.

She rose from the bed. Anger at herself from her dream, irrational as it was, held her in a strong grip. Pulling on her robe, she went to the "bathroom," but could still see herself and Arren Barkley beneath the tree, their arms entwined, kissing passionately.

When she returned to her room, her mood had not changed, and in fact had grown even more out of proportion while she dressed.

"What am I doing?" she asked herself, tucking the cotton workshirt into her buckskins. When that was done, she stepped into her boots, went to her dresser, and picked up her hairbrush. Deftly she brushed out her dark blond hair, ignoring the flashes of sun-created streaks radiating within the long, thick mane. When she was done, she twisted her hair and pinned it back. Glancing in the long oval mirror that had once been her mother's, she looked at herself quickly before leaving her room.

When she stepped into the kitchen, she stopped in her tracks. Steven Markham and Arren Barkley were sitting at the table, coffee cups in their hands, talking with Jenna and Kay.

Remembering the fear which had held her prisoner in her dream, Ti shivered. Slowly she walked to where Arren sat and stopped before him.

Faster than the eye could follow, her hand whipped out and slammed into his coffee cup, knocking it from his hand, sending it clattering across the room, spraying coffee in every direction. Everyone stopped what he was doing and stared at Ti. She didn't care as her eyes locked with his in a silent battle.

"You don't scare me one bit!" she spat. Turning her back on him, she walked out of the kitchen, slamming the door loudly in her wake.

"What the . . . ?" Steven said, wincing at the door's loud echo.

"Jenna?" asked Kay.

"I don't know," she said as she took off her apron and started after her older sister.

"Did you say something to her?" Kay asked, studying Arren Barkley's face and wondering why he was smiling.

"This is the first time I saw her today," he said truthfully.

"Well, whatever it is, I'd stay out of her way for a little while," Kay advised Arren.

Arren nodded silently to her and smiled. "Mind if I have another cup?" he asked pleasantly.

Outside, Ti was at the corral, leading Samson out,

when Jenna reached her. She ignored her sister and concentrated on the horse.

"Want to talk about it?" Jenna asked, stopping a foot away.

"No," Ti replied tersely, hoping Jenna would leave. But her sister stood her ground and waited patiently.

"Breakfast?" Jenna asked.

"Not with *him* there!"

"He's going to be here as long as we are. Are you planning to starve to death?"

"Jenna!"

"Ti, what happened?"

"I had a dream," she replied, still refusing to turn and face her sister.

"That's not what I asked. If you don't want to talk about it, I'll leave."

Ti turned to look at her sister. She shook her head and sighed. "I had a dream that upset me. He was in it, and I was mad at him."

"That's why you knocked the cup out of his hand?" Jenna asked, trying hard to understand her sister's words.

"Yes," Ti said. Then, as she stared into her sister's wide, doubting eyes, she began to laugh. She saw all their faces again, etched with incredulity at her actions. "Did you see Kay's face when I walked out?" she asked between tortured breaths. Suddenly Jenna laughed too, and they fell into each other's arms.

"But," Jenna said, gasping hard for breath, "that's still no reason for what you did!" she admonished.

Ti's face turned serious, and her eyes went out of

focus. "I know. I can't explain what happened, I don't know myself, but something's not right."

"With Arren?"

"With Arren, with the ranch, with Steven. I can't put my finger on it, but before we leave this ranch, I'll find out!" she declared as she slipped a foot into the stirrup.

"Breakfast?" Jenna asked again.

"I'm not hungry."

"Ti, you can't go out to the ranges without eating."

"It's still early. I'll have some food and coffee with the hands when I get to the north range," she said.

Jenna nodded, knowing that Ti would do just that, and the men who worked for them would not mind at all. Ti had proven herself more than once to the hands, and they treated her like the foreman she was. She worked, ate, and on occasions like round-ups, even slept on the ranges with the men.

"I'll be back for dinner," she told Jenna a second before she urged Samson forward.

"Just try to control yourself when you get back," Jenna called after her.

The sun was almost gone when Ti rode in. She reined Samson to a halt at the corral and bent over in the saddle to open the gate. Inside, she dismounted and unsaddled him, even as Billy, the stable boy, came up to her with Samson's feed. She happily gave over this chore to Billy and went into the house, glad the day was over.

She went directly to her room, took off her sweat-stained clothing and went to the "bathroom." There she stepped into the tub that Kay had filled only moments before, and sank into its relaxing warmth.

Each of the sisters had her jobs on the ranch. Ti's was making sure that everything ran smoothly, from the cattle and the men who handled them, to the buyers and the yearly cattle drives. Jenna's responsibility was the house and the accounts. Kay's was anything and everything. Their youngest sister was their backup. She would take Ti's place when necessary, or take Jenna's jobs and do them equally as well.

Among the three of them, the Bennett ranch had been running like clockwork since their father left for the war. But now, with Arren Barkley's arrival, everything had changed. *What was it?* Ti wondered again, trying to ferret out the misty feeling that bothered her.

"What?" she asked aloud. Shaking her head, Ti reached for the cake of soap sitting next to the tub. She lathered herself, washing away the Texas grit and trying to do the same for her thoughts. But no matter how hard she tried, she couldn't dismiss the visions of Arren Barkley's face from her mind, nor the remembrance of his strong hands on her back and his molten lips on hers. *And his utter disregard for propriety!* Forcefully Ti scrubbed herself harder.

When she felt clean, and had dried herself, she put on a simple white cotton housedress. The dress she had worn last night had been in deference to their guests. Tonight she would be comfortable, and also less revealing to Arren Barkley's sapphire eyes.

Leaving the "bathroom," Ti went directly to her father's office. There, amid the scents of leather and tobacco that would never leave, she sat at the desk and entered several notations into the ledger, detailing her activity for the day and marking down the loss of five steers. When she finished, she leaned back and glanced at the portrait hanging above the desk.

A young lieutenant stood proudly in his West Point finery. On his arm rested the white-gloved hand of his bride. Ti's mother and father gazed down at her affectionately, and a lump built in her throat.

Kay came in just then, breaking Ti's concentration with a one-word question: "Hungry?"

Ti nodded. "What happened around here today?" she asked as she stood.

"Nothing much except for the show this morning," Kay said, gazing at Ti strangely.

"Mine?"

"Yours. After you left, Arren and Steven rode out. They got back about an hour before you."

"They couldn't have gone to town," Ti said, thinking aloud more than talking to her sister.

"They didn't say where they went, and I didn't think it my place to ask."

"Still . . ." Ti said, wondering what they had been up to and why. "Kay, do you trust Steven?"

"Of course," Kay replied instantly, favoring Ti with a withering glance.

"And Arren?"

"Of c . . . I don't know, but he is with Steven," she said, her voice trailing off on the last words.

"Something's wrong. Dammit, Kay, I feel it!" she whispered as her eyes grew vacant.

"Ti, you can't fight Daddy!"

"But I can help him."

"Ti . . ." Kay pleaded silently, afraid of what she

saw in her sister's eyes and knowing the determination Ti was capable of when she decided to do something.

"Where are Steven and Arren?"

Kay's eyes sparkled for a second before she answered. "They're in the library having a drink."

"What's going on?"

"Oh, nothing really. Jenna insisted they relax there before dinner. Do you think Steven knows she's in love with him?" Kay asked suddenly.

"Kay . . ." Ti warned.

"Well, it's true. She is, we both know it."

Ti stopped herself from replying. Kay was right. It could be seen in the way Jenna's face glowed whenever Steven was near—just as it had since she was fourteen years old, and, Ti thought, as it always would. "At least she picked the right man," Ti whispered.

"Not—" But Kay cut off whatever she was about to say as she whirled around and went to the door. "Coming?" she asked, and left the office before Ti could say a word.

The evening passed swiftly, and night was full upon the Bennett ranch while five people sat in the salon discussing the future. Steven Markham and Jenna were on the divan. Kay and Ti sat in chairs that flanked the satin couch, and Arren Barkley sat across from them, relaxing in a large wing chair.

Ti had been watching him closely all evening, listening intently whenever he'd spoken. She was trying to find out something, anything, but nothing he'd said had revealed anything unexpected.

"Ti, I think tomorrow will be a good time to meet the men," Arren said in a low, authoritative voice.

Ti stiffened, but forced herself to relax. "I can have them come here," she volunteered.

"No, I want to watch them work and decide which of them I'll take with me."

"You'll need them all," she said defensively. "You do realize how many head of cattle you're driving?" she asked, unable to keep the sarcasm from her voice.

Arren smiled coldly. "It doesn't matter how many head there are if the men aren't any good."

"My father and I hired most of those men. Every one of them knows his job!" Ti retorted, anger turning her voice harsh.

"On the ranch," Arren agreed, "but the trail is a different story."

"Anywhere!"

"I won't argue with you, but I'm the one who'll be on that trail. I'm the one who has to trust each and every man with me. Anyone," he said, raising his voice sharply while he made his points, "anyone I have the slightest doubt about will not be going!"

"Just who the hell do you think you are?" Ti shouted. Her anger rose to burst the barriers she'd built, but she no longer cared. She stood to face him, her chest rising and falling rapidly with rage. "You think you can just walk in here and make whatever decisions you want to, don't you? What gives you that right? Or is it just your arrogance?"

"No," Arren whispered. His words were barely audible, but to each person in the room they were as loud as a shout. "Your father gave me that right."

Ti's breath left in an explosive gust. Her hands

balled into ineffectual fists at her sides, and her mind threatened to turn black. Spinning on her heels, she walked out of the room, out of the house, and into the night.

An uncomfortable silence settled in the room after Ti left, as each of the people stared at the others.

Then Jenna stood. "I'd best find out what's wrong this time," she said.

"No." Arren's single word shot through the room like a command. Jenna froze, and Kay stiffened. Both women turned their eyes on him, riveting him to the chair with their stares.

"Mr. Barkley," Jenna whispered, "you are still a guest in this house. Please act like one."

"My apologies. I didn't mean to sound preemptive," he said, smiling easily at Jenna and Kay. "But I think I should be the one to speak with your sister. It's me she's angry with."

"It's not you," Jenna said, her voice softening as she sat down next to Steven again. "Ti's been running this ranch since Father left—it's very hard for her to give it up now."

"I realize that," he emphasized, "but it's still my place to try to make her understand my position. Please let me try," he asked the two women.

They looked at him, and then at each other. Slowly Jenna nodded.

"Thank you," Arren said, nodding politely before he left the room.

"Steven," Kay said the moment Arren was gone, "how long have you known him?"

Steven Markham's eyes flicked from Kay to Jenna. "A while," he replied.

"Steven . . ." Kay reiterated.

"I've known Arren Barkley for a long time. Why?"

"Do you trust him?" Kay asked, ignoring his question.

"With my life," he replied simply. "So does your father," he added.

"Ti doesn't," Kay said.

"That's obvious. But she's wrong."

"She doesn't think so, she thinks she hates him."

"I think that's obvious also," Steven said with a smile.

"You're wrong, Steven," Jenna said in a low voice, speaking for the first time.

Steven looked at her and waited. Jenna took a deep breath and then went on. "Yesterday, when Ti met Arren, I saw something happen. So did you," she said to Kay. "It happened to both of them." Kay nodded, but it was Steven who spoke.

"What happened to them?" he asked.

"I think they fell in love."

"Jenna . . ." Steven said; his eyes reflected the shock of her words plainly. "Judging by the way Ti's acting toward Arren, I think she fell in hate."

Kay laughed at that, but Jenna's face remained serious. "That's just it. Ti's never acted like this before. She's fighting her emotions, and Father's orders are tearing her apart. Instead of understanding what's happened to her, she thinks she hates Arren because he's taking over her responsibilities."

"I can't believe that," Steven argued.

"I can," Kay said. "I saw it too, and I know Ti. She's not acting rationally, and the one thing Ti does is act rationally all the time."

"But it doesn't matter, does it? Nothing can be changed. Everything must go the way your father wants," Steven declared, and to the sisters' ears his words sounded both ominous and final.

A moment later, as the silence continued to deepen, Steven turned to Jenna. "You said they fell in . . . love."

"It was obvious," she said, using his own words to answer him. But when he tried to pursue the subject, neither Jenna nor Kay would discuss it. Instead they talked about the war and the end results that their father foresaw.

When Arren left the house, he paused on the porch to look for Ti. When he didn't see her, he walked down the three steps and headed toward the corral. There he saw only his horse, Steven's, and Ti's. Turning slowly, he walked toward the distant lights of the bunkhouses, hoping he would find her.

He was troubled about her reaction to him, and his own unaccountable behavior toward her. The memory of last night rose fresh in his mind. He'd acted hastily, but he didn't regret it. This evening's display of temper had only added more to his deepening regard for Ti. He'd never felt that way about a woman before, and he knew that one way or another he would pursue her until he won her. But he realized that now was not the time or place. Arren cursed the luck that had brought him and Ti together now rather than at a better time. He had a job to do, a dangerous one, and what he didn't need was to get involved with a woman, especially Sam Bennett's daughter.

But what a woman she was, he thought, feeling

again the softness of her breasts pressed to his chest
and the sudden softening of her lips when he'd
kissed them.

Easy, he warned himself. He stopped when he saw
Ti's white dress softly illuminated by the low wash of
moonlight. Taking a deep breath, he started forward
again.

When Ti had fled the house, she'd run as if
someone were chasing her, with her hem bunched in
her hands and her feet flying over the earth. Two
hundred feet from the house, she'd stopped. When
her breathing had calmed, she tried to organize her
thoughts.

She'd acted stupidly. She'd acted like some dim-
witted female whose emotions always ruled her
mind. Ti despised women like that. *But,* she thought
ruefully, *I did just that.*

What was he doing to her? She knew she must
obey her father's wishes. Even though she disliked
Arren Barkley, she could never fight her father.

Why did she dislike him? His arrogance, she told
herself. *His overwhelming good looks,* she added.
Yet, even while she thought these things, something
deep inside her stirred, and sensations she'd never
before experienced built within her body. Ti shivered and hugged herself.

"Ti." Arren Barkley's deep voice came from
behind her.

She stiffened and slowly dropped her arms as she
turned. She stared at him and her breath grew
shallow. The low haze of moonlight graced his
features and emphasized his looks. His eyes held

hers in a piercing stare until she thought she would scream.

"Leave me alone," she whispered.

"I came to apologize."

"For what?" she snapped. "You told the truth, you were right. I . . . Dammit, Arren, take your victory and leave me alone," she pleaded.

"Ti, I tried to tell you yesterday. I'll try again today. We haven't been fighting a war. There is no victory to win. I have a job to do, that's all. I didn't come here to hurt you, I came to help."

"Did you?" she asked, her voice low and her words distinct.

Arren gazed into her large green-flecked eyes for several long moments before he finally answered. "Yes."

"Then why don't I think so?" she replied.

"Ti, we can't spend the last days here fighting. Help me. Let me help you."

"Do you have any idea of what this is like for me?" she asked. Sadness tinged her voice and moisture welled in her eyes.

Arren saw her hurt, her pain, and wanted to reach out to her, but this time he stopped himself as his own memories flooded through his mind—his private memories of the early days of the war and of his own losses. "Yes," he whispered.

Ti heard truth in his voice, but she couldn't speak as a rush of sadness cascaded through her mind. A few seconds later she sighed softly. "I'm sorry, Arren. I'll try to help."

"That's all I'm asking."

"But, Arren," Ti said, her voice suddenly razor

sharp and cutting, "I promise you that if you do anything that will harm my sisters or my father, nothing in this world will stop me from coming after you."

Arren stared at her for a moment, her words echoing strongly in his ears. Then slowly a smile spread on his face. "We're not enemies, Ti," he whispered as he stepped closer to her.

"Don't," she warned, her hand held stiffly between them.

Arren stopped for only the barest second before he grabbed her hand. He held it prisoner while he looked deeply into her eyes. "Don't fight it," he said.

Ti held her breath as his words bounced crazily in her mind. Heat coursed along her arm, paralyzing her tongue. All she could do was stare into his eyes. Within them she saw depths that shook her to her very core. Then her hand was free.

Arren took a long, deep breath. "I won't take something that's not freely given. What I feel for you I've never felt before. But I won't take you against your will, even though I know you want me as much as I want you," he finished in a deep, intense voice.

Ti stared at him, still unable to speak. His arrogant words shocked her, even while they created a whirlpool of new emotions within her inner self. She wanted to hurl the denial of his words at him, but could not. Instead she watched him turn and walk away. She stood frozen to the spot for a long time after he'd disappeared, fighting with herself, telling herself that nothing he'd said mattered, that his words were only reflections of his own brash desires, but in the end, she wasn't sure about anything anymore, except the iron determination she'd seen in his eyes.

"Why did you do this?" she asked her father, who she knew was too far away to hear her whispered hopeless call.

Chapter Three

Ti HAD RISEN EARLIER THAN USUAL AND WAS IN THE kitchen before anyone had woken, drinking coffee and lost to her thoughts. She'd spent a restless night trying to comprehend her emotions. She'd thought about what had happened with Arren Barkley last night, and she didn't like what she was feeling.

By the time she'd fallen asleep, she still hadn't come to terms with it. His eyes had shown her his steel-willed determination, and she'd also seen a haunting specter lurking within their crystal depths. The determination didn't bother her—she had enough of her own—but the shadowy glimmer of the other made her pause.

Taking another sip of coffee, and twirling a stray strand of hair with her forefinger, Ti decided that trying to solve the mystery of her emotions was a futile exercise. It would be better to think about the massive undertaking of getting the cattle ready to be moved. She also decided to rethink her position against Arren Barkley, and try to believe what he'd said. His words had sounded truthful to her, and she had no real reason to think something was wrong. Perhaps it was just her own reaction to having her home and her life changed so suddenly.

"'Morning," Arren said when he stepped into the kitchen. Ti turned to face him, smiling tentatively, while trying to hide the chill rippling along her spine.

The first thing she noticed about him was his freshly shaved face. Then her eyes took in his massive chest, barely contained by a plain workshirt. The shirt was tucked neatly into buckskin pants that served to point out the slimness of his hips and waist. Ti couldn't help noticing the powerful muscles of his thighs bulge against the leather when he walked. He was hatless, and his dark straight hair gleamed in the low light cast by the lanterns. By the time he reached the table, Ti found her tongue.

"Good morning," she said as he sat. "Coffee?"

Arren smiled and raised his eyebrows. "To drink, or to fling?"

"Drink," Ti said, flushing at the memory of yesterday morning's outburst. "Arren, I'm sorry about that."

"Accepted. I'd love some coffee."

Ti went to the stove and poured Arren a cup of the dark liquid. When she returned to the table and handed it to him, Jenna appeared in the doorway.

"Is it safe?" she asked jovially.

"Jenna . . ." Ti warned.

"Do you have time for breakfast?" Jenna asked.

Ti and Arren both said yes, and as Jenna began breakfast, an uneasy silence settled in the room. By the time Jenna finished cooking, Kay and Steven had joined the rest of them. Breakfast was eaten with a minimum of conversation, and when they were done, Steven spoke.

"I have to go into town today to make some more arrangements," he said, letting his eyes sweep across everyone's face. "I should be back by tomorrow night."

"I'm glad to see you've decided not to wear your uniform," Ti remarked.

"Dumb I can be sometimes, but stupid? Never," he said with a good-natured smile. "Do you need anything while I'm there?" he asked Jenna.

She shook her head silently.

"I'd appreciate it if you could stop by Latham's and see if my new knife came in," Kay said.

"Kay, you've been waiting for that knife for a year. There's a war on, and you know as well as I that they're not shipping hunting knives from the East," Ti said, her voice tinged with annoyance.

"I can hope, can't I?" Kay shot back. Then she turned to Steven. "I broke the blade on mine," she said by way of explanation.

"I'll see," he promised.

"Ready?" Ti asked.

A half-hour later, Ti and Arren reined in their horses on the crest of a low hill. Spread out before them were thousands of head of cattle and twenty men.

"Good luck," Ti said, glancing at Arren's thoughtful profile. She realized she meant her words, and that surprised her.

"Thank you," he said. With her words, he'd sensed an easing of the tensions between them.

Inwardly he breathed a sigh of relief. Too many things had to be done, and there was no time to spend fighting her.

Arren winked confidently at her and urged his horse forward. Two minutes later they were dismounting in the midst of the ranch hands.

Ti called the men together and introduced Arren to them. They stared at him suspiciously and waited.

Arren took off his hat and ran his hands through his hair. When he put it back on, he was ready. "I guess I'll make this as simple as possible. I was hired by Sam Bennett to ramrod his herd to California." As soon as the words were spoken, a buzz rippled through the milling cowboys.

"Now, we don't have a lot of time, and I need to know which of you are willing to take the trail." Arren swept his eyes across their faces while he waited. Halfway through the group, they stopped on two men who were staring openly at him. He thought he saw recognition flickering in their eyes, but before he was sure, someone spoke.

"How long you figure we'll be gone?"

Arren studied the cowboy for a minute. He was young, maybe twenty, and his face was open and frank. "I don't know. If everything goes okay, we should make California within eight to ten weeks. You can get back by clipper. We'll supply your horse for the drive so you won't have to lose your regular mount. We'll also pay your fare back."

"Ain't it a little risky?" asked another, older hand.

"Life's a little risky," Arren replied tersely.

Ti, listening intently, heard the flint his words had

been etched in, and glanced apprehensively at the cowhand who'd spoken.

"I mean the Injuns. I ain't never heard of no cattle drive to California without an army escort."

"You have now," Arren commented dryly. "Or maybe you don't remember this country's at war."

Again murmurs broke out among the men, and Arren waited patiently until they stopped. Then he looked at all of them again before he spoke.

"Mr. Bennett authorized a bonus for anyone who makes the drive. Three months' extra pay," he said. Suddenly the men's eyes were riveted to his face, and he saw he'd gotten through to them. "For the next few days, while we round up the herds, I'll talk to each of you privately. Until then, you think about it."

"Three months' pay can't be spent if yer daid," commented the same man who'd spoken earlier.

"That's a fact," Arren replied simply. Then he turned to Ti and winked again. "All set?" he asked.

"All set," Ti replied. She turned to three of the men and motioned them to her. "Bill, Sam, Tom, I want you to cut out any unbranded head and get them together. We'll do the branding after all the cattle are put in the west range."

"Yes, ma'am," they replied in unison, and started toward their horses.

"Wait a minute," Arren called. The three stopped and turned to face him. "I might as well speak with you three first," he said.

A little while later, finished and satisfied with the men, he returned to Ti. "Tell me about those three," he asked as he stood next to her and watched the hands go about their duties, studiously ignoring both him and Ti.

"They've been working here for five years," she said. "They're good hands."

"Which of the hands were here during the last three years?" he asked while he looked about.

Ti gazed at him in an effort to understand what he was after. Finally she shrugged and answered. As she spoke, Arren continued to watch the men until he knew which men were new and which had been at the ranch for a while. Among the new hands were the two who'd caught his attention earlier.

By lunchtime Arren had spoken with eight more men and was planning on getting to the others before the end of the day. Joining the men while they ate, he watched not only them but also the way Ti interacted with them.

When lunch was over and the men started back to work, Arren called Ti to him. "You said there were another dozen hands working the fences?"

"I planned on sending word to them to meet us at the bunkhouses tonight," she said.

"Thank you," he replied, meaning it. He watched her mount her horse and ride off. Only after she was gone did he turn back to the men and the job at hand.

Arren reined in the bay gelding and dismounted. Standing at the horse's flank, he swept his eyes along the darkening landscape. The sun had set ten minutes ago, and night was falling quickly, spreading ominous shadows across the land. This meeting had been arranged the day before he and Steven had arrived at the ranch. Unless something was wrong, he wouldn't have much longer to wait.

Dropping the reins carelessly, he began to pace. He didn't want to be missed, especially since he seemed to have quieted Ti's suspicions about him. The last two days had gone well, and he didn't want to worry about something interfering now. Arren was playing a dangerous game, but he knew it had to be played.

And Ti. He'd been amply warned about her, but it hadn't mattered. For all her defensiveness, he'd seen the vulnerability in her eyes. But the one thing he hadn't expected was his own reaction to her.

Glancing around again, he thought about what had brought him to Texas, and why. He remembered the early days, when he'd thought the war would last only a short time. But he'd learned quickly how naive he'd been.

And then, when he'd come home on furlough, disobeying orders and sneaking through enemy lines for two days, he'd learned the horrible truth. It had been late at night when he'd reached the winding tree-lined drive that led to his home. But when he'd looked for the lights of the house, all he'd seen was darkness. With trepidation filling his mind, he slowly approached the house he'd been born in. When he reached it, he fell to his knees.

All that remained of Mountainview, the plantation that had been his family's for a hundred years, had been a few charred beams. Everything else had been destroyed. He'd sat there staring at the ruins until the sun had risen.

Then he'd walked through the property. Everything had been destroyed. The fields had been burned. The outbuildings and field quarters had been ransacked and were deserted.

He'd returned to the ashes of his home and had walked aimlessly through them. The sun had been high when he'd finally started out, but a glint within the ashes caught his eye and he bent to see what it was. A moment later he'd stood; a small circle of gold rested in the palm of his hand. The hot sting of tears and grief burned his eyes as he left the ruins and went to his horse.

He'd ridden boldly in the daylight, uncaring of any eyes that might have seen him, until he reached his destination.

The large white plantation house stood proudly amid the tall trees. The Virginia mountains framed it, giving it a beauty that even the war-ravaged land could not hide, but to Arren Campion Barkley, all he'd seen was that this plantation still lived.

He'd dismounted quickly, and ignoring the wide-eyed stares of the slaves working in the gardens, he'd run up the stairs and banged loudly on the door.

A moment later the door had opened. A pair of frightened blue eyes gazed up at him in shock. "Arren," she'd whispered.

"What happened?" he'd demanded, his voice harsh with grief.

"You can't stay here," she'd said. The fear in her voice made it tremble. "They'll find you and—"

"And what?" he'd yelled. "What happened to Mountainview? What happened to my family?"

"What did you expect?" another voice had said, a deeper, older voice.

Arren had looked up into the tightly drawn face of Samuel Maddox, and had seen all the hate and anger of the world within it.

"I don't want you here. I want you gone, now!" he'd ordered.

"When someone tells me what happened," Arren had replied, his anger unabated but under better control.

"They came at night . . ." Maddox had said, but he'd been unable to look Arren in the eyes.

"My parents?"

"They fought, but it was senseless. They were both killed. Your slaves were taken away, and everything was burned."

"And you did nothing?" Arren had whispered as his eyes locked with his neighbor's.

"What could I do? Let the same thing happen to my family? You did it to them! You!" he'd spat. "When you left, you left them defenseless!"

Arren had forced his hands to stay at his sides as he stared at them. Then he'd taken several deep breaths before he'd spoken. "Where are my parents buried?" he'd asked.

"I found their bodies the next day and saw to it they were buried in Mountainview's cemetery. Their graves are unmarked," Maddox had said.

Arren had stared at the man who had been his father's closest friend and at the woman he'd once been betrothed to. Then he'd stepped back and shaken his head.

"You will pay for this," he'd whispered. Then he'd left, mounting his horse and galloping away before he'd allowed himself the chance to think. Arren had known, deep down inside, that if he stayed any longer he would have struck out at them, and become just like them.

He'd ridden like a madman, and when night came, he'd realized what he must do. The fanaticism he'd been a witness to told him the war would not be over quickly, but would drag on mercilessly, killing thousands of innocent people like his parents. Yes, Arren had known then what he had to do, and known also how he would do it.

Before the memory grew stronger, Arren shook his head. The Texas night was fully on him now, and the moon had not yet risen. He could see no farther than thirty feet, but he heard a horse coming.

Carefully he drew his pistol, cocked the hammer and waited.

"Barkley," came a low, accented whisper.

"Here," Arren said, uncocking the Colt and holstering it. A moment later a tall dark-skinned man came into view.

"You are well?" the stranger asked.

"So far. What have you learned?" Arren asked the Indian as he stretched out his hand in greeting.

"The Apache are agreeable to safe conduct for the sum of five hundred head," the Indian said. Each of his words was distinct, as was the habit of a person who had learned another language and was proud of it.

"Five hundred . . . That's a lot," Arren replied.

"No. Each tribe's territory extends for hundreds of miles. They will pay whatever tribute they deem necessary to the other Apache tribes from the five hundred. Word is being sent now. Arren, it is a small fee to a people who hate the whites so ferociously."

"Our men?" Arren asked.

"They are doing well. No one has seen them, and their gray uniforms blend well with the land."

"Thank you, James," Arren replied, relieved that nothing had disturbed his carefully made plans.

"You trust the Apache?" Arren asked suddenly.

"As much as possible. Do not fear, they will abide by this agreement. It was sealed by the three chiefs in ceremony."

"I must return to the ranch," Arren said. "We will leave in seven days. Tell the men they are to follow the schedule I gave them."

Without another word, James Strong Blade mounted his horse and rode off. Arren watched him for a moment before getting on his horse. He and Strong Blade had known each other for many years, and he trusted the Indian implicitly. Wheeling his horse around, Arren started back to the ranch, again hoping that he would not be overly missed. But even as he rode, he was haunted by his earlier memories, and added to those were his thoughts of the future and his growing feelings for Ti Bennett.

Ti sat at her dressing table, the brush in her hand forgotten as her thoughts centered on the last two days. Since riding out from the ranch yesterday morning with Arren, she'd spent every minute watching and studying the man closely. There were many things that bothered her about him, and many things she liked.

The way he'd handled the men had been good. He'd gained their respect quickly by not painting a pretty picture about the cattle drive. At the same time, the insolence she'd seen in him had shown through in many ways, but the men didn't seem to notice it. To them, she thought, his arrogant mannerisms were the trappings of confidence.

She had been thankful, up until tonight, that for the past two days he'd been cordial toward her without overstepping his bounds. Every time he'd come near, she'd been afraid he would touch her again and try to kiss her. She had also come to fear herself, and the knowledge that she wanted him to. And tonight he'd brought that knowledge frightfully home to her.

Tonight, after dinner, when she'd been outside relaxing in the peacefulness of the evening, he'd come out and found her. They had talked about the coming trail drive until Arren had stopped her, and his hands had gripped her shoulders like steel bands.

Without a word, he'd drawn her to him. Her heart had skipped a beat, and her mind had become mired in quicksand. A sudden fire blazed within her mind, and she could not fight him. Her lips had parted under his, and the heated tip of his tongue boldly seared the inner warmth of her mouth. Her breasts had been crushed upon his chest, and her hands were suddenly on his back, her fingers curled, her nails digging into his shirt.

When he'd drawn his lips from hers, sanity had returned and she'd stepped back quickly. "What do you think I am?" she'd whispered as she fought to steady her breathing.

"A woman. A beautiful, desirable woman."

Ti had tried to shut out his words, tried to deny them to herself. "Leave me alone," she'd pleaded, balling her hands to stop their trembling.

"I can't," he'd whispered. But she saw he was standing still, and in an effort to save herself she ran from him, and had not looked back until she was in the safety of her room.

"Damn him!" she whispered to her reflection. Standing, her hair forgotten, Ti paced angrily, trying to rid herself of the knowledge that she'd lost control of her emotions and had responded to him like a silly addlebrained female.

When she could no longer berate herself for her actions, she went to her bed, turned down the wick of the lantern and got beneath the light summer cover.

There, in the quiet darkness, Ti tried to sleep. But she could not ignore the handsome, arrogant face floating above the bed, nor the burning memory of the second passionate kiss they'd shared.

Chapter Four

THE DAYS RUSHED BY LIKE THE OVERFLOWING BANKS OF a spring-flooded river. Ti knew that all too soon she would be gone. A week had already passed since Arren Barkley's arrival, and in that short time, nothing about her life was the same.

Just a little while ago, over a tension-filled breakfast, Steven had announced they would start for New Orleans in three days. Jenna, Kay, and Ti had stared at each other, and Ti had seen her own sadness reflected in their faces. The rest of the morning meal was finished in a heavy silence. But the silence could not continue, and the women faced the work ahead.

The day was hot, the sky clear, and the large sun rose to its zenith. Beneath it, the ranch was a beehive of activity. The bleating of calves and cattle could be heard floating in the air while the last of the herd was branded.

Everywhere Ti turned, new faces mixed with the

more familiar ones. Standing near the corral, she surveyed the ranch and shuddered involuntarily when her gaze fell on the two plains wagons that were being loaded.

"Ready?" Arren asked as he stepped close to Ti.

"Not really," she replied, gently stroking Samson's face. "Why did you hire so many new men?" she inquired, still not looking at him.

"We needed them for the drive," Arren said simply.

"That's not what I meant."

"What do you mean?" he asked, his tone turning harsh, forcing her to look at him instead of her horse.

Her eyes turned cold and challenging, and her voice was accusatory as she spoke. "You fired half our men and replaced them with new ones. Was it really necessary, or did you need to do it to establish your own power?"

"Yes," he said frankly, and saw her eyes flicker. "Yes, it was necessary. Ti, stop fighting me. I have a job to do, and I'm doing it the best I can. And, yes, I have to establish my authority over the men. We've got thousands of miles to cover, and without their trust and loyalty, we'll never make it! That's why I fired the ones who I knew wouldn't make it, and hired those who would."

"I still think you were wrong," she whispered, but her earlier convictions were weakened by the honesty of his answer.

"You're entitled," Arren replied as he swiftly mounted his gelding. "Ti, I'm tired of defending myself to you. Either trust me or stay out of my way!" With that, he spurred the horse out of the corral.

Ti stared at him in amazement, then quickly mounted Samson and urged him out, forcing him to close the distance between her and Arren Barkley's broad back. *Damn him!* she thought as his words and challenge rang loudly in her ears.

She caught up with him just as the ranch disappeared behind them. When she was abreast, she turned to look at his still tightly drawn features.

"I can't stay out of your way. Not until I leave. This is still my home!" Then, without letting the time between their last words and now interfere, she began asking questions again. "Where did you find these new men? I tried hiring a few months ago and couldn't get a single one."

"They were there—you just didn't have what they wanted," he responded.

Anger flashed, and Ti shot back bitterly, "Because I'm a woman?"

A sharp, barking laugh echoed in her ears. Then, with her face red with rage, Arren spoke. "I'm sure for some men, working for a woman wouldn't sit well, but the reason isn't that you're a woman, it's something else."

"What?" she demanded.

"A way out of Texas."

Ti had no reply for that. The very truth of what he said struck a chord within her mind. The men were getting tired of war and fighting, and it looked like the war would never end. That, and the waves of people fleeing the South, were making Texas an unappealing place for a lot of the men.

Yet within the many chambers of her mind, his words did not ring true. Texas had too few able-bodied men left, and there were too many new men who'd just appeared. They had to come from somewhere.

Ti and Arren rode swiftly, roaming across the many acres of the Bennett ranch. They would do today what they'd been doing for the past two days—ride the ranges in search of stray cattle.

Ti's mind was a constantly searching mass of thoughts as they rode. She tried to comprehend why her father was doing this, and why he'd chosen Arren Barkley to implement his desire. And also why she had this strange fascination for him, a fascination she could not rid herself of for more than a minute at a time.

At lunchtime they'd stopped to let the horses graze and cool off, eating the food Jenna had wrapped for them. Ti watched Arren closely while he ate, and suddenly found herself wondering what had made him so hard a man. When he finished eating, Arren smiled at her and leaned backward, supporting himself on his elbows.

As she put her food down, she saw something flicker near Arren. She froze and turned her head slightly. A wave of ice descended in her mind, but she forced herself to speak.

"Arren," she whispered, "don't move your hands." At the sound of her voice, Arren's eyes narrowed, but he listened to her. "A foot from your left is a rattler. When I say move, roll to your right."

Arren barely nodded his head, as he remained absolutely motionless. Slowly Ti unhooked the safety strap of her Colt and carefully slid the pistol out.

Moving her hands carefully, she cocked the weapon. She waited, her eyes on the flat head of the snake, chills rolling along her spine. Then she slowly lifted the pistol.

"Now," she yelled.

Arren rolled suddenly, and when he did, the sound of rattles filled the air. Ti pulled the trigger. The echoes of the gunshot rang out deafeningly. By the time she saw she'd hit the snake, Arren was on his feet, his own Colt in his hand.

Ti's breath was harsh as she stood. She'd hit the snake in the head and had killed it instantly. But even so, she shuddered when she walked toward it.

"Thank you," Arren said, his eyes going from the dead snake to Ti.

"I may not like you very much, but I don't want you dead," she said.

Arren stood still as she spoke. His eyes narrowed, and he shook his head. "A simple 'you're welcome' would have been appreciated. But then, anyone who can handle a pistol the way you just did can say whatever she wants." With that, Arren bent, picked up his things and went to his horse.

Ti watched him, a feeling of loss washing through her as he walked away. She hadn't meant to sound nasty, only to joke and relieve her own tensions. But she hadn't done that, she'd done something worse.

"Arren," she called, running after him. "I'm sorry," she whispered to his broad back.

"Are you?" he asked, his voice whiplike as he spun to face her. "Or is it that you've been pretending to be a man for so long that you don't know what being a woman is like?"

Ti reacted as if she'd been slapped. She stepped

back, her face reflecting the shock of his words, her uncontrollable temper flaring brightly. "You have no right!" she began, but he cut her off.

"Don't give me that high-and-mighty look. I've spent a week watching you. Everything you do is done to prove that you're anyone's equal. Well, lady, you are! But you lost something important along the way. We have work to do," he said as he turned and mounted his horse.

"Bastard!" Ti hissed under her breath. Then she went to Samson and mounted him. Silently she whirled Samson around and without a word rode away from Arren Barkley and the hot shame with which his words had filled her.

It was late at night when Ti returned to the ranch house. The corral, stables and barn were deserted. The only sounds were of cattle and the occasional whinny of a horse. Ti unsaddled Samson and let him loose within the corral before walking wearily to the house.

Her steps were heavy, as was her mind. When she'd ridden from Arren, hurt had filled her painfully. She couldn't bear to look at him or to be with him. The way he'd looked at her, his face taut with hatred and disdain, had been unbearable.

For the entire afternoon and evening, Ti had ridden and ridden, looking at the land she would be leaving soon, and wondering if Arren had been right in what he'd said. Had she forgotten what it was like to be a woman? Did she love what she was doing so much that she couldn't bear to give up the freedom she now had? Had her father taught her too much? All these thoughts cascaded in the whirlpool of her mind, making her rethink and doubt all she'd done during the past years.

Opening the front door of the house, Ti held her breath and listened. All she heard was silence, and she breathed a sigh of relief. She didn't want to speak to anyone, least of all Arren Barkley. Quietly Ti went to her bedroom and closed the door behind her.

As she undressed, she couldn't stop the erratic wanderings of her mind, and before her boots were off, she was once again lost in thought. She remembered the years before her father had left, and those since he'd gone.

But mixed with it all were Arren's words about her trying to prove herself. She hadn't been, she swore silently. *Never!* But she was acutely aware that she'd always been different from her sisters, and different from the other women she'd known.

For some reason, she'd never been interested in men, not the way other women were. And she especially didn't have time to play the foolish games that were a part of the ritual. Even when she was very young and her body had been starting to change, she'd been unable to watch older women make fools of themselves before the men.

Had he been right? Ti asked herself. His words filled her mind once again, and her shame returned. "Is it that you've been pretending to be a man for so long that you don't know what being a woman is like?" *No!* she screamed silently, but she could not chase away his words. *Had she ever known what being a woman was like? Had she ever been a woman?* Ti didn't know the answer to those questions either.

"What's wrong with me?" Shaking her head sadly, Ti remembered this same reaction when she was younger.

It had been when she'd turned sixteen and had her first experience at being courted. The son of a neighboring rancher had come calling. He'd asked her father's permission, and Sam Bennett had granted it. But the next day, Ti had gone to her father and spoken with him.

"Why do I have to see him?" she'd asked.

Sam had looked at her for a long time before he'd spoken. And when he had, his voice was soft. "Because it's time. Ti, you're a woman now," he'd said. "You have to think about getting married and having your own family."

"But I don't like him," she'd responded.

"That will change."

"No it won't," she'd promised.

And it hadn't. The young man had spent three futile months trying to get Ti to marry him. Ti had refused to do what she knew she was supposed to. She refused to simper and to act as if she couldn't think. She never gave in to protocol and let him impress her with the wit, charm and masculine abilities that he'd had so little of. When they talked, she'd never simply agree with what he said if she didn't believe it herself. She would argue her points, and usually win.

He'd finally given up and never returned. Almost a year later, Ti had gone to her father, worried about herself and her future. They had sat in his office, and Ti had poured her heart out. She'd told her father that there was something wrong with her. That no boy or man she had met had made her want to spend time with him. She was very upset, especially since Jenna had confided in her that she was in love. But Ti knew she couldn't tell her father about that. After all, Steven Markham was her father's assistant.

Sam Bennett had looked at her and smiled. "Ti, some women grow up quickly, some don't," he'd said. Ti had misunderstood him, and had argued that she was grown up, and almost seventeen.

"Not grown up physically, but some people take longer to know what they want. You're like that, Ti. One day you'll meet a man whom you'll fall in love with. When that happens, you will love fiercely, and all of this will be a funny memory."

"I don't think so," she'd said. For the next six years she'd never experienced anything that made her look at a man twice, not that she didn't have ample opportunity. Texas was young, and single women rare. The three sisters had more than their share of callers, but never once had Ti encouraged a second visit.

And then the war had come and Ti had no time to worry about men or about why none of them attracted her. She'd thrown herself fully into the running of the ranch and to making the men accept her as their boss, even if she was a woman.

Ti had dressed like a man, ridden like one, and worked as hard as, if not harder than, a man. She almost lived with them in her efforts to gain acceptance. And those efforts had paid off in the smooth and efficient way the ranch ran.

But still, no man had interested her, and she'd come to the conclusion that none ever would. Ti stopped her pacing suddenly, another thought striking inwardly at her mind.

When Arren Barkley had appeared at the ranch, everything in her life had changed. The moment she first saw him, even with the dirt and grit covering him, her heart raced and her stomach had fluttered. She'd never before experienced such feelings, and she'd pushed them violently away.

Whenever he touched her, something would happen inside, and even when she tried to deny it, her heart had fought against her. Thunderstruck, Ti almost moaned aloud as the truth began to emerge from her troubled mind.

For the first time in her life, Ti wanted a man to hold her, to kiss her and . . . And that man was Arren Barkley.

Ti shivered and turned toward the door. She crossed the hallway and, without knocking, went into Jenna's room.

Her sister was lying in bed. The lamp on her bed table glowed warmly while Jenna made notations in her diary. When her door opened, she'd looked up, and as Ti crossed the room, she'd put the diary and pen down.

"I need to talk to you," Ti said.

"Are you all right? What happened to you today?" Jenna asked. The worry of missing her sister at dinner showed on her face.

"Didn't Arren tell you?" she asked sarcastically. Ti saw a puzzled look cross Jenna's features just before she spoke.

"He said you two had another disagreement and you rode off by yourself."

"That's all?" When Jenna nodded, Ti closed her eyes. Then she told Jenna what had happened today, and when she finished, she stared at her sister. "Well?"

"Well what?" Jenna asked.

"Is he right?"

"Ti . . . Don't be silly—"

"I'm not being silly!" Ti declared loudly. "I . . . I don't know what I'm being," she admitted in a low voice. Before she could stop herself, tears rose up and spilled from her eyes. She stared at Jenna unbelieving, until she could no longer see her through the misty veil covering her eyes.

"Ti," Jenna whispered, opening her arms to her sister. Ti fell into them willingly, and let her younger sister hold her tightly.

When at last her tears stopped, she sat up again. "What's wrong with me, Jenna?"

"Don't you know?" Jenna asked, smiling softly.

Ti stared at her sister, trying to deny Jenna's words, but she could not. Slowly she nodded her head. "How?" she asked in a hoarse whisper that was more a plea for help.

"Nobody knows how or why someone falls in love. It just happens," Jenna said wisely.

"But not to me! And not with the likes of Arren Barkley!" Ti spat in a loud voice.

"To you, Ti, and 'with the likes of Arren Barkley.'"

"How did it happen?" she asked helplessly. "Jenna, I never felt this way before. What do I do? Dear God, Jenna, I'm scared."

Jenna gazed at Ti sadly. She took her sister's hand

in hers and squeezed it gently. "You'll do whatever you think you should, or have to."

"He'll be gone in three days," she whispered fiercely, "and so will we."

"But it won't be forever."

"Won't it?" she asked.

Chapter Five

ARREN LAY IN THE DARKNESS OF THE BEDROOM, TRYING to cut through the maze his mind was mired in. For the past two and a half years he'd worked and fought with the single-minded purposefulness necessary to survive the hell that this war was and to do the job he had chosen to do. But since his arrival at the Bennett ranch, he was no longer able to fully control his iron-willed resolve.

And it was all because of a woman! He'd promised himself that there would be no women, at least none that would mean anything to him. That until the war ended, and he'd found the peace he needed, nothing or no one would interfere or make him swerve from the dangerous course he had chosen.

He would not let himself again become the victim, and chance yet another loss. His parents had died partially because of him—because they believed in something the others had not. The woman he'd been brought up to hold above all others had been nothing more than a simpering fool who'd feared everything and who let the ideals of those around her become her own, rather than use her mind to decide what she wanted for herself.

More than his home had been scorched from him that day three years ago. The truth about himself, and about the people he'd grown up with, lived with and loved, had been burned indelibly into his brain.

He'd been taught the lessons of life that day, and had learned there was only one truth, and one truth alone. That truth was Arren Campion Barkley, his beliefs and his actions. From the moment he'd left the charred cinders of his home, he'd buried his past and promised never again to look upon it. From then on Arren Barkley had fought with vengeance. He'd kept his emotions tightly controlled, hoping that one day soon, men like himself, who did the unspeakable, would no longer be useful or needed. He looked forward to the day when there would not be a North and South, that being from one would not cause the hatred of those who came from the other. Only then would he be able to become human again, and set his emotions free.

A hollow laugh filled his mind but did not pass his lips. Arren shook his head to rid himself of his own demon, but it would not go. It laughed at him, pointing accusatorily, until he could not fight any longer, and forced himself to admit the failure of his logic.

All his noble thoughts had tumbled the day he'd ridden onto the Bennett ranch and seen Ti. Her confidence and determination, her beauty and strength, and above all, the quickness of her mind had struck him like the ball that had wounded him outside Chattanooga.

Never had he met a woman who had attracted him so powerfully, and whom he wanted to hold so badly. Besides having to fight the war that this country was so stupidly engaged in, Arren knew he'd finally met his own civil war, and was hard pushed to know how to win it. Because no matter what happened between him and Ti Bennett, he knew in the long run he would lose. And also the values he had been taught by his family as he grew to manhood held his desire in check: women like Ti Bennett were not to be used lightly and discarded.

In three days he would be leaving for California. Between here and there were a thousand chances he would be killed. Between the coast which he must reach, and the hot Texas sun, death waited for him as it had since the beginning of the war.

Forcibly Arren cleared his mind of his morbid thoughts and the overlying picture of Ti Bennett's large almond-shaped eyes. He willed his mind to become blank, concentrating on the method that James Strong Blade had taught him when they were both fifteen and the Indian boy had come to live at Mountainview to be educated by the Barkley family.

A smile formed on Arren's face, remembering James's arrival in Virginia. Arren's father had agreed to accept the son of the tribal chief as a favor to his old friend Thomas Fitzhughes, who was in charge of the Office of Indian Affairs and was trying to negotiate a lasting peace with the Navajo of the New Mexico and Arizona territories.

The boys had become friends in spite of the hazing Arren had to live with from his neighbors. While

James learned English, he'd taught Arren the language of the Navajo and Apache. In the four years they spent together, a bond had grown between them that was unbreakable.

In the peaceful quiet of the Bennett ranch house, Arren let his mind return to the lesson James had taught him as he opened his mind, let all thought flow free from it, and concentrated on nothing as he began slowly to unwind his tensed-up muscles.

A cool breeze filtered in through the window to caress Ti awake. Her mind rose through the foggy layers of sleep, until she stirred under the summer cover and opened her eyes.

She stretched languorously for a moment before willing herself to leave the comfort of her bed. But as the memory of last night returned, she knew that if she didn't move, she would again feel the doubts and conflicts that had plagued her so much since *he* came.

She rose quickly then, and drawing on her housecoat, went to the bath. When she returned, several drops of crystal water still on her face, she began to prepare for the day. It was a day that held no special plans for her. A day she'd decided to use to say good-bye to the home she'd fallen in love with when they'd arrived, and would love in her memory forever.

While she was looking at her clothing, the wave of doubts she'd been trying to avoid returned with their fullest impact. Ti closed her eyes in an effort to fight them, but they would not be beaten. Slowly she opened her eyes again.

"I *am* a woman!" she whispered to herself, again

denying the terrible words with which Arren had accused her yesterday. Taking off the light housecoat, Ti went to the mirror. Staring at herself, she saw the visible proof of her femininity. Her eyes appraised her full, well-shaped breasts before critically inspecting her narrow waist. She nodded her approval at the smoothness of her stomach and the soft flaring of her hips.

"I am a woman!" she repeated to herself, making the statement a litany. Going into her dressing room, she went to the rack that held her buckskins and lifted a pair of the tanned leather breeches. Suddenly anger filled her mind and she flung the pants away. "I'll show him!" she threatened the clothing.

Going back into her room, she went directly to her bureau. There she took a camisole and several undergarments out. Returning to the dressing room, Ti began to dress. When her undergarments were on, she added one item. A special underskirt that was split from the hem to an inch below the waist. After donning that, Ti walked to a rarely used cedar cabinet. Opening it, she sighed as the heavy scent of the wood tickled her senses. Slowly, reverently, Ti moved items around until she found what she was looking for and took it out.

"Thank you, Mother," she whispered, holding up the English hunt skirt. Her mother, who had died years before, had been an avid horsewoman, and because of Philadelphia's propensity for formality, had acquired several special items for her own comfort. This riding outfit was one of them. Moving gracefully, Ti drew on the split riding skirt. The skirt was unique in that it was really two skirts in one.

Each leg was encased within its own skirt, and standing, one gave the impression of having a full dress on, but when you mounted a horse, you could sit full saddle. Next came the underblouse of soft cream silk, and over that, the matching top to the skirt. The emerald-green color suited Ti well, and as she laced the bodice, she was aware of the whiteness of the tops of her breasts, almost overflowing the angular cut of the green material.

The full sleeves gave her arms plenty of mobility, and when Ti pulled on her special riding boots, she once again went to the mirror. The stranger looking back at her shocked her for a moment. Her mind played a trick, and she thought she was seeing her mother again. Closing her eyes, Ti shook away the vision even as she walked from the dressing room.

At her dresser, Ti brushed her hair until it fell in shimmering golden waves. Then she stood and prepared herself to meet the day.

In the kitchen, Ti paused when she saw the empty table. Her eyes flicked to the stove, where Jenna was working. "Good morning," she said.

Jenna turned, and Ti saw her eyes widen briefly. Then, with a soft smile curving her lips, Jenna spoke. "I forgot how much you look like Mother. The riding dress fits you perfectly."

"I . . . I have nothing to do today. I thought I'd take a ride this morning, then help you and Kay when I get back," Ti explained, wondering why she was suddenly making excuses for herself.

"Ti, I know how much it hurts for you to be leaving. You stay out as long as you want. Please," she added softly.

"Is Kay up yet?"

"Long gone. She went over to the Jacksons' to tell them we're leaving," Jenna explained.

"Why? So they can celebrate?"

"Ti!"

"Don't Ti me. Ever since the war started, the Jacksons have avoided us like the plague. We're Northerners, remember. Daddy's fighting their kin!"

"Kay and Lucy are friends. Nothing will interfere with that," Jenna told her, turning away so that Ti could not argue the point further.

"They'll put their cattle onto our ranges," Ti said, unwilling to let the subject be dropped.

"So? Until the war ends, we won't need the land. Ti, please, we have to accept Daddy's orders."

"Of course," she replied bitterly, "just like the good little soldiers he trained us to be. Dammit, Jenna, we could stay here. We can defend this ranch against anything!"

"Daddy doesn't want to take that chance. He wants us alive."

Before Ti could reply, footsteps sounded behind her.

"'Morning ladi . . ." Steven Markham began, but stopped when his eyes fell on Ti.

"Stop ogling me, Captain, and sit down!" Ti ordered.

"Yes, ma'am," Steven said. But before he did, he turned to Jenna again. "Good morning, Jenna," he said in a soft voice.

"Did you sleep well, Steven?" Jenna asked. Ti heard the tenderness in her sister's voice, and her throat constricted. She willed herself to pour some coffee and then slowly sip it.

"Thank you, yes," he replied just before he sat down.

Ti realized that as each day passed, Jenna's and Steven's feelings were coming out into the open more and more. She envied them, but at the same time felt sorry for them. It would be hard for them to part again, but Ti knew that would happen, even though Steven had not yet said so.

Suddenly the walls of the house began to encroach on her. She needed to be outside, to see the sky and feel the powerful muscles of her horse beneath her. She rose, a tentative smile on her lips as she looked at Jenna and then at Steven.

"I'll see you both later," she said, but before she could leave, another set of steps echoed in the hallway. Ti tried to move, but could not, as Arren Barkley entered the room and stared directly at her. Ti couldn't tear her eyes from him. She tried, but failed. Everyone in the kitchen disappeared except for the man who held her in thrall.

His eyes were steady on hers, and the tight line of his mouth only served to accentuate the strength of his face. The blue of his eyes seemed deeper this morning, and the breadth of his shoulders wider.

Ti realized she had to break the intensity of the moment. Willing herself to move at last, she turned and silently left the kitchen.

Outside, she took a deep breath and started to the corral. Before she reached it, Billy was at her side.

"'Mornin', Miss Ti. I already saddled Samson for you," he said with a smile.

Ti nodded to the young ranch hand, too caught up in her thoughts to see the look of admiration shadowing young Billy's face while she again tried to untangle her confused reactions to Arren Barkley.

"I seem to have an adverse effect on your sister," Arren said to Jenna as he went to the table. He would not allow the vision of Ti, dressed so differently and so beautifully, to enter his thoughts.

"Not really," Jenna said when she placed a large plate of food on the table and sat next to Steven. "Just a very disquieting one."

"Jenna," Arren said in a low voice, "what is she afraid of?"

Jenna stared at him for a moment. "You'll have to ask her yourself."

They ate silently until the sound of hoofbeats floated through the open window. "She's not going to the ranges dressed like that, is she?" Steven asked.

"No," Jenna replied, but her eyes were not on Steven; rather, they searched Arren's face. "She's going to say good-bye to her lands."

"She'll be back when the war's over," Steven said.

"She doesn't think so."

Suddenly Steven's hand covered Jenna's. "And you?"

"I hope I'll be back," she whispered.

"I promise you you will," he told her. Suddenly conscious of Arren's presence, Steven drew his hand back. "I think we'd better get a move on if we're going to make town today," he said pointedly to Arren.

"No," Arren replied.

"We have to," Steven argued. "The supplies will be waiting by now."

"Tomorrow. We'll leave before sunup and come back tomorrow night," he said in a tone that brooked no further argument.

"It's a long ride," Steven warned.

"Carver Town?" Jenna asked.

"Big Spring," Steven replied.

Jenna nodded her head. They both knew it would be a long ride. Big Spring, the largest town in the area, was not a one-day trip. "That's forty miles," she told them.

"It doesn't matter. I have to do something here today," Arren said as he stood.

"Mr. Barkley . . . Arren," Jenna said, her eyes locking tightly with his. "I believe she'll be on the northwest range, most likely near the stream."

"Thank you, Jenna." Arren walked to the door, opening it just as Jenna spoke again.

"Arren." The power within Jenna's voice made him stop. When his eyes met hers, she spoke in a bare whisper, but the underlying strength in her words reached his ears clearly. "She's confused and vulnerable. Don't hurt her, don't betray her. Because if you do, there will be no place on God's earth you'll be safe from me or my sisters."

Arren gazed into the steel her eyes had become and saw the truth of her words. Without answering her, he left the kitchen.

"Steven," Jenna said after Arren was gone, "you told me you trusted him with your life. I believe you, and I pray you're not wrong."

Steven stared at Jenna for a moment before speaking, and when he did, Jenna heard something in his voice she hadn't expected—admiration. "I've never met a man like him. Yes, I trust him, with good reason, but Ti doesn't. Why did you tell him where she went?"

"Why?" Jenna repeated with a shadowy smile on her lips. "Because Ti never met a man like him either." Then Jenna picked up her coffee and sipped it, silently hoping she'd done the right thing.

It was more like a late-spring day than early summer. Ti sat on the bank of the stream basking in the friendly radiance of the sun, while Samson, unsaddled, grazed nearby.

This was her favorite place, the place she always called her own. It was a safe and friendly spot she could go to, to hide from the world. But today, lying on a soft blanket, resting her head on the saddle, she found no solace. She didn't want to leave the ranch, and she knew intuitively that once she did, she would never return.

And it was *his* fault, she told herself unreasonably. Then she shook her head and squinted against the sun's rays. *No, it wasn't his fault, he was just obeying Father's orders. He had his job to do,* she tried to tell herself.

Ti felt like a foolish little girl while her emotions battled ceaselessly. She hated Arren Barkley for coming here and uprooting her life, yet she knew she loved him as she'd never thought it possible to love a man.

When she'd seen him this morning, she'd fled like a frightened child. She knew she'd dressed to show him up, to prove to him that she was a woman, but before she could speak, she'd run away. *Why?* she asked herself.

She had no answer.

Ti tensed as the sun was suddenly blocked and a shadow fell over her. She lifted her eyes and her breath caught when she found herself staring into the unending depths of Arren's eyes. They stayed like that, wordlessly, for untold aeons, until Ti forced herself to sit up and slow the racing of her heart.

"Why are you here?" she asked.

"Because you are," he replied truthfully.

"Can't you leave me alone? Can't you let me say good-bye to my home?"

"No."

"Damn you!" she swore. Standing swiftly, she faced him across the space of inches. She used every power she had to maintain control of her emotions, but his closeness robbed her of her chance.

Gently Arren took her in his arms and drew her close. His lips touched hers, and a gentle heat spread, winding a path deep within her.

Ti's mind rebelled against the touch of his hands on her back and his mouth on hers, but her heart beat faster, and it soon overruled her mind's feeble protestations.

With one last effort, Ti pulled her mouth from his and gazed into his eyes. She was almost lost within their whirling call, but she closed her eyes and fought to regain her balance.

"What do you want with me?" she asked when she opened her eyes again.

"You."

"You don't want me! You want a conquest! You want to make me bow down before you! You want to prove how much of a man you are!" she spat, flinging her words at him like blows of her fists as she pulled out from the circle of his arms and stepped back.

"Stop fighting me, Ti. Stop fighting yourself. I've never wanted a woman the way I do you," he whispered.

An icy rage swept through her, brought on by his arrogance. She took yet another step back, and as she did, her hand went unconsciously to her hip, her fingers seeking the handle of the Colt she'd not strapped on today. When her hand moved, she saw Arren's eyes follow it, and watched his eyebrows arch. Then she let her hands fall to her sides as she balled her fists ineffectually.

"Ti, I'm not a rattlesnake you have to shoot."

"And I'm not a woman, am I?" she asked, throwing his words of yesterday back at him vengefully.

"You're more woman than you even know," he whispered. He took another step forward, his eyes hardening when she raised her hands in the air between them, her fists still balled in anger.

Their eyes were locked in a silent combat that was louder than any words. Then Arren took another step. Her fists were almost touching his chest and she could feel the heat radiating from him.

His strong masculine aura threatened to overwhelm her senses, but she fought her emotions, stilling the sudden trembling of her legs as she defied him.

"Now you call me a woman?" she asked in a tight voice. "What has changed from yesterday? Is it because I'm not wearing buckskins that you want me? I'm still the same person I was yesterday!"

"I know."

"Why?" She hurled the word at him fiercely.

"Don't you know?" he asked in a hoarse voice.

"Damn you——" she cried a split second before his mouth descended on hers, his lips demanding and forceful in their need. She battled him, refusing to listen to his words, refusing to admit the truth of what he'd said. Refusing to yield to his needs, and hers.

She fought her body's betrayal of herself, pummeling his chest with her fists, fighting with everything she possessed. But the iron wall of his muscular chest and the heated brand of his lips stopped her. Then everything changed. A fire built within her very core, sending heat in racing waves to every part of her body. His hands were like burning embers rolling over her back. His thighs were like oak against hers, and suddenly she moaned. Her hands no longer fought him, but rather they slid to his sides and she could not stop herself from pressing against him to return his passionate kiss with her own.

The heated tip of his tongue entered her mouth and joined with hers. Deep within her throat, another moan grew. Then her hands were on his back, stroking, pressing, grasping and searching across the wide expanse of cotton-covered muscle.

Arren tore his lips from hers. Ti's sharply drawn breath echoed in the air as his mouth trailed its way along the side of her neck. Her legs were getting weaker, and she had to hold on to him, or she knew she would fall.

Slowly Arren lowered Ti to the very blanket she

had been lying on moments ago. But though he did, his lips and hands never left her and his kisses deepened into greedy, demanding pleas.

The minutes seemed like hours as they lay side by side, kissing hungrily beneath the clear blue sky. Then, even as the fire within her grew, Arren drew away. Slowly Ti opened her eyes and gazed into his face. His lips glistened with the moisture of their kisses, and his chest rose and fell, emphasizing the strain of each breath he took.

It was in that instant, with his head framed by the golden ball of the sun, that Ti knew she could no longer fight the need and desire within her. It no longer mattered that she doubted him—doubted who he was and what he was doing here. She knew only one thing with any certainty—that she loved him deeply and completely.

Arren's blood coursed madly through his veins. The desire he'd fought so hard to hold back threatened to take control of his actions. He moved his hand to her face and caressed her cheek tenderly. The beauty of her face engulfed him and drove his desire onward, pushing him to the very edge of sanity, making him forget his promise to himself, to not use Ti for his own needs.

"Ti," he whispered. Suddenly Arren could no longer think of anything but Ti. His hands went to the top of her bodice and began to undo the carefully laced material.

When the bodice was open and parted, and the cream underblouse bared, he lowered his lips to hers and kissed her deeply.

Ti tasted the sweetness of his lips and trembled

with the heat that flowed from them. The kiss lasted an eternity, and when it ended, Ti was ready to explode. Her breasts ached, and the fire which had been ignited deep within her grew stronger, reaching into the very core of her womanhood.

But again, the warning that had fled to the back of her mind returned, causing her to stiffen against his mouth. "No," she pleaded.

Arren drew back and silently stared at her. In his eyes she saw a multitude of things. The steel determination, the desire, the need, all flowed out to her.

"Whom are you saying no to? Yourself or me?" he asked. His voice was hard, demanding and honest. Then he shook his head. "From the moment I met you, I knew this had to be. I won't take you against your will, I can't. You have to want me as much as I want you. Ti, you have to trust me. . . ."

Ti searched every contour of his face while his words echoed in her mind. Yet it wasn't his words she heard; rather it was the way he said them, and the way he looked at her. The feel of his hand still lingered on her cheek, and suddenly she could not deny the hunger that was consuming her.

All her life she'd tried to live up to the ideals she'd seen reflected in her father's eyes. She'd had to do a man's job, and had forced herself to do it better than any man she knew. She'd driven herself mercilessly for years until she acted and thought like a man. Now she wanted to be a woman, to be held and loved like a woman.

"Arren," she whispered, fighting the sudden assault of tears that threatened to overcome her.

"Let it come, Ti," Arren said, drawing her close.

He did not kiss her, did not caress her; instead, he held her tightly to his chest, stroking her blond-capped head tenderly, knowing he was doing the right thing.

"Damn you, Arren," she cried, no longer able to stem the tide of her emotions. The tears of her confusion mixed with the fear of giving in to her weaknesses and overflowed her eyes to soak into his shirt.

"Don't be afraid of me," he whispered. "Don't be afraid of yourself," he told her as he drew her head back at last and lowered his mouth to hers.

Again his lips assaulted her even as his hands began to explore the lushness of her body. Flames raced across her breasts, and her breath turned ragged. His mouth slid along the side of her neck, and suddenly her hands were on him.

Their lips met again, and Arren drew her to him. "Arren," she whispered against his cheek as her hands pressed him closer.

Gently he separated them and slipped the bodice from her shoulders. Quickly he lifted the under-blouse and drew it off. Then his lips were on her shoulder, kissing the bare skin, sending tremors of desire through her.

Ti gasped when his hand cupped one breast gently. The firmness of his hand through the thin material of the chemise sent her desire rushing uncontrollably. Arren drew the chemise over her head until at last nothing barred the sight of her breasts from his eyes.

He laid her down on the blanket and gazed at her beauty. His mind whirled as his eyes devoured her.

Her soft breasts, full and peach-tipped, called to him, and he bent to heed their plea. Carefully he captured one peak between his lips and kissed it.

Ti cried out when his mouth touched the softness of her breast. Fiery lances pulsed within it, until another throaty moan gave her some release. Then his mouth left her breast and returned to the base of her throat, even as her hands wound into his hair and her lips kissed the top of his dark-capped head.

She could feel her blood rush past his lips, only to be heated even more by them. Her back arched against him, pressing her chest to his, and his hands began to explore her again. His mouth left her throat and traced a maddening path downward. When he reached her breasts again, she thought she would cry out at the sensations that held her in thrall. His hand danced across the tender skin of her stomach, and his mouth teased her rigid nipples wildly. Unable to stop the shudder of pleasure that swept her, Ti pulled his head upward, seeking his lips with hers.

She was conscious of his hands, caressing, stroking, exploring. The sensations he ignited in her were things never before imagined.

Then his hands were at the waistband of her riding skirt, and slowly, as if she were in a dream, Arren began to loosen it.

Slowly, maddeningly, he slid the skirt from her. Then his fingers touched the top of her boots and he stopped to gaze at her.

His eyes held hers for a long moment, and she saw the question within them. Reaching out, she touched his face. But he did not move; he was asking her and telling her at the same time. It was now her decision, and she knew it.

Hesitantly she smiled. Arren took her hand in his and kissed it softly. Then he moved, taking her in his arms, pressing the softness of her breasts against his chest and kissing her lips tenderly. A moment later he released her.

Ti laid her head back and closed her eyes as he slipped her boots off. Then she opened her eyes and gasped. Arren stood above her, dressed only in buckskin pants. The sun glistening over his powerfully muscled torso outlined the rippling muscles of his stomach. Her eyes fastened on his hands as they undid the buckskins. But when he lowered them, she closed her eyes again.

A moment later his burning skin was upon hers, and his lips began anew their exploration of her neck. Her hands would not stay still, as they too explored the vastness of his back. The taut, velvet texture of his skin sent ripples of delight upward through her hands, to explode in tremors within her depths.

She arched her back when his hand slid beneath her, to gently knead and caress her rear. New lances of fire shot through her at his touch, and Ti bit her lower lip to stop from crying out. Suddenly her riding skirt and undergarments were gone. When the full strength of the sun poured over her, she opened her eyes.

"I have never . . . You are incredible," he whispered in a desire-laden voice. Arren couldn't take his eyes from her as he drank in every inch of her beauty. Her full breasts only added accent to her narrow waist, and the gentle flare of her hips called to him in a tantalizingly sweet song.

His breath grew more strained while he tried to

impress upon his mind this sight, so that for all eternity he would never forget a moment of it.

Ti felt the full impact of his gaze. She was fearful until she read the truth within the blue circles. Then she began to breathe again, knowing that what was happening was right. They were meant to share this moment together no matter what the future held, Ti realized suddenly. Then Arren's eyes flickered, and Ti's breath caught. Slowly she lifted her arms, beckoning him to her.

In an ethereal whirling of desire and need, Arren moved gracefully to her. His lips covered hers, even as his body did.

A myriad of sensations ebbed and flowed through Ti's mind as pinpricks of desire swept across her breasts when they touched his chest. The hot brand of his male hardness pressed against her sensitive skin, but that was lost to her as his lips ran a blazing trail from her mouth downward along her neck. He pulled away slightly, even as Ti tried to keep him there, and his mouth caressed the tender skin of her breasts, lavishing them with heated kisses and exploring their lush contours with his tongue.

And yet again Arren drew away, only to return and take the pliant skin between his teeth and bite it gently. Then, when Ti could no longer stand the increasing wave of pleasure, his mouth drew in one stiffened nipple. The combined touch of his mouth and tongue broke the last strings of her control.

Her back arched and her fingers dug deeply into his shoulders, forcing his mouth harder against her breast as a rippling tremor shook her body. Endless moments later, Ti felt his strong fingers stroke along her belly, and then drop lower as they stopped to play within the downy covering of her femininity. They lingered there maddeningly before resuming their gentle explorations.

Arren luxuriated in the feel of her silken thighs under his fingers. His blood ran in torrents through his body, and his heart beat fiercely against the walls of his chest. He ached in his need for her while he slowly brought his fingers upward until they reached the moist warmth that awaited.

While his mouth lavished her skin with kisses, his fingers caressed her innermost places until Ti's throaty moans floated above his head.

Moving slowly, he raised himself above her and fitted his legs between her wondrously curved thighs. Although his desire was rampant, he held himself in tight control as his eyes met hers. He found her eyes gazing up at him unashamedly, and saw within their green-flecked depths a trust which he accepted gladly.

Carefully he lowered himself to her. His mouth found hers and he kissed her tenderly. Then he caressed each of her eyelids with his lips before returning to the softness of her mouth. Moving gently, Arren lowered his body further, willing control to every trembling muscle as he gently entered her.

Ti felt his heated entrance tear into her with a searing combination of pain and pleasure that sent scintillating lances of fire blazing in her mind. She tried to accept him, but her body stiffened against her will and he stopped. Her hands were on his back, her nails digging deeply into his skin, but she was held in a grip that made her powerless to do anything. Then, even as she fought against her body's reaction, a warmth began to emanate throughout her, and the pain of his first entrance dimmed. Her hands loosened, and her nails no longer dug into his flesh as the heated pleasure of the man within her spread.

Arren moved again. A sharp, quick snapping ripped within her. She cried out suddenly, her back arching, her legs tightening around him powerfully, even as he drew her firmly to him and held her there, motionless.

Slowly, with his length filling her, Arren moved again. Within her, the initial pain was gone, replaced by a throbbing, burning need controlling her every movement and leading her along the path that Arren's body was guiding.

She followed him slowly at first, avidly returning each of his kisses. Soon his body moved faster, and hers joined him. Rippling waves of pleasure wafted along her body. The damp touch of his chest against her breasts created sensations that lifted her higher and higher while Arren's deep, powerful thrusts became more and more demanding.

Her legs were around his hips, and she responded to his every movement with her own, joining him, taking him, and being carried by him in a breathtaking sharing she'd never thought possible. Suddenly Ti tightened around him, her arms and legs clutching him as she felt herself grow weak and strong in waves of pulsating ecstasy. She cried out, her mouth pressing against his shoulder, but she had not known she did as Arren moved within her. Then she exploded with the most intense reaction she'd ever known, again and again; her mind released everything in a torrent of giving that left her shaken to the very core, and unaware that with each breath she exhaled she called Arren's name.

He heard her cry out his name, and felt her grip him tightly. Suddenly Arren exploded within her, driving himself deeper and deeper until his body and hers became one.

Ti pressed her hands along the taut muscles of his back. For a brief second, what they'd just done flashed through her mind. But rather than feeling any shame at what had happened, she felt a warmth of love slowly filter through her mind. Whatever was to happen, would, but Ti knew that she loved Arren, and she would never regret this moment they had given their love to each other.

They lay together, silently gazing at each other and gently kissing. Then Arren slowly moved until he was on his side and drawing her against him again.

"I am a woman," she whispered as her eyes misted.

"A beautiful, loving woman," he responded.

"Arren . . ."

"Hush." His lips met hers and he tasted the saltiness of her emotions. In that moment Arren knew that nothing in this world could ever make him relinquish this exquisite woman, now that he had found her. It had nothing to do with the code of chivalry he had been raised with. It was a much simpler thing that held him.

The moment they had come together, once he had entered her, he had claimed her for his wife. And Arren knew that for him there would be no other.

But when he tried to tell her this, she covered his lips with her finger and rested her head on his chest. One hand caressed the smooth skin beneath it, outlining the ripple of muscles, and danced through the mat of dark curly hair, until she dipped her fingers lower and let them skip across his stomach. Suddenly her hand froze and she sat up. She looked at his stomach, and her eyes followed the path her fingers had. She saw a short, furrowed scar, and at his side, a dimpling of skin.

"You were shot," she whispered, her hand caressing the scarred skin gently.

"Ugly, isn't it?" he said as his fingers wound through her golden waves.

"I'm sorry." Her voice was low and filled with emotion. She bent her head to kiss the spot where the bullet had entered.

"Ti," he called.

"How did it happen?" she asked.

"In the war. Ti, come here," he ordered. She turned to him, about to ask more, but saw in his eyes that he didn't want to talk of it.

Smiling shyly, she slid along his length until her lips were on his and their tongues danced again.

Gently, lovingly, he caressed her back until his passion was again on the rise and Ti was responding in kind.

Before she could protest, Arren's mouth covered hers and another delicious shiver washed through her. The kiss lasted an eternity, until the fires he'd ignited earlier spiraled upward again. Her body melted along his, and even as his hands stroked the tender skin of her back, hers were doing the same.

The sweet taste of his mouth and the firm, tender

caresses of his hands drove any further thoughts
from her mind. They joined again, in celebration of
the love they had discovered, and Ti was carried
along in an explosion of passion, desire, need and
fulfillment that lifted her from the fertile ground and
brought her to the highest peaks of the world.

Chapter Six

THE SOUNDS OF THOUSANDS OF HEAD OF CATTLE echoed in the air, and the pinpoints of a million stars floated overhead in the clear West Texas night. The quarter-moon cast its soft silver glow over the land, painting a picture of peacefulness that encompassed all things.

Except me, Ti thought, walking restlessly under the pale moon. The warm night air caressed her gently, but her mind was too unsettled to enjoy it, as the memories of the day continually paraded before her eyes.

She could still feel the gentle heat of Arren's hands on her skin, feel the throbbing power he had filled her with, and remember the abandon to which she'd lost herself. Her love for him was strong within her, but the weakness she'd learned about within herself lingered in her mind.

The afternoon had disappeared in a haze of loving and of learning that Ti knew she would never forget.

The way he looked at her, the way he kissed her, and the way he made her feel, all combined to tell her that he had been right, and what happened to them had been meant to be.

She smiled at the moon as she thought about Arren. He'd fallen into a light sleep in the late afternoon, and she'd been content to sit there and gaze at him, watching the slow rise and fall of his chest until she laid her head upon it and listened to the even rhythm of his heart. She'd studied him and had impressed in her mind every part of him.

When he'd woken, they'd gone into the stream and played in the cool waters. At one point Arren had begun to speak about the future, but Ti had stopped him—they didn't speak about later, or about what would happen in three days.

But when they had dressed, Ti couldn't help wondering what would happen to them. Would today become a memory, one she would have to live with for the rest of her life, knowing she'd had loved once, and . . . ? *No!* she had commanded herself.

But she sensed that what had happened today was unique. She had not only proved herself to be a woman, she had become one. If she never knew another man, she had already learned the meaning of love, and of sharing that love.

When they'd returned home, night had fallen. Kay was back from the Jacksons' ranch, and Jenna had supper ready. When Ti had entered the kitchen, Jenna had given her a long searching look but had asked no questions.

Dinner had been pleasant, with very little conversation. Afterward, Jenna had entertained everyone on the piano, and by ten the night was over. But when she was in her room, Ti knew she wouldn't be able to sleep. Too much had happened to her today, and she needed to think it out.

She'd left the house silently, and walked into the darkness of night, letting her mind go to whatever corners it sought and ponder the reasons for her very existence.

Lost in thought, her mind replaying her first lovemaking over and over, Ti walked aimlessly until she stopped and looked around. She had wandered far from the main house and was in front of the ranch hands' stable. Standing to one side of the open door, she leaned against the rough-hewn wood.

As she again thought about Arren Barkley and her passionate reactions to him, the sound of two men talking reached her ears. She was surprised that anyone was up, and was about to see who it was, when she heard certain words, and froze, a tingling chill spreading along her spine.

The louder voice had a deep southern accent, and although Ti tried, she could not recognize its owner.

"He's no Yank! I told you when I first seen him that he was one of us."

"I still cain't believe it," echoed the other man, a Tennessee twang deeply embedded in his voice.

"Look, when we was sent here, we was told to keep our eyes and ears open. If anything strange happened, we was to get word back. Well, I think what's happenin' here is real strange, but we don't have to get no word back."

"Then why haven't you spoken to him yet?"

"Because we cain't do it here. Why do you think he's fired so many hands, but not us? He knows who we are and is jest waitin' till we're on the trail."

Ti listened to every word, trying not to let her thoughts run away, while dreading the possibilities of what the next words might bring.

"I still cain't believe it. How'd he get around General Bennett? And especially Bennett's stooge, the captain?"

"I don't rightly know, but I know one thing fer sure. Barkley is our man!"

At the mention of Arren's name, Ti's stomach twisted painfully and her mind threatened to go blank. Forcibly she made herself listen to what they were saying.

"Yesterday, when he was workin' out back . . . He had his shirt off. I saw his wounds. That's when I knew I was right. I'd seen those wounds afore!" the man stated.

"Lawd, there's a war goin' on. Lotsa men been wounded."

"Damn," he swore, and Ti heard the edge of anger in his voice cut through the air around her. "I seen him with Lee in Richmond once, ridin' right next to the general. But I'll tell you why I know it's him fer certain. The wound. Remember that Yank spy who stole him a train in Georgia, in sixty-two, and cut all the telegraph wires 'tween there and Chattanooga?"

"Sure, I was in Tennessee then. Everybody was sure riled about that—hung a bunch of 'em, too."

"Yeah. But when those spies was just outside of Chattanooga, they was stopped. I was there. There weren't many of 'em, twenty in all, but they put up a hell of a fight. When it was over, I had to help carry off the wounded. I'm a-tellin' ya, I carried that there Barkley to the hospital m'self. Damn near had a hole clear through his side. General Lee was there too, came up to the stretcher and looked down. He said, 'Captain, don't you die on me, I don't want to lose another Virginian.'"

Unable to listen to more, Ti stole quietly away from the stable. Her stomach revolted at the words she'd listened to, and nausea threatened to choke her. She fought to disbelieve what she'd heard. She tried to pretend she had imagined it, but the Southerner's words would not leave her mind. They haunted her, winding through the myriad pathways until they surfaced and resurfaced sickeningly.

Spy! they screamed in her mind. *Fool!* they laughed in her head. Suddenly Ti could not hold back, and began to run. She ran, taking deep, ragged breaths, until her eyes misted over and she couldn't see. She stumbled and lay where she fell, her head cupped in her hands as realization and truth exploded within her mind.

Pain lanced through her heart. Hot shame flooded her every sense. She'd been a fool. A stupid, lovesick fool. She had known intuitively that something was wrong with Arren Barkley from the beginning, but she'd ignored it to prove to him, herself and the world that she was a woman.

Well, she was. A foolish, gullible, weak, ignorant woman! And Arren Barkley was a spy and a traitor. He'd deceived her father, her sisters, Steven and herself. But she'd learned of his betrayal before it was too late. She would stop him from doing whatever it was he was planning—she had to!

"Bastard!" she shouted into her hands.

But how? she asked herself. Lifting her head and

wiping the wetness from her eyes, Ti drew in a deep shuddering breath. No more would she let her emotions gain the upper hand. That had been her undoing in the first place. She had forgotten she was trained to be a soldier, trained to keep her emotions under full control. Never again would she allow her heart to rule her actions.

As she made the vow to herself, she realized that to be able to stop him, she needed more proof than just what she'd overheard. She needed to know what he was planning. Rising from the ground with a new sense of determination swelling within her and over-powering the pain of the loss of her love, Ti started toward her house. She would find out what Arren Barkley was up to before they left for California. She would!

In her room, she turned down the wick on the lamp, and darkness blanketed the room, almost matching the darkness her thoughts were shrouded in. A moment later, silver moonlight filtered through the window and Ti breathed softly. She tried not to think about what had happened, but her efforts were in vain, as the memory of the day returned to haunt her with its visions.

She fought her heart, and fought her mind. She ignored the tears that spilled from her eyes when the pain lanced through to her very soul. She had given herself to him, and had done so with complete trust.

"Trust me," he'd whispered, and Ti had listened and believed. "Trust me," he'd whispered, and Ti had given herself to him willingly.

"Liar," she said to the night. "Liar," she cried to her heart.

* * *

"Ti."

She heard her name being called from afar, and pushed up through the darkness. Opening her eyes slowly, she saw a large silhouette sitting on her bed.

She sat up quickly, her breath catching in her throat, as Arren put his hand on her shoulder.

"Easy, I didn't mean to frighten you," he whispered as he leaned toward her and brushed his lips across her forehead.

"What?" she asked. She stared at him, trying to pierce the darkness of the room.

"I have to go to Big Spring to get the last of the supplies. I didn't want you to wake up and find me gone. We'll be back by tomorrow morning," he said.

Ti held back her words, fighting to keep her emotions hidden. She didn't want him to suspect what she knew; she must keep him off guard. "It's not light yet," she told him as she glanced at the window.

"If I want to have one more day with you before we leave, I have to go now. Ti, I . . ." he began, but stopped as his mouth covered hers and he kissed her deeply.

Unexpectedly, Ti found herself reacting to his kiss as strongly as she had yesterday, and even while the horror of what was happening filtered into her mind, her arms went around him. Her breathing grew heavy, and her lips parted at the gentle prod of his tongue.

Fire raced through her body. Her mind began to float away. Then he drew back, and she saw his chest rise and fall quickly as he tried to control his breathing.

"I've never met a woman like you before," he told her as he stood.

Then he was gone and Ti was alone. She stared at the door and forced her body to calm. When he'd kissed her, she hadn't expected her desire to burst forth so wantonly. She'd thought that after all the terrible things she'd discovered last night, she wouldn't be able to bear his touch. But she'd been wrong, and had learned another lesson. She couldn't trust herself when he was near. Ti's fists balled as she concentrated on banishing the feel of Arren's lips on hers.

Then another thought struck her. Why was he going to Big Spring for supplies? He could have sent some of the hands.

Suddenly Ti sprang from the bed. She lit the lamp and went into the dressing room. She dressed quickly, and when she had her boots on, she heard the sound of hoofbeats echo outside. Purposefully Ti went to her dresser and lifted the leather belt and holster. A minute later, the Colt was strapped to her hips and she was ready for what she had to do.

"I told you we should have gone yesterday," Steven said as he stood next to Arren, helping him saddle the bay.

"Steven," Arren said, holding the bridle in his hand and looking at his friend, "nothing was more important than what I had to do yesterday. Nothing! Now, stop worrying, I'll take care of things in Big Spring, and you go do that other errand. I'll be back by sunrise tomorrow."

"Dammit, Arren, we were both supposed to go," Steven protested.

"But we can't. Steven, I'm telling you those men have to be watched. If we're both gone, who the hell knows what they might do? I want them working and busy. Once I've got the herd on the move, I can take care of them," he said, unable to curb the edge of anger in his voice.

Steven looked at him for a long time before he finally nodded. "If I hadn't known you for as long as I have, I'd probably shoot you. Dammit, Arren, she's not some addlebrained farmer's daughter, she's Sam Bennett's daughter!"

Arren's laugh was coarse and grating. "You too? I thought all I had to do was watch out for the other two sisters."

"It's nothing to joke about, Arren," Steven warned sternly.

Arren looked into his eyes, and the smile left his face. "Steven, I won't hurt her," he said in a low, serious voice.

"See that you don't. Arren, you're my friend, but . . ." Steven shrugged and pulled the bay's cinch tight.

Arren gazed at Steven for a few seconds before he slipped the bridle onto his mount. Three minutes later he was astride the powerful gelding and looking down at Steven.

"Watch yourself in town," Steven cautioned just as two more men rode up. Arren nodded and spurred his horse on, followed wordlessly by the two cowhands.

On the porch, hidden in one corner, Ti watched Arren and the men ride out. When she saw Steven come toward the house, she went back to her room.

Taking out writing material from her dresser, she wrote a note to Jenna, not telling her what she was doing, but asking her not to tell anyone she would be gone. She knew Jenna wouldn't like it, but she'd do it, and when Ti returned, would demand a full explanation. By then Ti hoped to have one.

When Steven's door closed, she went to Jenna's room, put the note on her dresser and left the house.

By the time she reached the stable, the first gray tendrils of dawn were filling the eastern horizon. Inside, Ti started to gather her saddle, when a noise startled her. Whirling, the Colt drawn in one lightning movement, she saw it was only the stable boy.

"What are you doing up so early?" she asked.

Billy stared at her. Even in the low gray light, she saw his face turn scarlet. She waited a moment as Billy shifted nervously.

"I'm sorry, Miss Ti," he began, "I was gettin' my pa's holster and gun," he finally admitted.

"Why here?" Ti asked.

He shook his head slowly before he spoke, and when he did, his words were tinged with sadness. "When Pa went with General Sam, he left me his civilian holster and pistol and said if anything happened to him, they were mine. When all the new men started coming to work here, I didn't want them messin' with it, and you told me I couldn't wear it yet, remember?"

Ti nodded at his words, remembering clearly when she'd seen the fourteen-year-old boy cleaning the stables with the pistol strapped on.

"Well, I hid it in here, 'cause I knew the hands wouldn't find it."

"Why do you need it now?"

"'Cause I'm going on the drive. Pa ain't coming home. General Sam wrote me when it happened. And you all are leaving, so I asked Mr. Barkley if I could take the trail. He said I could."

"Billy, you're still too young," Ti whispered, seeing him as he was before the war, a gangly thirteen-year-old who helped his father around the ranch.

"I'm almost eighteen now. I'm a man, Miss Ti, and if I don't go on this drive, I'm going to join the army."

Suddenly Ti saw Billy as he really was. She nodded her head slowly, and was about to speak, when she had another idea.

"Billy, saddle your horse and meet me at the corral. Do it fast," she ordered.

Billy stared at her for a moment, then smiled. "Yes, ma'am," he said even as he turned and left the stable.

When Ti led Samson out of the corral, Billy rode up, and silently they rode from the ranch. It was an hour before Ti slowed the pace. While the horses walked side by side, Ti turned to Billy and spoke. "Billy, I want your solemn pledge you'll never tell anyone what I'm going to tell you."

"Yes, ma'am," Billy said, staring with wide-eyed excitement at her.

"My father asked Arren Barkley to take the herd to California, but I think there's going to be a lot of trouble," Ti said, putting into words the plan she'd formulated as they'd ridden from the ranch. She told Billy that she thought there was a Reb spy among the hands, and she was afraid they might try to steal the herd. She also told him that the reason they were riding today was that she needed to go to Big Spring to see if she could learn anything more.

Billy listened to her, and then gazed openly at her in question. "Why didn't you just go with Mr. Barkley?"

"Because he took two of the new men with him. One of them might be a Reb. That's why we're trailing them. Now, remember, not a word to anyone about this."

"Yes, ma'am," Billy said.

They rode at an easy pace for another hour, and then picked up their speed. By midmorning, Ti saw the tracks they followed were fresher, and she knew they were only a half-hour behind. She called a stop and they dismounted. Letting the horses rest, Ti unfolded a packet of smoked beef and shared it with Billy.

Ti reined Samson in, and Billy did the same. They were a half-mile outside Big Spring, and although it was Thursday, the road had a fair amount of traffic on it. They walked their horses to the side of the road and stopped at a large tree. There, as another carriage rolled past them, Ti gave Billy more instructions.

"You wait here for me, but if you see Arren and the men coming, make yourself scarce. Okay?"

"How long do you figure to be?" he asked.

"Not too long, I hope," she told him. Then she mounted.

Ti gazed at Big Spring as she neared the town. Although it was the largest town for hundreds of miles, it was not very big at all. Two dozen businesses and stores lined its single main street. The homes

of the business owners spread outward from it. Only
a few of the buildings were more than one story, and
the hotel was three. But the town was the heartline
for all the ranches in the area, and when you needed
supplies or news about the war, you came to Big
Spring.

At the edge of town, Ti guided Samson off the
main street and onto the smaller back street that
wound behind the buildings of the town.

She didn't know exactly what she was going to do,
but knew she couldn't sit back and watch the betrayal of her father's life. Reaching the back of the
general store, she tied Samson to a sapling. Then
carefully she walked around the store and stepped
onto the wooden sidewalk. She glanced up and down
the street before looking into the open door. There
were a few townswomen inside, but no men. When
she looked farther down and across the street, she
saw the two ranch hands loading supplies into a
wagon in front of the feed-and-grain store. Her eyes
searched the street again, until they fell on Arren's
bay tied to the hitching post in front of the blacksmith's.

Turning quickly when she heard footsteps behind
her, Ti went back through the alley. When she
reached the blacksmith's shop, she stopped again,
and carefully glanced into the open rear window.

Her breath caught when she saw the blacksmith
talking with Arren. Ducking beneath the window,
she tried to slow the racing of her heart. Then Ti sat
on the ground and listened to every word that was
said.

"At least that was taken care of. What else?" she
heard Arren ask.

"It's getting harder and harder to get the messages through. The last one was three days ago. The shipment is still on schedule. The English are getting worried, and they've promised even more help. You've got to make it to California in time. And you've also got to get those western troops provisioned. If you don't . . ." The blacksmith didn't finish, and Ti wondered what he was going to say. Nothing she'd heard so far confirmed last night's overheard conversation. The mention of the English, who were sympathetic to the South, was unimportant. But Ti wondered about the troops who needed provisioning.

"I'm going to split the herd. It'll be easier to get the cattle to the troops directly. The rest of the herd will be cover enough."

Ti almost gasped aloud, but stopped herself in time. *Split the herd. Will he . . . ?*

"I hope so, Barkley, but I'd be real careful if I were you. There's a lot of hate in the territories right now. When are you leaving?"

"Tomorrow or the day after," Ti heard Arren reply.

"Better make it soon. There were two men talking in the saloon about a bunch of graycoats they saw half a day west of here. You'd best teach your boys how to stay under cover a little better," he cautioned.

A chill raced along Ti's spine at the blacksmith's words. There was no longer any doubt as to who Arren Barkley was. He was a Confederate spy!

Moving with the utmost stealth, Ti returned to Samson, mounted him quickly, and rode out of town. Once she reached the main road, she spurred

Samson on, slowing only when she reached the spot where Billy waited.

"Let's go," she ordered, as she urged Samson on. Billy mounted and caught up with Ti quickly.

"Did you find what you were lookin' for?" he shouted.

Ti glanced at him for a bare moment and then looked straight ahead. Billy didn't need to hear her words; her face was answer enough.

They rode silently, and as the miles passed beneath Samson's hooves, Ti's mind raced on its own course. She'd thought herself in control when she'd ridden into Big Spring, but having her worst fears confirmed, and confirmed by Arren himself, had sent her spirits reeling once again.

In the past twenty-four hours her life had changed, and changed again. Her senses were bruised, battered and crying out for mercy. But she knew there was no mercy to be had.

She had finally found a man to love, and had given herself completely. She'd let all her barriers down in an effort to show her true self. Then she'd learned he'd deceived her, betrayed the trust and love she'd bestowed upon him.

More pain ripped through her, cutting deeply and knifelike, but she refused to cry out and release it.

Arren Barkley had used her—her body, her mind and her love. He was using her father also, for his own twisted ends. *No!* she screamed silently. *I will not allow him to win!*

Seven hours later, with the sun long gone, Ti and Billy reached the borderline of the Bennett ranch. Ti had been silent for hours, thinking of what she could do, until finally the first hint of a daring plan began to form. She thought about it, and looked at all aspects of it. When she was satisfied that it was the only course that could be taken, she made her decision.

"Billy, I've got a job for you."

"Yes, ma'am?" he asked, trying not to show in front of Ti how tired he was.

"First I want you to promise me that you won't say a word about it."

"Miss Ti, I already promised you that this morning," he reminded her.

"Things have changed. The job I have is dangerous, but you're the only *man* I can trust," she told him, emphasizing the word "man." Billy sat straighter in the saddle as Ti stared at him.

"I know who the spy is. At least one of them, and I'm going to have to protect my father's herd. I'm going to shadow the drive to California," she said.

Billy's eyes widened in disbelief. "But, Miss Ti, alone?"

"It has to be that way. Billy, when you're on that drive, I want you to keep your ears open. If anything funny happens, be ready. Don't tell anyone, not even Arren Barkley! Understand?"

"Yes . . . No, not really. Why not Mr. Barkley?"

"Billy, just listen to me. I'm asking you to do this for me and General Sam. Your father would never ask why, he'd just do it, wouldn't he?"

"Yes, ma'am," Billy said. It was true. His father had been General Bennett's sergeant and orderly for twenty-five years, both in and out of the army. He would do whatever General Sam told him.

"When we get home, you go about your business, and when you're on the trail, you watch out for things. If I need you, I'll find you."

"Yes, ma'am."

"And, Billy, thank you," Ti said warmly.

When they reached the ranch, Billy took her horse to the stable and she went directly to the house. Inside, she called to Jenna, and found both Jenna and Kay waiting for her at the kitchen table.

"Where's Steven?" she asked.

"At the bunkhouse talking to the men," Kay said.

"Good," Ti replied, exhaling sharply.

Then, as she stared at the two people she shared her life with, she told them what she had learned. She fought down her emotions, and gave her report in clear crisp words. She held nothing back, starting with Arren near the stream yesterday and ending with today's ride and her discovery at Big Spring.

When she finished, both sisters stared at her wordlessly, until acceptance filled their eyes.

At last, Kay spoke. "What do we do now?" she whispered.

After taking a deep preparatory breath, Ti told them.

Chapter Seven

THE LAST DAY AT THE BENNETT RANCH PASSED IN A flurry of activity that was at best a random mass of multifarious motion. Forty-odd cowboys packed their belongings and readied themselves for the long trail ride. Those who were not going packed their personal items and left the ranch, stopping first at the main house to collect their final pay and say good-bye to the Bennett sisters.

The women, throughout it all, crated and stored the possessions they would be leaving behind. It was a sad time for the three as they went about their duties silent and misty-eyed.

By late afternoon everything was done, and they began to implement Ti's plan. After Ti had told them what was happening and explained her idea to them, they had reluctantly agreed to go along with her. Now, as the three sisters stood in the kitchen, they laid out everything Ti would need and packed it in leather bags which would be attached to the horses.

"Ti, Daddy is going to be angry," Kay warned, but the severity of her warning was lessened by the excitement in her voice.

Glancing up from the bag she was packing, Ti let a shadowy smile play at the corners of her mouth. "And you would like to take my place, and accept Father's anger in my stead if I'd let you, right?" she asked.

Kay's eyes sparkled mischievously when they met Ti's.

"Sorry," Ti replied. Then her voice turned serious as she glanced from Kay to Jenna. "This is my fight. You two have your jobs," she reminded them. "You have to find out how Arren and Steven are connected, and you've got to get to Father and tell him what we've learned."

"Steven has no part in what Arren is doing!" Jenna said in a strongly emotional voice.

"I hope not, Jenna," Ti whispered.

Conversation stopped as each sister became lost in her own thoughts. Ti tried not to allow her emotions to surface, and forced herself to work even harder to keep that from happening.

Later, Ti stood in the center of her room looking about and wondering if there was anything else she wanted to pack.

She still sensed, deeply, that she would never return here to live. She didn't know why, but she accepted the fact without argument. On her bed was another leather bag. This one would soon be filled with the clothing she was taking with her on the trail.

Two cotton shirts, a spare buckskin top and breechs would have to suffice. Undergarments, a pair of soft moccasins she'd traded for with a wandering Comanche, and two cakes of soap would join the clothing. She knew she'd have no need of anything fancy, and couldn't afford the space, even if she'd so desired.

Moving slowly, Ti entered her dressing room and looked at the empty racks. All that remained was the dress she would wear tonight, and her clothing for tomorrow, plus one set of buckskins.

She'd already decided that for appearance's sake, and to keep Steven off guard, she would wear a dress when they left the ranch, rather than her buckskins.

When night descended, it found Ti lying in her bath, letting the hot water relax her tensed muscles. Her head was against the edge of the tub, and her eyes were closed. She tried to keep her mind free by concentrating on the beauty of the "bathroom," but once again failed.

Visions of Arren rose to taunt her. The way he'd smiled, the way he'd held her and the way he'd whispered in her ear when they'd loved poured through her mind. Her heartache at discovering his treachery only added to her misery. His haunting blue eyes floated above her, and she wavered dangerously under their impact.

"Stop," she pleaded, and rose gracefully from the bath. She toweled herself and put on her housecoat before returning to her room. There she sat at the dressing table and prepared for her last meal in her home.

She held her hair up, moving it around until finally

twisting the long blond waves to the back of her head and securing the soft mass with two pearl-tipped hairpins.

She went to the bed and lifted the garment on it. Smiling suddenly, Ti began to dress. Tonight, for some reason, reminded her of other nights, before the war, when her father had guests, and the sisters had dressed formally. It had always been fun.

Tonight's meal was their farewell. She, Jenna and Kay had decided to dress for the occasion. But Ti knew she would also have to act for the occasion. She hoped her overtly feminine dress would help divert some of Arren's attention and make her job easier.

She put on the two petticoats and the silk chemise before stepping into the gown. But Ti realized she would be unable to do it herself. Replacing the gown on the bed, she went through the dressing room and into Kay's bedroom.

She found her sister half-dressed also. "I need help," Ti said, glancing at the dress Kay was struggling with. It was a shimmering green taffeta gown, high-necked and elegant, and Ti knew how nice Kay looked in it.

"Help me finish," Kay asked.

Nodding, Ti went to her sister and started to lace the bodice. Ten minutes later, Kay was dressed.

"You look lovely," Ti told her honestly.

"Thank you," Kay replied. "And now you."

In her room, Ti stepped into her own dress. Kay adjusted the bodice, shifting the chemise until she was satisfied, before lacing up the bodice, and stepped back.

Turning, Ti glanced at her reflection in the oval

mirror. The full skirt billowed out until its hem gracefully swept the floor. The bodice emphasized the slimness of her waist. Its rounded top dipped daringly across the top of her breasts, showing off their creamy fullness to the best advantage. The blue silk emphasized the light shade of her skin, but Ti knew there was something missing.

She went to the dresser, opened the top drawer and withdrew a golden chain. She held it up, gazing at it reflectively.

"Yes," Kay whispered.

Slowly Ti unclasped the chain and held it out for Kay. The cool feel of gold on her neck sent a chill along her spine. Her eyes fastened on the brooch, lying atop the valley created between her breasts, and looked at the black-onyx silhouette of her mother's profile. It was indeed the perfect finishing touch. Turning, she looked at Kay.

"Perfect. Ti, you're beautiful," Kay said. Suddenly Ti's arms were filled with her sister's form, and she pressed her close. A moment later they drew apart, and Ti saw the mistiness in Kay's eyes.

"What's wrong?" she asked.

"I'm afraid," Kay whispered.

"The trip to New Orleans won't be dangerous," Ti began, but stopped when Kay shook her head.

"For you. I'm afraid for you. Ti, are you sure about your plan?"

"Yes," Ti said, shaping a confident smile on her lips. "It has to be done, and I must do it. Kay . . ." But she couldn't finish as her own emotions welled powerfully within her. Instead, the sisters embraced warmly again before leaving to help Jenna.

At eight o'clock, dinner was ready. The three

sisters went into the main salon, where Steven and Arren waited. Ti's breath caught involuntarily when her eyes fell on Arren.

He was dressed simply, in far contrast to what Ti was wearing, but even so, he cut an extremely handsome figure. His broad chest was covered with a low-collared cotton shirt, and his dark breeches fit snugly, without concealing the powerful thighs Ti knew they encased. His hair was combed neatly back from his face, and the scent of soap emanated from his skin.

Fighting the sudden trembling of her legs, Ti forced herself to break his stare and look at Steven. He was dressed similarly to Arren, and looked quite handsome.

"If I had known, I would have made sure to bring my finery," Arren said as he stepped close to Ti. His eyes swept across her features, drinking in her beauty, and again impressing it in his mind.

"You have no need of finery," Ti said without thinking. Blood rushed to her face, and she turned quickly away.

"No," Arren whispered, "there is nothing wrong with honesty."

His words struck her sharply, and it took all her willpower to hold her tongue. Taking a deep breath, Ti faced him again and smiled hesitantly.

Arren took her hand and, using the same low voice, spoke again. "You become more beautiful with each day I know you."

Shivers raced along her arm, and warmth spread within her. Again Ti forced control on herself, willing her body to stop its betraying reactions to him, and silently pleading with her heart to obey.

Finally Arren released her hand and stepped back.

He complimented each sister in turn, and then, with both Kay and Jenna smiling at him, their emotions well under control, everyone went to the dining room.

Dinner, illuminated by two double-tiered candelabra gracing the table, was a silent affair. The somber mood of the women was reflected in the air as they ate for the last time from dishes that would be stored in the cellar until one of them returned to make this house a home again.

Ti, sitting across from Arren, ate slowly and tried to keep her face expressionless. Jenna had prepared a roast, and had opened a bottle of their father's favorite French wine.

As they sipped it, Ti noticed Arren's face change. She watched carefully when he sniffed the wine and then took some in his mouth. Lowering the glass, he stared at the dark red liquid for several seconds. "Excellent," he commented. Ti saw the faraway look in his eyes just before he recovered and gazed at her. "A hundred years ago, my mother's family owned a vineyard in France. It had been in the family for generations."

Ti glanced at Jenna, and they exchanged surprised looks.

Steven turned to him, his eyebrows upraised as he studied his friend. "Since when is Barkley a French name?" he asked, half in jest.

"Campion," Arren replied. "My mother's family was Campion."

"Then you still have family in France?" Kay asked.

"No. My mother's family fled their lands and came to America. But I've always wanted to . . ." Arren stopped himself from saying more. He took a deep breath, and another sip of the wine. "Sorry, I didn't mean to prattle."

Silence again descended over the table as the five continued their meal. When it was over, Jenna insisted the men go to the library and enjoy a glass of her father's brandy while the ladies cleaned up.

Afterward, Jenna played the piano for Steven, and Kay retired to her room. Arren sat next to Ti, and Steven stood at the side of the piano. When Jenna finished, she gazed up at Steven, and an imperceptible signal passed between them. A moment later Jenna and Steven left the salon and walked out into the night.

When the front door closed, Ti's nerves began to hum. She knew the next few minutes would be crucial, and steeled herself for whatever was to come.

Arren turned to her, and saw the tension in her face. He tried to smile reassuringly, but couldn't.

"Ti," he said, drawing himself straighter in the high-backed chair, "when the war is over—"

"No," Ti said suddenly, stopping the words she sensed were coming. She couldn't listen to more lies. "I've not asked you for anything. I'll not do so now. When the war is over, we shall see what it brings."

Arren was momentarily taken aback by the intensity of her words. He stared at her, wondering how to say what he needed to. But before he could, she spoke again.

"Tell me about your mother's family. Why did they lose their lands in France?"

"Do you really want to know?"

"Yes," she whispered truthfully. She wanted to know, and she also needed something to hold back the inevitable confrontation that was yet to come.

Arren's eyes took on a faraway look as he began to speak, and the strong emotions in his voice startled Ti. "The Campions were winemakers for hundreds of years. They made the finest wines in the region, and were wealthy and titled. Then, because of their religion, they became the persecuted."

He saw Ti's startled reaction and quickly continued. "They were Huguenots, and were among the most despised people of France. They lost their land in the ongoing battles of religion and politics, and were forced to flee their home. When they arrived in America, they had only a small part of their fortune. My great-great-grandfather spent many years trying to learn the soil of his new country and grow his grapes again.

"But he couldn't get the results he wanted. He was forced to give up and find a way to provide for his family. He did, and they prospered."

Before Arren had finished, she'd seen something flicker across his face, and suddenly saw a different man. "What did he do?" she asked, drawn completely into his story.

"He became a merchant, importing fine wines. He did so well that he ended up with a fleet of ships traveling the world in search of wines to bring to this country."

"My father spoke of the Huguenot persecutions once. He said they were terrible. He likened it to the slavery here," Ti ventured, caught within his story.

"From what has been told to me, there is a

parallel," Arren agreed, and paused for a moment.
There were things he wanted to tell her, things he
knew he shouldn't. "When it's over," he began, and
he saw Ti understood what he meant. "I want to
begin a new life."

Ti waited breathlessly to hear what he was about
to say. Her heart beat loudly, and she was afraid he
could hear it. *Tell me!* her mind demanded. Was he
going to speak the truth now? she wondered.

"When it's over," he repeated, his eyes lingering
on hers, "I want to continue what my ancestor
started. I want to make wines, great wines."

Ti's mind spun at his words. She had thought he
was going to be truthful, but she had been wrong.
She forced herself to regain her composure, and
exhaled slowly before she spoke. "Wines?" she
asked, dumbstruck.

"I had all his diaries, all the Campion family
records. They're lost now, but I remember them
perfectly. I read them all the time, and I know
exactly where in this country I can grow the grapes
which are needed."

"Where?" Ti asked in a whisper.

"California," Arren replied. "Ti, if I live to see
the war's end, I will start my life over again in
California."

She hadn't heard everything he'd said; her mind
had stopped when she'd heard him say "if I
live . . ." Confusion reared its ugly head as she tried
to comprehend what was happening to her. She had
to hate Arren Barkley. She must. But when he'd
spoken of death, she'd turned cold with fear.

Arren saw her face drain of color and he cursed
himself for speaking so foolishly. He went to her,

drawing her to her feet, and stared into her green-flecked eyes.

"What?" he asked.

Suddenly conscious that she was being held by him, and being surrounded by his powerful aura, Ti pulled away. "I won't listen to anyone who talks of dying!" she said, trying to hide the real reason she'd reacted so strongly.

"I'm being realistic," he said in a low voice.

"Only optimists are survivors," she snapped, quoting her father.

"Like you?" he asked.

"Arren . . ."

"It was only a manner of speech. After you see the amount of death I have, you become armored against it. I'm a survivor, Ti, just like you. And, Ti, I'm coming back for you."

The conviction of his words was like a granite wall. She fought her heart's quickened beating, and grasped for a slim thread of control. "Forget me, Arren. We have different needs, different ideals."

Suddenly Arren's hands were on her shoulders, and his eyes burned into hers. "Never!" he said in a hushed voice. "Are you telling me that what happened between us means nothing to you?"

"Nothing? Damn you, Arren, it meant everything. But you said it already. I am a survivor, and I know what my future must be," she stated boldly, unable to hold back any longer.

"Do you? You're saying that your future is not with me?"

Ti saw his eyes harden when he spoke, and as a tendril of fear crept into her mind, her own temper rose in defense.

"Take your hands off me," she commanded, challenging him directly. "I don't want your hands on me! I don't want you!"

"Stop lying to yourself," he growled, pulling her roughly to him and crushing his lips on hers.

Ti struggled in his grip, but she was powerless to stop him. His mouth bore intensely down on hers, cruelly pressing against her soft lips. Yet within the pain of his kiss, a molten fire began to burn. She fought him, keeping her lips in a tight line, but his tongue stabbed through the resisting barrier and entered her mouth.

Her mind screamed in protest, but even as it did, fire erupted within her very core as her body responded to him. Suddenly his hands were in her hair, and her head was pulled back sharply, forcing her to stare into the crystal of his eyes. There she saw his determined intent.

"No," she said, her lips curling to expose her gleaming white teeth, clenched in rage.

Arren didn't reply; his blood was running hot, and his need and desire for this woman overcame his senses. "Say anything you want. But your body is telling me the truth," he whispered, his voice low and steel-edged.

Ti tried to deny his words as she thought of who and what he was. She struggled, trying to pull away, but could not. Suddenly his fingers tightened, and she was pulled into his arms again.

"No!" she cried as his lips again crushed hers, bruising them in his need. Slowly his lips softened against hers, and unable to help herself, Ti responded to his kiss. A volcano burst forth, sending rivers of lava shooting through her body and turning her mind into a sparkling kaleidoscope of color.

An eternity later, Arren drew his mouth from hers. "I'm still the same man I was two days ago," he told her in a gentle voice; the hint of violent anger she'd seen in his eyes was gone, replaced by a gentle blueness.

You're not the same, she wanted to say, but knew she could not.

"And you're the same woman. Ti, I need you," he whispered.

Ti knew she should find a way to stop what was happening, but there was only one way to deny herself to Arren, and that was impossible. She couldn't tell him what she knew. She had to keep her silence. She was trapped, and had no way of freeing herself. Her own desire forced her deeper into the trap, and she despised the way his treachery spilled over to contaminate the love she'd so naively given him.

Sinking against his chest, she fought her rising tears. Then he moved, and Ti was suddenly lifted from the ground. Her face was buried on his chest, even as he carried her from the room.

Ti kept her eyes closed while Arren carried her through the house. She hated herself for having to give in to him. She hated him for forcing her, and she vowed again, even as she felt the resurgence of her desires, to repay him for the pain and humiliation he was burying her in.

And then they were in his room. The low glow of the bedside lantern filled the room with a ghostly light. He set her on her feet and gazed into her eyes.

"Arren," she protested, but the word was barely audible as she fell deeper under his hypnotic spell. Gently this time, Arren covered her lips with his. Heat exploded in her mouth, and the probing tip of his tongue found hers and caressed it endlessly.

Unable to fight the rising of her own desires, Ti released the bonds she had been trying vainly to maintain, and let her desires burst free.

Arren's hands cupped the back of her head, and the strength of his fingers sent a tremor through her body. Slowly his hands began to play on her back, and the heat within her grew. And a new aching need centered low within her. She pressed her hips to him, even as her hands curled and her nails dug into his shoulders.

Arren tore his mouth from hers and stepped back. His eyes roamed her face before they dropped to the full swell of her breasts. "I must see you," he said in a husky voice.

Before she could move, his hands were at the laces of her bodice, opening and pulling them free. The material parted, and Arren quickly slipped the sleeves from her arms. Ti stepped back as the gown fell to the floor, and then stepped completely out of it. Her breasts rose and fell forcefully beneath the scant cover of the chemise.

Holding herself proudly under his gaze, Ti finished what he'd started. She had to do it herself; she had already lost too much control. She removed the petticoats and accompanying garments, and, holding his desire-laden eyes with hers, took off the chemise. When at last she stood before him, clad only in the golden chain around her neck, she held her head high while her blood pounded loudly in her ears.

Arren stepped across the pile of clothing and drew Ti to him, caressing the silken skin of her back and kissing her lips hungrily.

Ti stiffened as his lips grew more demanding. Her rage at his betrayal turned suddenly and tunneled inward, where it met her desire and joined, expanding with it to erupt in a blazing overflow of passion and need.

Explosion after explosion tore through Ti, and she was soon totally lost within her passions as her body shook against his. She could feel the heat of his swollen manhood through his breeches, and could not stop herself from pressing against it.

Then her feet were off the ground again, as Arren lifted her, still pressed to his length, and walked to the bed. He set her on it, and quickly undressed.

This time Ti did not take her eyes from him, and watched as he took off his clothing. Her blood flowed hotter when she gazed at the wide expanse of his dark-haired chest, and when he stood naked before her, his manhood thrusting outward, almost bursting with desire, she raised her arms and urged him to her.

Arren came willingly. When his lips met hers, her hips thrust wantonly against him. Ti felt the spreading wetness between her thighs, and the incessant ache of her need. She cried out when he pulled away, and moaned throatily when his lips pressed lightly on the sensitive skin of her stomach.

Pinpricks flowed from wherever his lips touched, and her hands wound through his hair, fighting desperately to bring his mouth back to hers. Gone from her mind was his betrayal, the war, anything, except the magic of his body and hers.

Suddenly her wrists were imprisoned by one of his large hands. He stared at her for a long, silent second before lowering his lips without releasing her arms. Slowly, as her skin turned to liquid fire, his mouth rose upward. His tongue rasped, catlike, across one full breast before he took the already stiff tip within his mouth.

He teased her peach-tinted nipple with his tongue, and felt it grow even tauter in response. He held her wrists effortlessly, denying her their use as he lost himself within the taste of her skin.

Ti's back arched when his teeth closed on her nipple. She shuddered when he left it, crossing the soft hill of one breast to torment the other. She moved under him until her legs were on each side of him and she could feel his hard muscles on the delicate skin of her inner thighs. She raised her hips again, even as his teeth bit her other painfully rigid nipple. She cried out, trying to capture the velvet lance pressing so hotly against her thigh. She moaned in anguished need when Arren drew his mouth away.

And then her hands were free. Again she tried to hold him to her, but he was gone. Suddenly his lips touched the inside of her thigh and she gasped as more pinpricks coursed along the oversensitive skin. His hands caressed the soft skin, and his lips roamed freely.

"Arren . . ." she called, her voice hoarse and throaty in a whispered plea, her only desire being that he join her now. Her fingers again wound through his hair, but they could not bring his mouth to hers.

Then she screamed, deep in her throat, when his

lips danced across the portal to her womanhood. Her hips arched upward uncontrollably, and she felt the tip of his tongue dip within.

Lances of pleasure shot upward as he penetrated within the delicate warmth. His lips and tongue caressed and demanded acceptance while he tasted of her deepest treasures. Her body trembled wildly, and her hands turned to fists, while her head twisted from side to side at this new and most intense of assaults to her senses.

His hands held the muscles of her buttocks firmly. His fingers gripped her flesh tightly, refusing to allow her to move. Then another explosion began to build, and with each movement of his tongue, her muscles tensed tighter. Waves of hot pleasure washed through her, her breathing was loud in the air and she could not hold back. Her hips rose forcefully against him. She cried out helplessly when a new warmth spread its cloying tendrils through her, turning her every breath into the sweetest of tortures. Then Arren drew his mouth away. She gasped at the loss, and then cried out at the touch of his lips trailing up her stomach, kissing her skin tenderly. He lavished each breast with adoration, until finally he was gazing into her eyes.

The warmth that had caught her had not left, and the ache within her had grown even more intense. Ti had no control of her actions, and wanted none. The passion that held her refused to let her free as it shut off all thought of her life before this moment. Her hands grasped his hair and pulled his mouth to hers harshly, meeting the ferocity of his passion with equal quantities of her own. Her lips were crushed against her teeth, but all she felt was the lava her blood had become. She accepted his tongue, and caressed it with her own.

She drew back and took his lower lip between her teeth. His hands were everywhere, beneath her, between them, caressing, grasping. Then his fingers dipped below her downy hairs and explored her moist interior. She moaned and bit his lip as her back arched against him.

She tasted a new warmth in her mouth, but was unaware it was his blood as her thighs rose alongside his. Then he pulled away, and rose, poised above her.

Their eyes locked for endless moments, until at last Arren lowered himself into her. At the touch of his throbbing staff, her body stiffened in memory of their first time. But there was no pain as he slid easily within her waiting and wet sheath.

Again, a low cry was torn from her lips when he buried himself fully within her.

A brilliant flare of light cascaded before her eyes. She raised her hips, urging him deeper and deeper within her. Her legs locked around the back of his muscular thighs, and her teeth sank into his shoulder as another wave of pleasure shook her unmercifully from head to toe.

Then his hand was in her hair, pulling her head back sharply. He stared into her eyes, and as he did, his body began to move. He thrust himself deeply within her, and drew back tantalizingly. Then he did it again, and again, and again, until all that there was, was Arren.

He filled her, and pushed her, and carried her with him. She cried out with each powerful thrust, trying to free her head from his hold.

Her nipples rubbed against the hair of his chest and turned as hard as diamonds. Pleasure flowed from them in rippling waves while he guided Ti along their passionate journey. Ceaselessly he moved within her, his manhood swelling and growing until Ti thought she would burst.

But still he would not stop. Suddenly Ti's body arched again, her eyes widened, and her legs tightened painfully around his. Heat burst within her, turning into a sheet of flames that consumed her body.

Her mouth opened to scream, but her cry was silent. Then her body shook and trembled with the release of passion and desire that swept her away to another world.

But still Arren moved within her, holding her against him, sheathed within the molten wetness that gripped him so tightly. He saw her eyes widen, and released her hair. Drawing her mouth to his, he hungrily devoured it.

Then she was shuddering against his frame. She opened her eyes when she felt the heated lance within her grow harder. Suddenly she was moving again, as more and more incredible waves of ecstasy built within her. Again and again he lifted her to explosive heights before she saw his eyes change and felt his rhythm alter. With his hands beneath her, he thrust harder until she felt him tense and burst forth, coming powerfully within her.

Their labored breathing was the only sound in the room, that, and their mingled heartbeats. Ti tried to calm her heart and mind, but could not. Her body had betrayed her, and she had not fought it. She knew now, with dread certainty, that she could never come near him again, because to do so would leave her his slave.

Never before had she been so overwhelmed by anything or anyone. Ti was shaken anew by this knowledge, afraid of what it meant to her.

Then Arren moved. She unlocked her legs, biting her lower lip as she did. The warm air of the room brushed across her sweat-dampened breasts and she sighed at this freedom. Then he pulled her into the crook of his arm and gazed down at her.

"I love you, Ti. Remember that, believe that," he said. "And I'll be back for you," he whispered.

A chill spread over her. She knew he meant it, and she wasn't sure that she didn't want it.

Then he kissed her.

Chapter Eight

THE SUN IN THE CLEAR BLUE SKY SEEMED ALMOST LOW enough to touch, and the man who rose and stretched gazed at it in awe. Then Steven Markham shrugged, picked up his blanket and shook out the dirt.

Turning, he saw Jenna standing over the small fire and smelled the coffee she was brewing. He drew his eyes from her figure, and saw Kay still in the blanket she'd pulled over herself last night. But when he looked for Ti, her blanket was gone. Sniffing the coffee-scented air, Steven walked toward the fire, but stopped, frozen to the spot, as a warning rang in his mind. He spun to look at the hobbled horses, and a chill of premonition covered him.

"Where is she?" he asked Jenna.

Jenna turned, a slow smile spreading on her lips. "Good morning, Steven," she said in a husky whisper.

127

"Where's Ti?" he repeated, staring hard into her eyes.

"She had to go."

"Had to go . . ." Steven echoed, barely able to say the words. Slowly his anger grew. "Had to go?" he questioned, his voice loud in the quiet Texas morning.

"Steven," Jenna said in a low voice, trying to think of some way to calm him down, "it is for the best."

Steven couldn't believe what was happening. He couldn't accept the fact that he'd lost one of the people General Bennett had ordered him to protect.

"It's far from the best," Steven said in a tightly controlled voice. He turned quickly and went back to the wagon. There he took out his saddle and checked his Henry rifle.

While Steven and Jenna had talked, Kay had watched from the comfort of the sleeping roll. But when she saw Steven walk away, she knew there would be a problem. She watched him carefully, and when he had the saddle in his arms, she spoke. "Where are you going?" she asked.

Steven paused, the saddle heavy in his hands as he looked down at Kay. "To stop your sister. To bring her back."

"No." The single word hung in the air until Steven shook his head and started toward the horses.

"Steven," Kay called.

He was stopped by something in her voice. Turning, he found himself face to face with her Colt. He stared unbelieving at her, and then he got mad!

"Steven!" Jenna shouted when he threw his saddle to the ground and took a step toward Kay.

Steven paused in mid-stride. He was unafraid of Kay, but the urgency in Jenna's voice held him back. Then, glancing at Jenna, he saw Kay relax. He moved swiftly, and in a split second Kay's gun was knocked from her hand. Steven held her long hair in his fingers and twisted her head back.

"Don't ever do that again," he hissed as his foot covered the barrel of the gun.

"Let her go," came Jenna's voice. And Steven again froze at the icy tone within it. Without releasing Kay, he turned to face another Colt, held by yet another Bennett sister.

"Jenna, put it down."

"Let her go," she said, fighting against herself, and hating what she was doing to the man she loved.

"Jenna, I have to go after Ti."

"Let Kay loose," she repeated.

Steven stared at her, gazing deep into her green-flecked eyes. He knew she wouldn't shoot him, but he also knew he must maintain some semblance of control.

"Put it down, or shoot me," he said in a whisper.

Jenna stared at him, the Colt steady in her hand. Then slowly she lowered the barrel and closed her eyes against her weakness.

Steven released Kay but did not take his foot from the Colt. "Why?" he asked, looking from Jenna to Kay.

Jenna turned back to the fire and poured coffee into a cup. She brought it to Steven before speaking. "How long have you known Arren Barkley?"

"Jenna, answer my question!" he ordered.

She looked at his face and then at the white-knuckled hand gripping the cup. Taking a deep breath, and closing her eyes, Jenna answered, "She went back to protect the herd and to help you and our father."

"What?" The word was more an explosion than a question as Steven looked from Jenna to Kay and back again.

"Ti found out that Arren Barkley is a Confederate spy," Jenna said at last.

"Oh, no . . ." Steven whispered.

Jenna saw the color drain from his face at the impact of her words. "We knew he had you and Father fooled—"

"Fooled? Dammit, woman, he had no one fooled except you! You're right," he spat, "Arren is a spy."

Jenna and Kay both gasped at his words. They glanced at each other, and a warning look passed between them. "You knew," Jenna stated in a subdued voice.

"Knew? Dammit, Jenna, of course we knew. When did she leave?" he asked suddenly.

"Last night after you fell asleep."

Steven shook his head sadly; he knew he couldn't go after her now, there wasn't enough time. He had to go on. Everything depended on his reaching New Orleans on schedule.

A flash of anger rushed through him, and he flung the coffee cup away. "Yes, Arren Barkley is a spy, just like me, just like your father! But he's a Federal spy! Arren and I went through the Point together. We graduated together! Dammit, Jenna, he's on our side!"

"But . . ." Jenna began, but the shock of his words filled her mind and turned her speechless.

Steven went on as if Jenna had not spoken.

"Arren became a spy in sixty-two, after he learned his family had been killed by his neighbors because he was a Union officer. He utilized his background as a Virginian, and infiltrated Lee's army. To the Rebs he was a true Southerner and a cavalry captain. He fought with the Confederate Army, but the information he sent back to us helped win battles! Arren Barkley is what we call a double agent. And," he said as his voice calmed, "he works for your father. Jenna, Kay, General Sam Bennett is the army's chief of espionage. He has been for two years."

Kay stared at him for a long moment after he'd finished, trying to comprehend the enormity of what she'd just heard. Bending, she picked up her Colt and wiped it on the hem of her dress. "Why is he taking the cattle to California?" she asked, accepting what he'd said and storing the information away until she could better think about what she'd just learned.

"It's what is called a cover story. He's doing several important jobs. First, he's supplying the western outposts with beef. Second, he's stopping the Rebs from stealing the cattle and shipping them to the front. But most important, and his real mission, is to reach California undetected.

"By the time he gets to the coast," Steven continued, "he'll have half a battalion of troops and will be fighting possibly the most decisive battle of the entire war."

"In California?" Jenna asked.

"The British have designed a new weapon. It is devastating. Even now, the manufacturing is being completed, and a shipment is being readied. It will be sent to California, and from there, the Confederates plan on making a sweep to overrun the western outposts, take the territories and states for themselves, and build the most massive army ever seen. If we don't stop it when the weapons arrive, there will not be a United States of America in two years."

Silence fell heavily among the three as the sisters digested what Steven had said. Hesitantly Jenna spoke. "Ti?"

"God help her. She's going to be caught in the middle. Arren is using your father's herds as a cover so that the Confederate soldiers who are going to the coast, both by ship and in small groups overland, will not realize who and what Arren is," Steven whispered.

"Ti's not stupid. She'll see what's happening and know what to do," Kay said confidently.

"Will she?" Steven asked. "One of the reasons that Arren fired so many of the hands is that we knew—your father knew—that one of them was a Confederate spy. But we don't know if we found the right one."

"You didn't," Jenna told him, and then related the story Ti had told her about the two men she'd overheard in the stables.

"Then we'd better hope Arren finds out about him soon. But in either event, Ti's life is in danger. And so is mine," he whispered.

"Because Ti is following them?" Kay asked. "She'll survive. We know that!"

"No," Steven said, "because if anything happens to her, I'll have to face Arren myself."

"What?" both sisters said at the same time.

"Just before we left the ranch, Arren came to me

and asked that I watch over Ti until all three of you are on the clipper to Philadelphia." He paused for a moment, then walked to the first wagon, where he took out a cloth-covered packet. Turning, he unwrapped it slowly and smiled at Kay. "He asked me to give you this," he explained as he held out a gleaming hunting knife. "He said that you had been waiting too long for one, and he had an extra."

Kay stared at the wide-bladed knife a moment before reaching for it. Then Steven gazed deeply at Jenna. "And I was to give this to Ti when she was on the ship," Steven said as he held up a simple gold ring. "It was his mother's wedding band. He wanted Ti to hold it until he came back for her. It was Arren's way of telling Ti he was coming back to marry her."

Jenna stared at it, and then at Kay. Slowly she went to Steven and took the ring. Her eyes filled with tears, and she was unable to stop their flow. "I'm sorry, Steven, we thought we were doing what was best," she said. Suddenly she was enfolded within the security of his strong arms, and buried her face into his chest.

Across from them, Kay fought to stop the tears that rose, but she too failed.

Ti reined in Samson, and Kay's mare stopped as well. She stood in the stirrups to gaze at the land before her. The sun beat down powerfully, but she ignored it as she had been doing for the past two weeks. She searched the land, and then looked at the low-hanging dust cloud that proclaimed the herd of cattle moving in the distance.

For two weeks she had been shadowing the cattle

drive, venturing close only at night to see what was happening. The one thing she'd noted, and this she'd discovered on the third night after she'd found the herd, was that their ranks had swollen by at least twenty more men.

But still there had been no signs of the Confederate troops she'd heard the blacksmith talk about.

Shaking her head, she urged Samson forward, and guided him down the low hill. Ahead of them she saw the mighty peaks of the San Andreas Mountains. Within the next week, the herd would reach the Rio Grande River. Ti wondered where Arren would go from there.

Although she rode with ease and confidence, Ti's eyes never stopped moving. For two weeks she'd watched everything around her, knowing that death might come at her in an unexpected fury. Anything was possible out here. Indians were one threat, mountain men another, and wild animals yet a third. But underlying it all were the roving bands of ex-soldiers who had turned away from both their country and its laws.

The New Mexico Territory was an awesome and wild place, mostly unsettled, with harsh, jagged mountain ranges and flat arid plains. But the very ruggedness of the land was what made it beautiful.

While Samson picked his way down the slope, Ti's thoughts returned to weeks ago and the last night at the ranch. A tremor passed through her body, but she fought it away. Not one day had gone by that she did not remember the passionate, frantic lovemaking which had been her and Arren's farewell.

That night, when her anger had turned into passion, and she'd unleashed its full fury on him, she'd learned more about herself than she'd ever thought possible. And she'd also learned that her love for him was total and absolute. It had shaken her and filled her with shame. How could she love a man who represented everything she despised? How could she live her life with that knowledge? She couldn't. She knew, even as her body had been shaken with the spasms of her passion, that she and Arren would never live a life together.

Instinctively Ti knew she would never love another man with the depth she had for Arren. It saddened her, but she had no choice. Her biggest agony was her fear that one day she might have to face him and kill him in order to save the cattle and her own self-respect.

No more! she commanded herself.

Beads of sweat rolled between her breasts, and Ti was suddenly conscious of her need for a bath. It had been four days since she'd been able to wash, and she desperately wanted to do so.

Four nights ago, when the herd had stopped for the night, Ti had found a small pool, half-hidden in the side of a stone-faced cliff within the Sacramento Mountains. There she'd greedily undressed and submerged herself in the cool mountain water. She'd lain in the pool for a long time, letting the water caress her skin. Then she'd washed herself and her two light cotton shirts. She'd spread them out on the rocks afterward, and by morning they had dried. But the unexpected luxury of the bath had made her crave the comforts she'd given up.

Forcefully Ti shook away everything except the cattle in the distance as she reaffirmed her reasons

for being here, and let her determination grow
again.

When Ti reached the bottom of the hill, she urged
Samson on. She didn't look back, and because of
that, she didn't see the spotted horse that occupied
the place she'd been at moments ago. Nor did she
see the sun glint off the rider's coppery skin and
long, gleaming black hair.

Ti rode for hours until the sun was almost gone
from the sky and the herd in the distance had
stopped moving. She sat in the saddle until she was
sure that the men who drove the cattle were pitching
their camp at the edge of the Rio Hondo River. She
admired the way Arren followed the various rivers
and streams in order to keep the cattle well watered
and strong. She hoped that most of the head would
survive the barren stretches of desert to be crossed
before reaching California.

Dismounting in the cover of several stunted trees,
Ti hobbled the horses and unpacked them. Then, as
she had done every night, she laid out her supplies
and chose what she would eat. While she did this,
she took inventory and realized she would soon have
to leave the trail for a day to hunt for more food and
to cook it where her fires would not be seen.

She sighed, sitting at last, and began to eat a
section of jerky. Ignoring the toughness of it, Ti
reminded herself of its value in keeping her alive.

Under cover of the stars, Arren walked near the
edge of camp. He waited to make sure no one
noticed him leave, and when he was satisfied, he
slipped from sight and walked quickly away.

He heard the low call of a bird, and a moment

later a dark figure appeared. "Good evening, Arren," said James Strong Blade.

"And to you," he replied. "Anything?"

"That group of men is still parallel to you. Perhaps thirty or so. I got close last night, but I couldn't learn anything."

"James, I have a bad feeling about them," Arren said.

"Arren, there's something else . . ."

"What?" he asked, staring into the jet eyes of his friend.

"There's another rider trailing you," he told him.

Something in his voice warned Arren that this piece of information was different. He waited, but James was playing his silent-Indian game.

"And?"

"Nothing. She's staying back out of sight. I've crossed the trail a few times in the last two weeks, and today I thought I'd better see who it was."

Arren began to shake his head, until he realized what James had said. "She?" he echoed, as a sudden premonition formed in his mind. "Describe her," he ordered.

When James was finished, Arren exhaled sharply. But he'd known even before James had spoken that he would hear Ti Bennett's description. "Damn her! What is she doing? James," he said, putting his hand on his friend's shoulder, "I have another job for you. Watch her, make sure she stays safe."

"I'm only one man," James replied, shaking his head.

"Twelve years ago you taught me how to be in two places at once, or so it appeared to others. I think you'll find a way to do it."

"Arren, I'm only a dumb Indian," James said with a smile that matched Arren's. "She means a lot to you?"

"Everything," he said simply.

"Then I will do my best."

"Thank you. We'll talk tomorrow night?" he asked.

"Two nights," James replied before he disappeared into the night.

Shaking his head, Arren started back to the camp. Halfway there, he froze at the sound of footsteps nearby. He drew his Colt, and when he saw a figure silhouetted before him, held it high. "Don't move," he whispered.

The man froze and turned to face him. Arren stepped closer, and lowered the gun. "What are you doing out here?" he asked harshly.

"I thought I heard somethin', and I was checkin' it," Billy replied.

"Never alone. I told all of you that you were never to go anywhere alone."

"Yes, sir," Billy said in apology.

"Come on, let's get back," Arren said, smiling at the boy, glad it had not been one of the men. He would have been hard pressed to explain why he had broken his own rule. But even as he walked to the camp, Ti's face rose up before him.

Why? Why was she following them?

When he reached his bedroll near the supply wagons, he sat and stared at the many fires burning. He tried to understand what was happening, and wondered again what Ti was up to.

He remembered clearly that last night and the early-morning hours when he'd held Ti close to him.

She had been strangely silent, and her lovemaking had been explosively passionate. He hadn't realized it at once, but as the morning had neared, he'd noticed a distance growing between them.

"I love you, Arren," she'd whispered into his ear. Then he'd felt the warm tears that fell from her eyes land on his cheek. He'd sat up and looked at her for a long moment.

"Then you've decided I will be back for you?" he'd asked.

"I hope not," she'd whispered.

"Dammit, Ti, after what we've discovered together, how can you say that?"

"How can you look at me and ask that question?" she'd replied, staring coldly at him.

"Will you please make sense?" he'd almost shouted, trying with all his power to control his anger.

"I can't. Just accept it," she'd said. Then her fingers had strayed to his scarred side, and she moved to lie across him and gaze at the old wound. With one finger she'd traced the short path of the bullet, until her finger had dipped into the small crater where the ball had finally entered. Gently Ti had replaced her fingers with her mouth, and kissed the spot.

When she'd sat back up, she had stared at him. "I'm glad you survived Chattanooga," she'd whispered before her pliant lips sank onto his and her softly curved body had pressed urgently against him. Further words had been stopped, and together they had given and taken of each other until they crested yet another peak together, and floated back to the bedroom they had never left.

With the suddenness of a rifle shot, realization

flooded his brain. When she had kissed him, all his thoughts had fled, and his only desire was to make love with her once more before he had to leave. Only now, weeks later, had he thought about what she'd murmured, and a cold chill swept through him.

"Damn!" he whispered. "Damn!" he repeated, cursing himself for being so stupid. He had never told Ti where he'd been when he was wounded. She had found out somehow, and Arren knew it hadn't been from Steven. He knew why Ti was shadowing him. She must think him a Confederate. "Damn," he whispered once more.

"I'm coming back for you," Arren whispered. Ti jerked awake as the words echoed in her mind. She'd been dreaming again, the same dream which haunted her nightly. Arren holding her close, filling her with himself and telling her he would be back for her.

Throwing the blanket back, Ti stood and stretched. She was dressed in her buckskins, and glanced toward the east. The sky was growing light, and she figured it was almost six. Slowly she walked to the edge of the stream and knelt before it.

Staring into the crystal waters, she saw herself. Her face was even more tanned than before, and her hair hung in messy waves. She closed her eyes and dipped her hand into the water.

Ti wet her face, and went to her supplies to get a cake of soap. She undressed and stepped into the stream, where she washed herself thoroughly, scrubbing away all the dirt and grime of the past days. When she was done, she dipped her head beneath the water before washing her hair. The water cascad-

ed from her hair and skin just as the sun broke over a
far mountain peak. She gazed at it, watching its
gentle beauty, until at last she began washing her
hair.

Ten minutes later Ti was dressed in buckskin
breeches and a cotton shirt. Her hair was still wet,
but she'd combed it out, and the sun was drying it
rapidly.

She was distant enough from the herd to have a
fire, and the coffee she brewed was the first she'd
had in a week. Her only regret was that she would
have to eat more jerked beef. Suddenly Ti craved
anything, anything except what she'd been living on
for two and a half weeks. And she wanted to talk to
someone—Jenna, Kay, anybody!

Ti tried to think of something else, but the memory of that last sad day, when they'd left home, rose to
torment her painfully. The overwhelming despair
which had hovered over the wagons had grown more
intense with each eastward mile. During the ride, if
any of them had as much as uttered a single word,
tears had sprung from their eyes. It was as if their
lives were ending that day.

By evening Ti had realized that there was nothing
that could be done, and had forcefully shaken away
the sadness and tried to ease Kay's and Jenna's hurt
as well.

It had been a hard day and a harder night. They'd
waited until Steven had fallen into a deep sleep, and
then had taken the bags they had prepared for Ti.
The three sisters led Samson and Kay's mare away
from their campsite, and then, under the bright
stars, they'd had a tearful, painful farewell.

Forcing away her self-pity, Ti again dipped into

the well of her resolve and brushed aside her sadness. But she couldn't. Something was going to happen, and she sensed it would happen soon. She was just finishing a piece of beef and trying to figure out her next step, when she heard hoofbeats in the air.

Moving quickly, she kicked out the fire and drew the Colt. Then she waited to determine the direction of the sound. A moment later she breathed easier. The hoofbeats had passed.

Her heart raced, and she tried to slow it. She gathered her supplies and tied them to the mare she was using as a packhorse. She saddled Samson and carefully walked him from the campsite, looking for the trail the unknown riders had taken.

An hour later Ti crested a low rise and stopped. Below her was a group of riders. She looked around and saw the low dust cloud from the herd to her left and realized that the riders were parallel to the cattle drive.

Wondering what was going on, Ti decided to shadow this new group until nightfall and then see who they were.

With her mind made up, Ti looked for another trail she could use to follow both groups. Then she remembered her promise to hunt for food today.

"Tomorrow," she said. She had only enough food for tonight. Tomorrow she would have no choice.

Chapter Nine

TI ATE THE LAST OF HER BEEF WHILE GAZING AT THE darkened landscape. She was in the lower foothills of the San Andreas, with fifty miles of waterless, sun-baked ground separating her from the Rio Grande River.

The early night hid well the rough terrain she was ensconced within. Patches of buffalo grass and stands of small cactus were the only vegetation amid rocky, hard slopes. The high peaks were behind her, but the multihued rock walls of the rugged mountains she'd just crossed stretched for miles to the north and south of her.

Just before the sun had set this evening, Ti had looked westward and seen an open gray-brown expanse. She realized that tonight would probably be the last sleep for two days. If Arren didn't push the herd day and night, he would lose many head to the heat of the day. But sleep was the last thing on her mind. She also needed to find out who those other men were, the ones she'd seen this morning.

When she finished eating, she walked to Samson and the mare and fed them more of the precious grain she had brought with her. The next two days would be hard on them too.

She stroked Samson's neck, and was rewarded by the gelding's gentle push against her palm. She hugged the horse as another wave of loneliness washed through her. Willing it away, Ti took a deep breath and walked toward a low rise.

Staring toward the south, she tried to see if the small band of men had lit a fire, but couldn't penetrate the darkness. A myriad of stars hovered in the sky, but the moon had not yet risen to its high throne.

Ti returned to her blanket and sat. She would wait a little while longer before going to the spot she had scouted earlier, above where the men had camped.

Willing her tired muscles to relax, she tried to make her mind go blank, but a restless energy filled her. She took the Colt from its holster, and using a small piece of cloth from one of her bags, cleaned the dust of the trail from the pistol.

An hour later the moon started its ascent into the heavens, and Ti rose. She saddled Samson, and with the call of birds and insects floating on the night air and the radiance of moonlight illuminating the ground before her, she started toward the second camp.

When she was within walking distance, she dismounted and dropped Samson's reins over his head. They were in the midst of a small grassy area, and while she was gone, she knew Samson would stay to graze contentedly. She walked several hundred feet and stopped.

Searching all around her, Ti looked for the best avenue to reach the campsite unseen. Stilling the nervousness that suddenly drew her muscles tight, she walked slowly forward. There were no trees to hide behind, but the craggy ravines and jagged ground suited her needs well.

It took her another fifteen minutes to cross the last hundred yards. Voices floated to her ears, but they were unintelligible gargles. Forcing her breathing to stay calm, Ti ran low between two outcropping rocks.

She climbed a small rock crest overhanging the campsite and knelt. The men's voices were loud in her ears as they sat on the ground. No fire was lit, and no matter how hard she tried, she could not distinguish the clothing they wore.

Ti shivered when a gust of wind swept across her and the suddenly cool night air rushed over her skin. She was about to look for another vantage point closer to the men when she heard the sound of an approaching horse.

The horse and rider passed beneath her, galloping into the camp. The rider dismounted quickly, and Ti tensed.

"Captain," the rider called.

"Here," came the reply.

"They're settled in for the night, and this spot is well hidden, if'n you want to light a fire," the rider said.

"Thank you, Sergeant," the captain replied. He

ordered a small fire lit, and as two men worked on it, the captain and sergeant walked toward the spot Ti overlooked.

"What did you learn, Sergeant?"

"Well, sir, word is that they're going straight across the river. Be crazy if they didn't."

"Is that what *he* told you?" the captain asked.

"Yes, sir. Said that they would push the cattle without stopping—had salt and three wagons of water just for that purpose."

"Good. That'll make our job easier. We'll let them get across the waste before we take them."

"Yes, sir," the sergeant replied, stopping eight feet below Ti's eyes.

She held her breath until she thought her lungs would burst, and then took only the shallowest of breaths. Her mind was flooded with their words, and then, when the clouds covering the moon floated away, both men were illuminated by its silver light.

Ti's heart raced when she saw the dark uniform the sergeant wore, and almost called out, but held herself back. These were soldiers who were trained to react to surprise. Coming to them out of the dark might earn her a bullet.

Ti exhaled softly when the two men walked back to camp and to the fire that now crackled warmly. When she was certain no one would see her, she left the overhang and made her way back to Samson.

During the short ride back to her campsite, Ti thought about what she'd heard, and another realization came to her. They had one of their men in Arren's camp. One of the Union soldiers was with Arren, and that was how they learned where the herd would be and where it was going.

Reaching her camp, Ti dismounted and for the first time in over two weeks was encouraged that something might happen to save the cattle, to help her father and expose Arren Barkley for the traitor he was.

With exhaustion numbing her mind, she lay down and closed her eyes. She fought and won yet another battle as she banished Arren's face from her thoughts and slipped into the welcome darkness of sleep.

Only three fires remained alive as Arren walked the perimeter of the camp. Most of the hands were sleeping, except for the ten on guard duty. Those ten and the ten who would relieve them were not men from the ranch. They were professional soldiers whose battle experience ranged from the devastation of Virginia and Pennsylvania to the unorthodox and deadly Indian campaigns before and during the war. Arren had handpicked each of the soldiers and knew their value. He would need them, both on the trail and when they faced the Confederates in California.

Above Arren the stars shimmered brightly, and the few clouds visible were whisked quickly on their way by the swift mountain winds. By now, Arren thought, Steven would be on his way to intercept the shipment. No, he warned himself, don't think about it. There were too many variables, too many things that might go wrong.

Thoughts of Steven brought on memories of Ti. The way she felt against him, the way she looked, sitting proudly on her horse's back. Why? Why hadn't Steven stopped her?

Concentrating on the here and now, Arren walked

up to one guard and nodded silently when he passed him. He was going to meet James, and he hoped his friend would be on time; there was much to do tonight if the next step of his plan was going to work.

Three minutes later the low call of a crow reached his ears, and Arren looked toward the sound. "A crow?" he asked when James appeared.

"As good as any," the Indian replied in jest.

"How is she?"

"Sleeping, and still between you and the others."

"They can't wait much longer. When do you think they'll hit us?" Arren asked.

"Not until you reach the river. Perhaps then. If they wait too long, you'll reach Albuquerque."

"They also can't follow us on the flatland. They'll have to take another way. They'll probably be there before us," Arren said thoughtfully.

"But they'll be surprised, won't they?" James asked.

"I hope. Is everything ready?"

"My people have done what they have promised. They have made peace with Cochise and the Chiricahua, against the advice of our great shaman, who foretells that this peace will cost the Navajo their lands," James said in a suddenly tight voice.

"And you believe that?" Arren asked, surprised at his friend.

"Because I speak your language well and because I have been educated at your university does not change my beliefs. Yes, Arren, I believe that. The old medicine man deals in superstition and fear, but behind that is knowledge. I too can see that soon my people will have nothing. No, when your great war is over, if not sooner, attention will again be turned to the Indian. I do not think we will survive this attention."

Arren was stunned by his friend's words, and by the force of them. "James, we will not let it happen. Promises were made—"

"And will be broken. Arren, let us stop this foolish talk. The sands have been read. The great Moqui priests have spoken. We must accept their decisions."

"Superstition!" Arren declared.

"Religion," James whispered. "But no matter, for the first time in our history we are at peace with the Apache. Cochise will not let us free. His hatred of the white man will infect my people." Arren tried to interrupt him, but James waved him to silence.

"The warriors of the Chiricahua and Navajo wait to guide your men and cattle across the Arizona Territory. They will bring them to the edge of the Mojave, to await you."

Arren nodded. His plan was working well. He would split the herd before reaching the Rio Grande. Half his soldiers would go with the Indians. The other half, and the cowhands from the ranch, would go with him and follow the Rio Grande to Albuquerque, where he would leave that herd for the army post to distribute to the western forts. There he would also meet the platoon of cavalry that was waiting, and leave the ranch hands there. He hadn't discovered yet which of them were the Southern agents, and once he left New Mexico, he couldn't take any chances. They would all stay in Albuquerque, while he and his men turned west again. Hopefully, this splitting of the cattle would confuse the men who were chasing them, and the others that they would be crossing paths with.

There was only one other thing that must be done. "How is she?" Arren asked.

"Efficient," James replied. "She is good. She knows what she is doing, and is not afraid."

Arren gazed at his friend. Educated or not, James was still an Indian, and his friend's words were the highest of compliments.

"Is she? But she still can't cross the desert unseen by the others. We're going to get her tonight," he said.

"That is wise," James conceded.

"Is it?" Arren asked, wondering just how wise he was being, and just how stupid he'd been in Texas. Turning, Arren called to the guard. He told him he was riding out, and would return later.

When his horse was brought to him, he mounted quickly and met James a hundred yards from camp. As Arren followed his friend, he wondered what Ti's reaction would be.

Ti stiffened under the blanket. She held her breath and listened intently. Something had woken her, but she wasn't sure what. A tingling at the nape of her neck sent warning calls to her mind. She breathed shallowly, waiting, her hand moving slowly toward her side.

A twig snapped and Ti froze. She kept her eyes closed, lest she give whoever was there warning. Indian? she wondered. Trapper? Her nerves screamed, but she held herself back and waited.

Arren moved quickly across the rocky ground.

When he was five feet from Ti, he paused. Only her hair and eyes were visible outside the blanket, but that sight was enough to bring his dormant passion to the fore.

He had missed looking at her, missed the gentle fury that surrounded her, and missed the touch of her against him. Slowly Arren came to her side. Bending, he drew the blanket low enough to uncover her mouth.

Then he kissed her.

Ti sensed someone standing over her and forced herself to stay still. By barely lifting her lids, she was able to make out the outline of a man. When warm breath brushed across her face, her hand tightened. Suddenly her mouth was covered.

Her eyes flew open and she found herself staring into Arren's face. He drew back for a moment, a smile playing on his lips, before he lowered his head again and kissed her deeply.

Fire erupted instantly to race through her body. She stiffened, fighting against herself and the man above her, forcing her lips to stay in a firm line and hide her response.

Arren drew away and exhaled sharply. "You stupid little fool," he whispered, ignoring her wide-eyed glare. "What the hell are you doing out here? Don't you realize that anyone, an Indian, a renegade, anyone could have done what I just did? You could be dead, or worse!" he said, anger and concern making his voice rise sharply.

Before Ti could answer, his hands were in her hair and his lips crushed down on hers. It happened too fast, and Ti was unprepared. His lips were molten, and seared her to the core. But again he drew back.

"Pull back my blanket," she whispered breathlessly.

Arren did, and when his eyes flicked to the cotton shirt that barely contained her full breasts, he heard a click. Then he was staring into the barrel of her Colt.

"If you were an Indian, or a renegade, or anyone, you would be dead," she told him simply.

"What are you doing here?" Arren asked, ignoring both the pistol and her words as he stood.

Ti moved swiftly, rising also and keeping the Colt between them. "Protecting my property!"

A curtain of red dropped across Arren's eyes. With it, reason and sanity fled. Anger took control of his mind, and he took a step toward her. Before Ti could move, Arren spun. His booted foot arced up, and the Colt was torn from Ti's hand. Before she could react, Arren completed his turn. His hand snaked out, catching her wrist and spinning her in a circle that ended with his arm around her neck and her back pressed tightly to his chest. His arm was like a steel band, and she could not move.

"Listen to me!" he hissed in her ear. "You've been fighting me from the moment we met. Stop! I'm not what you think," he told her.

"The hell you're not!" she spat when she felt his arm loosen for a brief second. Swiftly she dipped her head and closed her teeth on his skin. She bit, and Arren's arm jerked away. Without waiting, Ti jumped clear of him and spun to face him, her rage heavy in her mind, making her arms tremble uncontrollably.

They stared at each other, their breathing loud in the air, each waiting for the other to move. "I know exactly what you are. You're a Reb spy, and I'm not going to let you get away with this!"

Fighting the fear that gripped her, and crying inside at what she knew she had to do, she dropped her hand to the hilt of her knife.

"Is that what you really think?" Arren asked, staring openly into her eyes. He saw a range of emotions flicker through them before her determination reappeared. "Don't," he warned when her hand dropped low.

Launching himself from the balls of his feet, Arren dived at Ti. The knife was out, flashing deadly in the air before him, barely missing his arm as he twisted in the air. He landed heavily on his shoulder, rolled and regained his feet before Ti recovered from her thrust.

Ti's mind went numb when Arren dived at her. Her hand moved of its own volition, her years of training guiding it without conscious need, until she knew it would strike its target. Within her, something snapped, and as Arren's body twisted from her, her wrist flicked away also, the blade missing him by a hair's breadth.

Confusion ravaged her mind as she again faced Arren. She didn't want this, but she had no choice. Steeling herself for yet another attack, Ti lifted onto the balls of her feet. She watched only his eyes, waiting for the telltale signal.

She saw him blink, but as he did, her arms were pinned to her side. Again, reacting instinctively, Ti pulled her feet from the ground in an effort to take whoever was holding her down. But it didn't work, and all she got for her efforts was a bruising crush.

"Thank you, James," Arren said, taking a deep

breath and stepping toward Ti. He took her wrist tightly in his hand, and shook the razor-edged knife free. When it fell to the ground, James released her.

"Traitor! Liar!" Ti spat, her rage lending her words ferocity.

"Again you are wrong about me," Arren said with a smile.

Ti stared at him helplessly while she rubbed her wrist. Glancing down, she looked for both her Colt and her knife but did not see them. Then she saw Arren take a step toward her, and spun, willing her legs to carry her away.

She made it ten feet before her head was jerked back painfully, her long hair caught by Arren's hand. "Stop fighting me!" he said in a low, deadly voice that made Ti turn to look into his now hard eyes.

"Only when I see you dead!" Jerking her head back, she tried to break his hold, but failed, as pain lanced through her scalp.

"As you say," Arren said angrily. Without releasing his grip on her thick mane, he turned to James. Speaking rapidly in the Indian's own language, he told James to gather her things, pack them on her horses and take her to Albuquerque and the army post.

James nodded his head, but his eyes stayed fastened to Ti's hate-tightened features. "Is that wise?" he asked, still speaking in the Navajo dialect.

"It is our only choice."

"Those men?" James asked.

"We have nothing to worry about until the Rio Grande. I'll work it out."

James grunted doubtfully and turned to gather

Ti's things. Arren slowly released her hair and she started to back away.

Ti had listened to them speak, but had been unable to understand a word. But when she saw the Indian bend to her belongings, she sensed what had happened. When Arren released her, she tried to step away. His fingers were like a vise as they grasped her arm, and she couldn't help wincing at the sharp pain.

Angrily she swung her free arm at him, her small hand balled in a fist, but Arren caught it in his own.

"Enough," he ordered in a low voice. He released her hand, but not her arm. Then he pulled her along with him, until they were a good twenty feet from James.

He turned her to face him, and slowly released her arm. She stared at him, hatred pouring from her eyes.

"You're wrong, Ti. In your heart you know the truth," he whispered before he bent and kissed her.

Ti stiffened against his kiss, but when his hands wound around her back and drew her closer, the pain and humiliation of her defeat fled. Her passion exploded, once again betraying her weakness to him.

She moaned deep in her throat, and pressed her lips heatedly to his. The hardness of his body against hers sent tremors racing madly. When they parted, Ti gazed into his now soft eyes and fought her emotions down. "I hate you," she whispered.

"You love me!" he told her. "And one day you'll learn to trust me." He stepped back, his hand imprisoning her arm once again. "It's time," he told her.

"Where am I going?"

"Someplace safe," he said, fighting the pain that sending her away was causing him, but knowing that until this was over, he had no choice.

"New Mexico is part of the Union, not the Confederacy," she told him.

"Really?" he said, exasperated with her tenacity to cling to her stubborn idea. "So am I."

"No more lies! I won't listen to them," she said, her voice harsh as she futilely tried to free her arm.

"No, you only listen to what you want to hear."

Ti heard the strangeness in his voice, but shrugged it away, as her anger at him and the memory of her body's betrayal refused to let her hear the truth.

"James," Arren called in English, "take care of her. Ti," he whispered in a voice meant only for her ears, "I love you."

The Indian led Samson and the mare and his own horse to them. Arren grabbed Ti suddenly and lifted her to Samson's back. It was then she noticed Samson's reins tied to James's horse. She sighed, hoping that would be the limit of her bonds. When James urged the horses on, Ti turned to look at Arren. His eyes held hers in a torturous gaze until she could no longer see through the mists that veiled them.

Long after Ti and James disappeared into the night, Arren stood in the deserted campsite. He knew he must change his plans. Without James as his scout, he would be blind to where and when the Confederate band would strike. But he also realized that with Ti safely taken care of, he could concentrate solely on his mission.

Arren shook his head sadly. Ti must have left Steven before he'd had the chance to give her the ring. If he'd done so, then she would have known. But she didn't, and in her present state of mind there would be no possible way of telling her or getting her to believe him.

"Damn this war!" he spat. Turning, Arren mounted his bay gelding.

It was only a few hours before sunrise when he finally fell into a light and troubled sleep. Throughout it, visions of Ti holding a knife to his chest haunted him and caused him to toss and turn restlessly.

But when dawn came, and he rose, he pushed all thoughts of Ti from his mind. Today they entered the terrain called the dead man's route—Jornada del Muerto—the barren, waterless trail between Mexico and Sante Fe.

With those chilling thoughts filtering through his mind, Arren began his day.

Chapter Ten

THE HOT NEW MEXICO SUN BEAT DOWN UNMERCIFULLY on Ti's head. The hat she wore helped some, but she wished for some shade. When she glanced at James, she saw he seemed unaffected by the heat. Seeing that, Ti willed herself to ignore everything and keep her face as stoic as the Indian's.

The day had gone slowly, and with the sun hanging halfway between the horizon and its zenith, Ti wondered when they would make camp. They'd left the mountains two hours ago and entered a vastly different terrain. The hard ground of the desert made Ti long for the cooler mountains behind them.

Ti had spent the morning trying to find out where they were going, but James had not answered any of her questions. The only words he'd spoken were commands, and those were very rare. He had untied her reins from his horse and had made a simple statement: "Don't run away."

Having seen the futility of her hopes in his eyes, she had slowly nodded. But still, whenever she tried to question him, he acted as if he hadn't understood her.

Ti unhooked her canteen from the saddle horn and took a needed drink. From the corner of her eyes she saw James look at her.

"How much farther?" she asked.

"A day and a half," he said. He almost smiled, but stopped himself when a look of discernment flashed across her face. "But not in the desert. We will reach cooler land by morning."

"Thank you," Ti said, genuinely glad he'd told her something.

For the rest of the afternoon they rode without further words. When the sun dropped, and the low-hanging mountains that had been in view through the afternoon loomed closer, James called a halt.

He hobbled the horses and told Ti to unpack her bedroll. When that was done, she saw him staring at her and holding a length of rope.

"Will I have to tie you?" he asked.

"No."

"Then I have your word you will not try to escape?"

Ti bit her lower lip nervously. To an Indian, a promise was sacred, just as it had always been to her. Taking a deep breath, and hating herself, she nodded.

"Good," James whispered. He went to his horse and took down a cloth-wrapped bundle, and as Ti watched him, her stomach growled. This morning

James had shot three rabbits while they rode toward the desert. Now he was going to prepare them.

Ti watched for a few moments while he cleaned two of the small animals and readied them for the fire. Then she turned, aware that the Indian watched her, and began to gather kindling for the fire.

Ten minutes later the fire roared to life, and while the Indian cooked their meal, Ti went to Samson and the mare and unsaddled them, fully aware of James's eyes following her every movement.

For a few minutes, as she worked with the animals, Ti forgot about the situation she was in, until the scent of roasting meat reached her nostrils. She turned to see the two rabbits over a nice fire. When she finished, she returned to the fire and waited until the food was ready.

They ate in silence, and when they were done, Ti could not stop the yawn that struck. Her eyes were closing slowly, and her limbs were heavy. She stood and looked at James; then she walked into the darkness.

"Do not go far," he cautioned.

Ti did not reply as she went about her toilet. When she returned, she saw James had not moved, and was grateful for his trust. Yet, she regretted it also.

Opening up her bedroll, Ti readied herself for sleep. "James," she called once she was safely ensconced within the blankets.

"Yes?"

"How far from the Rio Grande are we?"

"We will reach it early tomorrow," he replied.

"What tribe are you of?"

"The Navajo," he said truthfully.

"The Navajo are not on the side of the Confederacy," she stated.

"My people are not on any side. It is not our war," he told her.

"Then why are you helping Arren?" she asked.

"Because it is necessary. Because he is my friend."

Ti was silent for a moment while she digested his last words. Knowing the pointlessness of going on, she turned her back to him and closed her eyes.

Ti kept her breathing steady to give the effect that she had fallen into a quick sleep. But even though she was very tired, she made herself stay awake. There were things to think of, and plans to make. She knew what must be done, and the longer she waited and the more distance that separated the herd from her, the harder it would be.

The Rio Grande was near, and that meant she must find a way to escape from James. She let her mind run free, while idea after idea filled her head. Finally she saw only one possibility, and knew that before the sun rose she would try to make it work.

Slowly, setting her waking time in her mind, Ti drifted into sleep, to rest and prepare herself for the morrow.

Ti woke suddenly. She opened her eyes and gazed around. To the east, bands of purple were dissolving into gray. The thoughts that had filled her mind last night returned, and she carefully turned her head to look for James.

Damn! she thought. He was already awake, sitting

on his blanket and gazing up at the sky. She had wanted to startle him from his sleep. Now she hoped his being awake wouldn't affect her plan. Taking a deep breath, Ti prepared herself for the worst.

"James," she whispered hoarsely. James turned and stared at her. "I . . . Help me," she pleaded, making her eyes grow wide as she looked at him.

He saw the fear on her face and moved swiftly and quietly to her. "What?" he asked, stopping three feet away.

"There's something at my feet," she told him.

"Easy, be easy," he whispered. "What is it? Snake?"

"No," she said. "Small . . . Scorpion."

"Do not speak. The vibrations from your voice will affect it," he said as he took another step toward her. "Where is it? On your foot?"

"Under," she whispered.

"Good. Listen carefully. I will go to the bottom of the blankets. When I nod, draw your feet up quickly. Do not hesitate!"

Ti nodded and watched him. He went to the blanket and bent, his hands hovering a bare inch above it. Ti knew the next seconds would spell the difference between success and failure. She eyed his hands, and then gazed at his waist. His knife was still sheathed.

She saw him nod. His hands flew lightning fast to the blanket and Ti drew her legs under her. The blanket was in the air and Ti rolled and stood two feet away from James. He shook the blanket quickly before letting it fall to the ground. Before it reached the earth, Ti moved.

Her arm shot out, and her fingers grasped the

knife's handle. Before James realized what she was doing, the tip of his knife was at his throat.

"No scorpion," he said slowly, his back stiff while he waited for her next move.

"No scorpion," she replied. She pressed the tip harder against his neck when she spoke again. "James, I don't want to hurt you, but I cannot let Arren steal my father's property. No!" she spat, digging the knife sharply into his neck, stopping him from making the move she'd been prepared for. "Don't make me hurt you," she whispered.

When James's muscles eased, she spoke again. "I have never broken my word to anyone, and I am ashamed and sorry I had to do so to you, but my life and property are at stake. Now, walk backward, slowly," she ordered. She kept just the right distance between her and James, so that he could not trip her and get his knife back; all the while, the tip of it served to remind him of her power over him.

When they reached the horses, she told him to lie facedown on the ground. He did so, and while he stared at her, his face as stoic as ever, she went through the bags until she found her Colt. Ti checked the chamber and then cocked the pistol.

"Please stay like that," she ordered. Carefully, never letting her eyes stray from him for more than a moment, she saddled Samson. When that was done, she packed the mare and checked the Henry rifle. All the while, her eyes continually returned to James's prostrate form.

"Where are you going?" he asked when she'd finished.

"Back."

"You don't know where they are."

"Yes I do. They're halfway to the Rio Grande. I'll find them by tomorrow at the latest," she informed him smugly.

"Perhaps," he replied, his dark eyes never once blinking as he stared at her.

"Definitely! I will leave your horse near the foot of those mountains," she said, pointing westward.

"Leave him loose," James asked.

"He may run away."

"Better that than being tied for the big cats."

Ti nodded and went to his things and took his rifle. Then she dropped his knife within the pile, and went to his horse. She led the Indian pony by its rope halter, and tied it to the mare. Mounting quickly, Ti looked at James once more.

"I will leave the rifle when I am out of range," she promised.

"Stop," James said as he turned and sat. Ti's finger tightened on the trigger, and James froze. They stared at each other, until finally Ti shook her head.

"Don't move again," she warned.

"Don't do this," he told her. "It is too dangerous. You don't know what you will be walking into."

"Yes I do. I only hope I'm there when the Federal soldiers take Arren at the Rio Grande," she swore vehemently.

James blinked, and Ti saw a strange expression cross his face. Then it was gone, and his eyes were again unblinking. Ti urged Samson forward, beginning her journey to the river to seek her revenge on Arren Barkley.

When she was a few hundred yards away, she stopped and looked back. James had not moved. She dismounted and placed the rifle on the ground carefully. Mounting Samson again, Ti rode toward her destiny, knowing that for the time being she was free and doing what she had promised herself she would.

Ti had pushed both herself and the horses in her effort to find Arren. She knew time was of the essence and wanted to be there before anything happened. By the time night fell, Ti had become very tired. After she'd left James's horse in the foothills, she'd gone due west. An hour later she had reached the Rio Grande. Turning south, she followed the banks of the river, constantly pushing the horses forward.

The only time she left the banks was when she saw evidence of an Indian pueblo nearby. Then she would circle the area, bypassing the small villages, before returning to her landmark and forging ahead.

When the sun had set, Ti reached the foot of another low-lying mountain range running along the river. But with nightfall, she could not negotiate the hills, and had been forced to stop. There, in the darkness, she'd gone down to the river, and using a burning branch as a torch, hunted for her dinner.

She held the torch over the river's surface in one hand, and the Henry rifle in the other, its stock firmly butted against her shoulder. When she'd seen the flicker of a fin within the rifle's sights, she carefully squeezed the trigger.

A half-hour later she cooked the trout over a small fire, and after eating, she'd fallen into the sleep of one who is truly exhausted.

By the time the sun had risen, Ti caught another

fish and had eaten it. Feeling stronger from both her meals and her sleep, she started off again.

Late that next afternoon, Ti crested a jagged incline and pulled sharply back on Samson's reins. She whirled him around, and when she dropped a few feet back, she dismounted quickly and crawled stealthily to the edge.

Below her, and off to the side, Ti saw the thousands of head of steers lazing about the banks of the river. Her heart beat quickly, and her mind unwound. She'd found them, she realized, and she hadn't been too late.

Returning to her saddlebags, she took out a pair of binoculars. Focusing them on the men below, she tried to find Arren. A moment later her breath caught as his face filled the lenses. He looked tired, dust was on his face, and the handsome lines around his eyes seemed deeper than they had at the ranch. A wave of sadness gripped her mind painfully, but she forced it away and moved the field glasses from him.

She cursed her own reactions at again seeing his face, and concentrated on the scene below her. But as she finished sweeping the binoculars, she realized something was wrong. Again she looked at the herd. It was too small. Not even fifty miles of desert could have taken that many head. Somewhere in the middle of the desert, Arren had split the herd! Then she remembered his words to the blacksmith in Big Spring. Again Ti realized she was too late.

She moved the glasses to look at each of the riders. Slowly, as she went from face to face, another fact surfaced. Almost half of the new men whom Arren had hired in Texas were gone! Yet all the original ranch hands remained.

But even with half the new men gone, Arren still had enough men to put up a good fight against the Union soldiers who Ti knew were somewhere close.

Patience, she reminded herself as she moved the glasses to find Arren again. She watched him, her mind numb with her discoveries, while he talked with Billy. Billy, she cried silently, wondering if she could somehow reach him and let him know she was near.

But there was no way. The area Arren had picked was impossible for that. One side was a sheer wall of multicolored rock rising for a hundred feet. Across from it was the river, and on either side was hilly but open land. No, there was no way for her to sneak in.

Standing, Ti dusted the front of her clothing and went back to the horses. Ten minutes later she was on a small plateau, deciding on a new plan.

She needed to find the Union soldiers. But how? she wondered. Two hours later she was still pondering her course in the darkness of the newly fallen night. She shrugged and stood, searching around her for any sign at all.

It had taken her almost an hour from when she'd stopped looking down at Arren for his ghost to leave her mind. The moment she'd seen him, she'd felt herself assaulted by her memories. Even now, they lingered in a corner of her mind, threatening her with their return.

"No!" she cried to the night. Whirling, she walked toward the opposite edge of the small plateau. There she once again looked down, but froze.

She saw two small campfires in the darkness below and realized she'd been sitting right above the Union platoon all this time. With her heart racing and her mind tugging her in two directions at once, Ti ran to the horses.

She jumped onto Samson's back and spurred him on, knowing that if she thought about it for too long she might change her mind. All the determination she'd felt when she'd escaped from James had threatened to flee at the sight of Arren's face. So she moved toward the camp, moved toward succor from her own mixed emotions, knowing that once she reached them, she would be free of his haunting image, and her choice would be irreversibly made.

Ti rode boldly, sitting high in the saddle, when she approached the camp. She passed the first guard post and held one hand high to show it was weaponless. Within a flash, her horses were surrounded and she faced a dozen musket and rifle barrels.

"I must speak with the officer in charge," she said, moving her eyes from face to face, trying to see each of the men in the darkness.

"Git down," one of the men ordered, gesturing pointedly with the barrel of his musket.

Ti obeyed the command; but when her feet touched the ground, two men grabbed her arms and held her tight. She struggled against them, but was unable to move.

Suddenly the group of men parted, and a tall, gaunt man appeared. She saw gold braid at his neck and breathed a sigh of relief.

"What's going on here?" he asked as his eyes widened at the sight of a woman and his face registered disbelief.

"If you'll tell your men to release me, I'll explain," she snapped. The captain nodded once, and Ti's arms were loose. She crossed her arms and

massaged the spots where the men's fingers had
bitten cruelly into her flesh. Then she stepped
toward the officer and held out her hand. "I'm Ti
Bennett," she said.

The officer stared at her extended hand and then
moved his own to his hat. He lifted it for a second
and dipped his head in a formal greeting. "Captain
Joshua Maddox," he said. "Now, what do we owe
this unexpected pleasure to?"

Ti let her untouched hand drop to her side without
taking her eyes from his. The lean, almost hungry
planes of his face were held tightly. His lips were
thin, and his chin showed several days' stubble. His
ocher eyes bored into hers while he waited.

"Captain Maddox, I have been following the same
people you have. I've spent weeks trying to figure
out a way to stop Arren Barkley from stealing the
herd and supplying the Confederacy. I want to help
you stop him!"

Captain Maddox looked at her, and Ti saw his
eyes flicker strangely. Belatedly she realized that her
story must sound ridiculous. But before the officer
could speak again, Ti added one important fact.
"Captain, my father is General Sam Bennett. Those
are his cattle that that spy is stealing."

She saw Captain Maddox's eyes widen again before he gained control. Then he nodded. "Have you
eaten yet, Miss Bennett?"

Ti breathed a sigh of relief. "No, sir," she told
him.

"Hastings, McColough, see that Miss Bennett is
fed. Sergeant, you other men, come with me. Oh,
Hastings, watch yourself with the young lady, no
improprieties," he said with a smile. But Ti missed

the meaningful glare that Maddox fixed him with as she sighed in relief.

"Yes, sir," he replied. The two soldiers took Ti to one of the fires, and after she was seated, filled a plate with stew and handed it to her. Grateful, Ti smiled her thanks and began to eat. While she did, she watched the officer and his men as they talked twenty-five feet away from her.

One thing, and one thing only bothered Ti. Every man who'd spoken had a southern accent. Although many men in the Federal Army were from the South, it seemed strange to her. But her hunger, and the satiating of it, took her mind from that subject.

When she'd finished her second portion and set the plate down at her feet, the group across from her broke up, and Captain Maddox and the sergeant walked toward her.

When they reached her, both men sat down, and Maddox dismissed the other two. After a moment, a pleasant smile graced his face, and he spoke in a low voice.

"Miss Bennett, I hope you'll accept my apologies for our hasty treatment, but the last thing we expected was for someone to ride into our camp, especially a woman."

"I understand," Ti replied, favoring both Maddox and the sergeant with a smile.

"Good. You know, my first thought was that you were one of Barkley's men. We've been tailing him for a long time."

"Then you know what he's up to?" she asked.

"Yes, ma'am, and we're here to stop him."

"Did my father send you?" she asked.

"No, ma'am, General Grant gave me my orders directly. Arren Barkley's been one spy who's become a painful thorn in our side. He's pulled the wool over a lot of eyes, and our orders are to stop him."

"How—?" Ti began, but Maddox cut her off.

"How did I know where to find him?" he asked. Ti nodded, and Maddox went on heatedly. "I've been looking for him for years. I had hoped to face him on the battlefield, but Barkley's not man enough to fight like a soldier. He's a sneaking spy, and if necessary, he'll die like one!" Maddox paused for a moment when Ti stiffened in response to his outburst.

Ti willed herself not to react further, and pushed away the anger that rose so quickly when he'd called Arren those names.

"Sorry for letting myself get carried away, but I've a personal score to settle with him. I followed him from Washington when he left for your ranch."

"I see," Ti whispered. "Then Captain Markham is a spy too?" she asked, half in fear of his answer.

"I don't believe so. I think he was fooled as much as your father and the other men of Lincoln's counsel."

Ti stared at Maddox, thankful for his words exonerating Steven, but crying inside with this further proof of Arren's betrayal and deceptions.

"He's very convincing," she whispered.

"Yes, ma'am, he is."

"When are you going to stop him?"

"Soon, very soon," Maddox whispered, and a cold chill raced along Ti's spine.

"Captain, can I ask you something personal?"

"By all means," Maddox said expansively.

"I've noticed that you and your men have strong accents. Why is that?"

Maddox laughed and exchanged glances with his sergeant, who was smiling broadly too. "That's real simple, ma'am. Myself and my men are from the Shenandoah Valley, but each and every one of us hates what happened to our country. When war was declared, my men and I put our beliefs ahead of anything else. We're an all-Southern fighting unit, and proud of it."

"So am I," Ti said after hearing his explanation, "and very glad, too."

"Well, ma'am," Captain Maddox said as he stood, "Sergeant Wallace will see to it that you're made comfortable for the night. We'll be moving out again at dawn."

"Thank you, Captain, I appreciate everything you're doing."

"Yes, ma'am," he said, tipping his hat before walking toward his men. Sergeant Wallace smiled at Ti and showed her where to put her things. Then, when she was in her sleeping roll, she felt safe for the first time in a long while, and fell into a sound, peaceful sleep.

Across the camp from her, Maddox and Wallace talked quietly; neither of their eyes left Ti's sleeping form as they discussed their plans.

"I think we should get rid of her," Wallace whispered.

"No, Sergeant, you're dead wrong. We'll leave her at the camp tomorrow night, and after we've dealt with Barkley, we'll keep her. I think General

Lee might like to have Sam Bennett's daughter as a hostage."

"I don't know," Wallace said.

"But I do. First we get Barkley!" he hissed. "And when we get that traitorous son of a bitch, I'm going to hang him myself."

Chapter Eleven

ANOTHER HOT NEW MEXICO DAY HAD FLOWN BY AS TI, riding next to Captain Maddox, followed Arren and the herd. They had ridden parallel to the cattle drive, separated by low rolling hills. By late afternoon Ti realized they were closing in on the flatlands she'd crossed yesterday.

She told Maddox where they were, but all he did was nod. A few moments later, he spoke. "They'll be making camp in another hour," he informed her.

Ti accepted his word, knowing that he had a spy in Arren's midst, and again sat back in the saddle and forced herself to relax.

Just as she'd had bad feelings about Arren when she first met him, she was now experiencing doubts about Joshua Maddox. The more she thought about his words of last night, the more she wondered about their truth. But as farfetched as they seemed, there was to be no other explanation.

The only other piece of information she'd gleaned

from the silent, sullen officer was that he'd known Arren for a long time, longer than the war. It was reflected in the way he'd spoken to Ti earlier in the day, telling her that he and Arren were deadly enemies. *But why?* she wondered. *Had it been the war, or something else?*

A half-hour later, Sergeant Wallace called a halt and rode back to Maddox and Ti. "This looks like a good place to stop," he said.

"Very well, Sergeant," Maddox replied.

Two minutes later the men had dismounted and were efficiently setting up camp while Ti and Maddox stood to one side. Then Wallace walked to them. "I guess I'd best go ahead and get the report," he ventured.

"All right, Sergeant, but be careful," Maddox warned. Wallace went to his horse and opened a saddlebag. Ti stared as he took off his army shirt and put on a plain dark one in its place. His pants were faded and almost indiscernible, but his shirt, with the bold sergeant's insignia, would stand out too plainly. When he was finished, he mounted his bay and rode off in the low light of dusk.

When Ti turned back to the men, the cooking fires were already lit and food was being prepared. Maddox left her side and walked to the men. When he stood in the middle of the camp, he spoke loudly.

"Eat well," he said, his eyes scanning their faces intensely. "And prepare your weapons. When the sun rises, we strike!"

A cheer went up, and Ti shivered at its violent sound. She turned from the group and walked a little away.

"Why did it have to be this way?" she whispered in an ineffective plea.

It would be a long night, she realized as darkness spread across the land. She tried to fight that very darkness from claiming her thoughts, but failed, and gave in to it one last time.

Sensing a presence behind her, Ti looked up. Maddox's shadowed features smiled down at her for a brief moment before he bent to hand her a plate.

"Thank you," she whispered when he joined her on the ground.

"You're welcome. You know," he began, favoring her with a long glance, "I still don't understand why you took it upon yourself to follow Barkley."

"I had to," she said, stirring the food on her plate aimlessly. "He betrayed my family."

"He does that well," Maddox said in a tight voice. "He . . ." Maddox stopped as the echo of hoofbeats floated up to them. His hand was on his pistol grip, and he rose slowly, even while several of his men ran to the perimeter of the camp.

Ti saw the tension leave his body when the mounted figure of Sergeant Wallace came into view. The sergeant halted his horse next to Ti and Maddox and dismounted quickly. "All set. I spoke with—"

"Sergeant!" ordered Maddox.

Wallace stiffened and then looked at Ti. "Yes, sir," he said in a tight voice.

"Very good. At ease, and come with me."

Ti watched the two men walk away, conscious that Maddox had stopped the sergeant from saying anything in her presence. Then she realized that he was about to speak the name of the man they had in Arren's camp when Maddox had stopped him.

Shrugging her shoulders, Ti started to eat the tasteless food on her plate.

Later, after she'd had a cup of what the soldiers called coffee, she sat among them, listening to Maddox detail tomorrow's raid. He outlined the area and showed them where each sentry would be.

"I want this to be quick and clean," he ordered. "If there's too much shooting, we'll lose half the herd in a stampede. It has to be fast, they outnumber us almost two to one, but the cowboys won't fight. Concentrate on the soldiers. Do you understand that?"

The men shouted their understanding, and Maddox smiled at them. "All right, we leave at midnight to get into position. Each of you has been assigned a job. Don't let me down," he said as he finished.

"Captain," Ti called suddenly.

"Yes, Miss Bennett?" he asked, cocking his head and gazing at her with a suddenly lean and hungry look.

"You haven't assigned me my duties," she said, holding his gaze with her own challenging stare.

"I don't quite understand."

"I think you do. I intend fighting with you and your men. Where do you want me positioned?" she asked.

"Ma'am, I don't think the battlefield is the proper place for a woman," he said in a low but firm voice. Within it, Ti heard all the decrepit morality of the Old South come forth.

"Captain, I'm not a fuzzy-headed belle. I can fight with the best of your men. I can help you, and I intend doing just that," she stated boldly.

"No, ma'am, I'm afraid I can't let you do that.

Why, the general would have my hide nailed to the war room's wall."

"I am going!" Ti spat.

Maddox's features tightened into a cruel mask, and he nodded his head in one quick jerk and Ti's arms were seized roughly. "As I said, Miss Bennett, you will not be fighting with us, but when I get back, you can help me," he said. Ti shivered when he'd spoken those last words. His eyes had turned cruel, and she suddenly knew what he meant by helping him.

Summoning up all her strength, Ti again tried to pull free from the men who held her arms. Then, unable to gain her freedom, she sagged within their grip. Her eyes stared mercilessly into Maddox's, and hate flowed from them.

"And," Maddox went on, "after you've *helped me*, you can *help* the boys. There's a few of them that's never had a Yankee woman before!"

Raging fury sped through her body, and the enormity of what was happening took her breath away. Her mind was numbed by this revelation and the sudden changing of her circumstances, but she fought against it. Drawing on her last thread of sanity, Ti made her legs hold her upright.

"I'll kill you for this," she whispered.

"Kill me . . ." he echoed as he walked toward her. "You filthy Yankee pig! You and Barkley and all you simpering, meddling fools couldn't kill me. Your soldiers have tried to do just that since the war started. And I'm supposed to be afraid of some Yankee slut?" he asked.

Maddox stopped, his face a bare foot from hers. Ti felt his words hit her like blows. His breath whipped across her face, the evil in it souring her stomach and sickening her. She took a deep breath and stared at him.

"Yes," she whispered. Then she moved. Both her booted feet arched up as she used the hard grip of her captors' arms to support her. A muffled thud sounded in the night, and Maddox's low animal growl spewed from his lips. The men dragged her back from their captain, even as he fell to the ground. A deadly silence enveloped the camp, and everyone waited until Maddox sat up. He groaned when he did, and his eyes shot sparks of hatred at Ti.

Then she smiled at him.

"Hold her," he bellowed, drawing himself painfully to his feet. One hand supporting his injured manhood, he walked toward Ti. "You *will* live to regret that," he whispered.

Ti started to speak, but stopped as his arm drew back. Fear and hatred filled her as his arm whipped forward. Pain shot through her head, and then a merciful blackness descended, taking both his face and all other thought from her mind.

After Maddox had hit her, he ordered her tied tightly, and assigned one of his men to guard her. Then he again went over his plans, until every man had repeated his duties twice.

While this was happening, Ti struggled back to awareness, and found herself tied in such a way she couldn't move. Rather than fight her bonds, Ti lay still and listened intently to every detail Maddox gave. But eventually the pain in her jaw, combined with the pain in her heart and mind, threatened to choke her with self-hatred.

She'd done the unthinkable: she had become the

one to betray everyone. Arren had been what Steven had said, only she'd been too stubborn to believe him. Not even the memory of the overheard conversations helped to soothe her shame and humiliation. Stinging tears welled in her eyes, and she welcomed their arrival. Arren's death would be because of her, and she would be helpless to do anything about it.

Maddox was a madman—she saw that clearly—an insane Confederate who was a fanatic on the trail of some sort of vengeance.

And she had led him to Arren. *Stop!* she ordered herself. *Find a way to get loose! Find a way to warn him!*

But when she struggled against her bonds, she could do nothing. "Give up, missy," came a voice from behind her. She craned her neck and saw one of Maddox's men sitting five feet away. "Ya'll ain't going nowhere, so you might as well relax."

When she returned her eyes to the others, she saw Maddox walking toward her. "Welcome back, Miss Bennett. I'm glad you're awake for me to say good-bye. But don't fret none, I'll be back to give ya'll a sample of what a Southerner, a real man, is like."

Ti bit her lip and held her tongue in check while he stared at her. He laughed suddenly and spun on his heels. "All right, men, let's get us those Yankees!" With that, everyone except the man guarding her left the camp to get in position for the morning attack.

"You might as well get some sleep, missy," said her guard, "'cause after the captain's been a-fightin', he gets a terrible appetite for a woman, and it hain't gonna matter whether ya'll are a Yankee or not. When the captain's finished with you, it just hain't gonna matter," he repeated softly, his eyes growing large as he looked at her.

Ti shivered again, uncontrollably. Then she willed her body to stop and conserve her strength.

Hours passed with the swiftness of years while Ti waited patiently for her guard to doze. She was still on her back, her hands tied and trapped beneath her, pretending to sleep, but through her almost closed eyelids she watched every move the man made. Finally his chin dropped onto his chest, and when the even rise and fall of his chest proclaimed him asleep, Ti began to work on the ropes. A half-hour later, with her wrists raw, Ti knew she would never get free. She almost gave up then, but the memory of Maddox's leering face and the knowledge that if she didn't warn Arren, all would be lost, spurred her on.

She bit her lip against the pain, but didn't stop. Suddenly a hand was on her mouth. She tried to scream but couldn't. Then a voice was whispering in her ear. "Be still."

Ti stopped fighting, and the hand was gone. She took a shallow but needed breath and waited, but heard nothing. Had she imagined it? A thud rang out suddenly, and she watched her guard topple sideways.

Her eyes widened even further when she saw the man stand up in the spot where the guard had been sitting. Her tongue was paralyzed, and no matter how she tried to speak, nothing came out.

Then James Strong Blade went to her, and using the same knife Ti had held on him two days before, quickly sliced the rope. Sitting up and rubbing circulation into her arms, Ti swallowed and gazed at the Indian.

"Why?" she asked in a hoarse whisper.

"I gave my word to Arren I would watch over you, but now it seems I must do the same for him."

"But I broke my word to you," she reminded him, unable to think of anything else to say.

"Yes," he replied, "that's the white man's curse and disease, lying. However, I think you learned your lesson. Especially when it comes to knowing who is friend and who is enemy."

Ti looked at him for several seconds, listening to his words and letting them settle in her mind. She had never before met an Indian who spoke so eloquently, and wondered where he'd gotten his education. She almost laughed at the ludicrous meandering of her mind, but stopped. Instead, she simply said, "Thank you."

"Tie the man up tightly," he ordered. Without further hesitation, Ti did his bidding, and when she was finished, James had her horses and weapons waiting.

"Now, tell me what is going to happen."

Ti did, detailing everything that had been said while she checked her pistol and the Henry rifle. When she was finished, James looked at her.

"It is almost dawn. They will be attacking soon."

"Then we must leave now," Ti declared, mounting her horse quickly and waiting for James to do the same.

"In a minute," he told her. She watched him go to Maddox's supplies. Using his knife, he sliced every bag open, letting the grains and other foodstuffs fall to the ground, kicking and scattering as much as he could while he worked. When he was finished, he went to the water supply, and again used his knife to make the waterskins unusable. When his destruction was complete, he returned to Ti's side and mounted his pony.

"How did you find me?" she asked.

"Within two hours after you left me, you were never out of my sight. Remember, an Indian's horse is his life. There are no big cats near the desert. But if you had tied my horse, it would have taken three more hours to reach him." And then Ti saw James's lips move, and for the first time she saw him smile.

"You lied to me," she whispered.

"We're even," he replied. Then he urged his horse forward.

The predawn sky was beginning to lighten when Ti and James crested a rocky knoll. It was light enough to see everything, and when Ti's eyes swept the lower ground a hundred yards away, she saw several of the Rebel soldiers moving up on the sentries they'd been assigned to overrun.

Without delay she drew the Henry from its sheath and saw James doing the same. "Wait," she whispered. James held back his fire, but his sights never left the man below them.

Ti knew their timing must be perfect and that the surprise from behind the Rebs must be swift and devastating in order to give Arren and his men time to defend themselves.

"I'll go left, we'll meet on the other side."

James held the man steady in his sights. He smiled once without looking at Ti. "Be swift, be sure, be brave," he whispered to her, repeating the very words that he and his people always spoke before going into battle. Ever since he had begun to follow Ti, weeks ago, he knew that besides her being a woman, she was also a warrior.

"Now!" Ti yelled, pulling the trigger and spurring Samson forward. Her shot and James's rang out in unison. She caught a fleeting glance of her target falling, and then looked for the next one. She fired quickly, reloading as she rode low in the saddle, just the way her father had taught her. She yelled, and heard across from her James's own chilling cry as he fired shot after shot at the Rebs. Then pandemonium broke loose. The Rebel soldiers no longer hid. They were charging madly, firing directly into the camp.

The sentries fired back, and finally Ti heard more shots being returned from the center of Arren's camp. Then there was no time to think, as all hell broke loose around her.

The sound of thousands of frightened steers echoed in the air. *Stampede!* Ti's mind cried. But even that thought was wiped away as one of Maddox's men rode toward her. Ti swerved Samson, ducking low just before the man pulled his trigger. From beneath Samson's powerful neck Ti pointed the rifle and fired. The Rebel fell from his saddle and rolled on the ground. Then there were no more men to face, and Ti whirled Samson around and charged toward the camp.

Dust was thick in the air as the cattle broke free. Sounds of fighting mingled with the thundering hooves as Ti raced toward the center of battle. Just before she reached it, James was at her side. His rifle was raised high above his head, and another wild and savage war cry emerged from his throat.

Arren stood with his back to one supply wagon, his Colt in his left hand, a rifle in his right. He shouted a constant stream of commands, yelling at the cowhands to stay low, while he directed his own men in the battle.

The surprise would have worked, he realized, except for the warning shots. He'd been standing near this very wagon, waiting for something to happen, as he'd known it would. Only his soldiers had been warned; the cowhands had not. He had been expecting this attack since yesterday, and now that it had come, Arren hoped he had not misjudged the enemy's size.

James's wild call had shaken him, but he gladly accepted whatever help was here. But when he'd begun to fire at the enemy, he'd seen a sight that sent fear plummeting through his heart. Ti Bennett swept along the left flank, firing at the enemy with deadly accuracy. Before he could even think of a way to get to her, the cattle had begun to stampede. He'd screamed at the cowboys to go after them while he fired at his attackers.

Then the sounds of fighting began to lessen, and Arren took a deep breath and reloaded the Henry. Then again, James's war cry ripped through the air, and Arren spun. Two of the cowhands were coming toward him, their pistols raised and ready.

As a shot whizzed by his ear, Arren fell to the ground, spinning sideways and returning the fire. He saw a tall man fall just as he rolled again to face the two others.

The one on the left fired, and the bullet narrowly missed him. Arren lifted the Colt, then froze. James and Ti were riding toward him, and the two men were trapped between them even as they drew a bead on him. Suddenly both men jerked forward. Their bodies twisted in the air before they fell into the dirt as Ti and James rode past them, their rifles still smoldering from the last shots fired.

Ti charged forward while James's cry echoed in her ears. Time stood still as everything and everyone seemed to move in slow motion before her eyes. Then she saw the two men between her and Arren. She saw, too, Arren turning, firing and rolling on the ground. He was defenseless for a split second, and Ti knew it might be his last. She barely had time to aim the rifle at the man in front of her, but did, and fired as more shots resounded in the air. She saw the man spin around from her bullet's powerful slam, and then he was gone, and she was riding to Arren's side.

He stood just as she reached him, and when she slipped her foot from the stirrup and jumped, she landed in his arms. James too reached the ground at the same instant, and placed his body between them and any other enemy.

But the only sound she heard above the racing of her heart and her tortured breath was the thundering of ten thousand steers stampeding madly away from the bloody arena. There were no more gunshots, and an eerie semisilence filled the air.

Then Arren's mouth was on hers, and she hungrily returned his kiss with tears of happiness and fright overflowing her eyes. Slowly, carefully, their mouths parted and they gazed deeply into each other's eyes.

"I love you," she whispered.

Before he could reply, one of his men was at their side. "It's over, sir," he said, freezing, his eyes going wide in surprise at the unexpected sight of a woman in Arren's arms.

"Good. Lieutenant Tremain, gather the wounded and make fast the prisoners," Arren ordered.

"Yes, sir," Tremain replied, but could not take his eyes from Ti's face.

"Lieutenant!" Arren snapped. "I'll introduce you later. Now, move!"

A small giggle escaped from Ti's lips, but Arren's fierce expression stopped it quickly. "Well, you do have to admit it's unusual to find a woman in the commanding officer's arms in the middle of a battlefield," she said.

Suddenly Arren's lips parted and a low laugh rumbled through. "I love you," he whispered.

Then the pandemonium around them resumed, and Arren was forced to release Ti and join his men in the search for both the survivors and the dead.

While he did, he wondered at his luck and at the fortune that had brought him and Ti back together. But that thought was wiped from his mind when he stared down at an unconscious man. His breath hissed out dangerously. He bent to inspect the man's face closely, until he knew he'd not been mistaken.

"Maddox," he whispered. Kneeling, Arren looked at his bloodied head and saw it was a glancing shot, nothing more than a surface wound. Quickly he searched the man, making sure he had no hidden weapons. Then he lifted him across his shoulders and went to where the other wounded were being brought.

"Simmons," he called to one of the men. The soldier came over to Arren and took the man from his shoulders. "I want this one separated and cuffed. He's the leader," Arren said.

"Yes, sir," Simmons replied, walking away and putting Maddox down several feet from anyone else.

Arren turned to see Ti, her Colt drawn, escorting the man she'd shot when he'd tried to kill Arren. When she'd forced him to sit with the other prisoners under the watchful eyes of two of his men, she walked over to Arren.

"That was Maddox's man in your camp," she said.

"I know."

"Then why did you . . . ?" She paused as understanding came. "You were expecting them to attack, weren't you?"

"Yes, but not the way they did. If it hadn't been for you and James—"

Ti smiled, cutting off his unnecessary words. "Arren, where are the rest of the cattle, and your other men?"

"Halfway to Arizona, I hope," he said, guiding her away from the ears of the prisoners, to explain what he and James had done.

When he was finished, she turned to him, her eyes growing hard and challenging. "Why didn't you tell me in Texas?" she asked.

"I couldn't, there were too many ears around, and the way you acted toward me eased any suspicions that the men may have had."

"I see," she replied, understanding what he said, but still disliking it. "When would I have found out? In Philadelphia?"

"No," he whispered. "In New Orleans. Steven had something for you."

"What?" Ti asked. Her intuition rose and made her heart race without her knowing why.

"Sorry," he said with a half-smile. "You'll have to wait until you see Steven."

Before she could protest, he kissed her again, and the question flew from her mind as the love she felt for him filled her completely. But slowly reality returned and they parted.

Arren stood back and surveyed the carnage of his camp. While he did, Ti slipped away to attend the wounded and do what she could to help.

Chapter Twelve

THE DAY PASSED IN A STREAM OF NONSTOP WORK. Ti attended the injured, helping two of Arren's soldiers clean and dress the wounds of those they could, while Arren, the soldiers and the cowhands spent the day rounding up the steers and getting them back to the camp.

Of the dead, four were Arren's men and thirteen were Confederate troops. They were buried side by side on the banks of the Rio Grande, in a solemn service led by Arren. Ti cried quietly when he'd spoken, and even now, hours later, his words still rang in her mind. "They are buried together in a strange land, but although they were enemies when they lived, death ends all hate and war, and in death, they are joined together in friendship and peace."

By suppertime everyone was tired, and as they ate, silence descended on the camp. When the meal was finished and several of the men went to bathe in the river, Ti and Arren slipped away. They walked along the edge of the river, enjoying the peace and tranquillity of the early night. She too had wanted to bathe, to cleanse herself of the dirt of days and the stink of battle. Arren had agreed to take her from the prying eyes of the men and to stay with her while she washed herself in the river.

They'd had little chance to talk during the day, and although Ti was tired, and saw the same in Arren's face, she needed to be with him, to walk, and to talk. Bathing was not the most important thing on her mind right then. There was so much that had to be said, and so many questions that needed to be answered.

They stopped when the sounds of the camp could no longer be heard, and sat on a rocky perch a few feet above the river.

"Arren . . ." Ti began, moistening her lips with her tongue while searching for the right words. "I feel like such a fool, getting myself caught by Maddox, and for not believing in you," she said.

Arren cupped her cheek with his hand, and then gently stroked it. "If you were any different than you are, I wouldn't love you. What happened wasn't your fault. It was the way things had to be. I had my orders from your father. I couldn't change them."

"I was so angry at you. I hated you while I loved you," she said truthfully. "When I overheard those men talking in the stables, I thought I would die. It was the same day that we . . . It was when we were at the stream," she finished in a low voice.

Arren gazed at her for a long time. He had no idea when she'd found out about his supposedly Southern loyalties, but he knew now. Before he could say anything, Ti went on.

"Then I followed you into town—"

"Followed me?" he echoed.

"Yes, Billy and I followed you. He waited for me outside Big Spring, and when I went in, I overheard you speaking to the blacksmith."

"Then you must have been really confused. One day you hear two men talking about me being a Confederate, the next you hear me talking about the Union Army."

"No," Ti said, shaking her head.

"No?" Arren asked, puzzled. He remembered speaking to the blacksmith, who was the general's local agent in West Texas. They'd discussed several things, but mostly the effect of the war. "What exactly did you hear?"

Ti told him what she'd heard, until Arren started laughing. "I can understand why you thought me a Southern spy. Of course I had some of my men in the hills. Where did you think all the new hands came from? They were my men, and they were wearing Reb gray to keep safe."

"I figured that out last night when I discovered who Maddox really was."

"How did you know about Chattanooga?" he asked. "I never told you where I was when I was shot."

"The wound?" Ti smiled and shook her head. "When I overheard the men talking that first night, one of them said he carried you to the hospital. He even said General Lee stopped them and commended you. Is that true?"

Arren nodded slowly as the memory of that day flashed brightly in his mind. Then he told Ti of John Andrews' daring raid. Andrews, who had stolen a train and cut all the telegraph wires from Georgia to Tennessee, was one of the bravest men Arren had ever met. He told Ti he had been with Lee's staff when it happened, and when the train neared Chattanooga, he'd gone, presumably to fight, but in reality he'd gone to help them escape. The only problem was that one of the Yankee spies with Andrews didn't know him and had shot him.

"I can't believe it. You were shot by someone on your own side?" Ti asked, shocked.

"It happens every day. Especially when you're not who you're supposed to be. It's part of the hazards, but it's a necessary risk."

"Oh, Arren," Ti whispered. He kissed her then, a gentle, soft, warm kiss that showed her his love. A moment later she drew away.

"Did Maddox hurt you?" he asked, his eyes searching across every inch of her face.

Ti shook her head quickly. "No, I hurt him, though." Then she told him what had happened, and what she'd done. When she was finished, Arren looked thoughtfully at her.

"He's insane," he stated.

"I know. I saw it. Arren, why does he hate you so much? It's more than the war," she added.

"Yes, it is," he responded. He was silent for a moment, and when he did speak, his voice was flat and unemotional.

"Joshua Maddox is a fanatic. His family and mine have been neighbors for generations. I was engaged to his sister before the war. It had been a prearranged match. But I was always different from the others. I guess our mutual dislike, Joshua's and mine, started when James came to live with me . . ." Arren related then the story of James Strong Blade, his mysterious education, and his unbreakable friendship with Arren.

"You're a very special man, Arren Barkley," Ti whispered, but Arren did not seem to hear, and as he continued speaking, a chill raced along Ti's spine.

"When I graduated from the Point and returned home, Samuel and Joshua Maddox informed me that it was time to fulfill my obligation and marry my fiancée. But I had learned that Amanda was far from the woman I wanted. She never used her brains, was afraid of everything and couldn't carry a conversation with a frog. So instead, I managed to get assigned to a post in Texas. I spent three years there, not because I was a coward, but because I was trying to find a way to save my family's reputation. I met your father for the first time then.

"But," Arren said, his voice growing stronger and his eyes returning to Ti's face, "Joshua Maddox wouldn't let it end gracefully. He wrote me scathing letters, demanding that I return and marry his sister. His Southern cavalier's pride was hurt, and he wanted the marriage to take place, or to face me in a duel.

"When my tour ended and I returned home, rumblings of the war were strong. At Mountainview, I found my family afraid for the very future of the country. But they were also adamant that the way of the South was wrong. It was something we believed strongly in, and despised the system of slavery.

"A week later I received my orders to report for duty. I knew that war was coming. Before I left, I decided to see Amanda and tell her I couldn't marry her. I would face the Maddoxes and let their wrath fall where it would, but before I could say anything, Joshua informed me that he was leaving that very day to form his own Confederate company. He asked me to join it, and I refused.

"He was angered, and demanded to know why. I told him that I was already in the army of my choice. He went berserk, calling me a traitor, and attacked me. Before either of us was hurt, we were separated. But it was that day that I saw the madness in his eyes.

"He screamed and ranted and forbade my marriage to his sister. His father tried to stop Joshua, but couldn't, and finally told me that he agreed with his son. Joshua swore he'd avenge the insults to his family that he imagined me responsible for. I left after that, and did not return home until the war was a year old. Then I learned that Joshua had indeed avenged himself."

Ti stiffened when Arren spoke those last words. They'd come at her like a whip, and something within them wrenched at her heart.

"What happened?" she whispered tensely.

"Joshua Maddox and his Rebel company raided my plantation. He burned my home to the ground, killed my parents and took all the field hands and returned them to the slavery my family had freed them from years before."

"My God," Ti said, gazing into the misty depths of his eyes. "How could he?"

"It was then that I became a spy," he continued, ignoring her question. "Because of my accent and my background, it was easy to infiltrate the Southern armies. It was more difficult, but not impossible, to get the information out. That's how I've spent the last two and a half years of the war," he finished.

Ti, her mind overwhelmed by the mass of information she'd learned in the past half-hour, couldn't say anything. The pain, suffering and heartache that had poured from him had reached her and made her feel the same. Suddenly she was in his arms, holding him, and being held by him. For the first time in three weeks, Ti was in the arms of the man she loved, and nothing else mattered.

Their lips met and what started as a warm and gentle kiss soon turned into the fieriest of passions and the most tender of expressions. When they finally separated, both breathed deeply and the desire reflected on Arren's face was mirrored across Ti's.

Slowly Ti stood and looked around. Then she smiled and whispered, "Bath."

Arren rose with the folded blanket in one hand, and with his free hand took her to the edge of the river. There, with no embarrassment, they undressed and stepped into the waters of the Rio Grande.

The quarter-moon spilled silver light upon them, and the stars winked to accent the night. To Arren and Ti, the sky was a comforting sheet that enveloped them peacefully while they washed the day's dirt from each other's bodies.

Ti could not take her eyes from him; even while she lathered his broad back, she could not get her fill of looking at him. His smooth skin and taut muscles excited her and at the same time filled her with a sense of security she'd thought gone forever. Finally

Arren turned to her, and with hands far gentler than she ever thought possible, he lathered her skin and cleansed both her body and her mind.

When the soap was rinsed from their bodies, they stood silently in the waist-deep water. Time stood still as their bodies pressed together and their lips molded into one.

After an eternity, Arren lifted Ti and carried her to the waiting blanket. He placed her gently on it, and joined her there, pulling her against him and losing himself in the heat of her satin skin.

His mouth became a hungry searching entity that would not be denied. He kissed her deeply, then drew his lips from hers to travel along her damp neck, drinking the river's water from her skin and feeling the flaming satin respond to his touch. Greedily his mouth roamed across the breasts he'd dreamed of and needed, as he kissed and caressed them endlessly.

He reached one dark tip and slowly drew it into his mouth. Her hands wound through his hair, and her low cry floated to the stars. Ti's skin was alive beneath his hands and mouth, and Arren's passions soared.

His fingers traced random patterns on her stomach before dipping to the damp downy hair at the joining of her thighs. He caressed her firm thighs, savoring the feel of the creamy taut skin covering the muscles of her legs. Its smoothness drove him wild as he took her other nipple in his mouth and lavished it with love.

Ti could not lie still under his ministrations. Her desire, passion and love rose to command her actions and directed her trembling body to obey her mind. Her hand, still in his hair, demanded his attention. She forced his mouth from her breast and brought his lips to hers. She kissed him fiercely, as a deep moan rumbled in her throat. Then she moved, and suddenly Arren was lying on his back. She was above him, kissing him as her breasts were crushed against his chest.

Then it was she who tore her mouth from his and hungrily kissed his neck. She felt the corded muscles beneath his skin, and felt also the blood rush past her lips. She slid along his length, her lips caressing every inch of skin they could find, biting and teasing the heavy mat of hair covering his chest, until her mouth stopped on his own desire-hardened nipples. She kissed each one lovingly, drawing it into her mouth for a moment to tease it with her tongue before leaving it to go to the other.

But not even that satisfied her yearning to know every inch of him. She slid lower, her breasts rubbing along his length enticingly, her nipples getting even harder as her mouth and tongue lavished him with every caress possible. She outlined the ridges of his stomach muscles with more kisses, until her lips tasted the river's water within his dark curly hair, and she felt his manhood press against her hotly.

She could not stop herself from traveling farther down his body. Her fingertips caressed and massaged his strong inner thighs, and her lips followed their path. Her nails drew slow circles on his tender skin a moment before she nipped at a trembling muscle in his thigh. Then her hand rose to encircle his lengthening staff.

She felt a tremor flow through his body when she

grasped him, but paid it no heed. Her hand stroked his length, and the heat from his manhood turned her fingers to lava.

Her lips soon followed her hand, and she lavished him with more and more kisses, until his heated velvet spear seared her mouth and tongue.

Then Arren's hands were in her hair, and his hoarse moan covered them. Still she refused to follow his call as she showed him the full strength of her love. Then, maddeningly, she retraced her path toward his mouth, kissing the same muscles and skin as she tantalizingly covered his body.

With the moon washing them in gentle light, Ti rose and gazed deeply into Arren's eyes. "I love you," she whispered. "I want you," she cried.

Lowering herself to him, she accepted the hard lance of his manhood within her. Astride him at last, she cried out when they joined, and her mouth crushed harder against his. She stopped as heat flowed to every part of her body, and opened her eyes, drawing her mouth from his.

She saw him looking deeply into her eyes, while his hands stroked her back. Then she began to move upon him, and with each movement, a trembling, tingling wave of pleasure entered her. Ti rode him, filling herself with his hardness and giving him all her warmth. Suddenly she sat up straighter. Her body tightened, her neck arched and her head was flung back. Her eyes opened to see the stars whirling above her as incredible wave upon wave of flowing heat shot through her.

She gasped when Arren moved again, but he did not draw out from her. He sat, holding her to him, his mouth devouring the soft skin of her breasts.

Then his lips were on her neck and her breasts were pressed tightly to his chest as he sat up and pulled her against him. Her legs wrapped around his waist, locking tightly, and again the most intense of joinings seamed them together.

Arren took his mouth from her neck when her legs wrapped around his waist, and gazed into her open eyes. Their bodies were locked together, and their eyes glowed with love as they sat immobile.

"I love you," Arren whispered, half in plea, half in statement. He moved within her, his hands caressing her back firmly, his hips rising against hers. She felt the power and strength of her man within her, and joined with him to move upward on a heated soaring flight that brought them both to the highest peaks their love had ever known.

As they moved together as one, their eyes never closed, never wavered, while their bodies fulfilled the needs of each other. Then Arren's mouth closed on Ti's, and their tongues wove together. Her breasts were pressed tighter to him as they began another ascent to the heavens, climbing higher and higher above the world, until their bodies tensed, trembling when they exploded in a breath-shattering climax of love and sharing that bespoke to each of them, without the need for words, the depth and truth of their love.

Ti's head fell slowly to rest on Arren's shoulder, while her hands ceaselessly wandered along his back. Her breathing would not slow, nor would the rippling, flowing sensations filling her body ease. He still filled her with himself, and she refused to move.

Her breasts were on fire, and pressing them tighter against him did not help.

She lifted her head and kissed him deeply, before sliding her mouth along his cheek until she reached his ear. "I missed you, I love you and I will never let you go," she swore passionately.

Arren's hand went to her hair, and he gently but firmly drew her head back until she was looking at him. "For the rest of our lives," he stated. He kissed her deeply and tasted the warm sweetness of her lips and tongue. His breathing turned ragged, and the intensity and pleasure of her heat and moistness caressed him and coaxed him to grow stronger.

Again desire built and lent strength to his body. He moved quickly, spinning them, and lifting Ti without releasing her. Then they were lying down, with Arren above Ti, her legs still lightly locked and her hands pressing hard on his back.

A wave of passion flowed through Arren's mind, and he was again lost within the magnificence of the woman he loved. He moved slowly, thrusting gently, until he could not hold back, and as Ti urged him on with whispered cries and words, he let himself free, and guided them along another journey of love, until again they rose above the tallest peaks, joined together in love.

Their mingled cries reached out as Arren grew harder within her. Ti's hips thrust against his in a pattern as old as time, yet as new as their love. Everything was gone from her mind except the two of them. Suddenly her body tensed, and another volcanic eruption tore through her. She felt Arren explode again, filling her with warmth and heat, until they lay quiet and content beneath the warm western sky, their bodies bonded together, as were their hearts and minds.

Ti wiped the dust from her eyes and glanced around. They had been on the move for nine hours, and had stopped only once for the noon meal, before heading north again. The dropping sun no longer beat down unmercifully, and Ti gave silent thanks for that.

She was riding on the right flank with Arren and James. The herd was strung out for almost a half-mile, with the cowhands and soldiers flanking its edges, while the Rio Grande River did the same on the left. Of the four supply wagons, only two were being used for supplies. One held the five severely wounded men and the three less badly injured men who were watching over them. The fourth wagon held Maddox, whose flesh wound had not done much damage, and his men. One of Arren's men drove the wagon, while yet another rode behind it, his rifle always at the ready.

Throughout the morning and afternoon, whenever Ti passed near the wagon, she saw Maddox's hate-filmed eyes stare out at her. Whenever she passed the wagon, she shivered.

"We'll be in Albuquerque tomorrow afternoon," Arren said. "And you'll be able to sleep in a real bed."

"That would be nice," she replied wistfully. "And you? The men?"

"The hands will stay with the cattle tomorrow night, along with half my men. The others will come with us and bring Maddox to jail."

"How long will we be there?" she asked, gazing at

his blue eyes and trying hard not to fall under their spell.

"Two nights. Then I have to get on the trail again."

"We," she said quickly, challenging him with both her stare and her tone.

"We'll discuss it in Albuquerque," Arren said. Before Ti could reply, Arren spurred his horse toward one of the outriders.

"We!" she shouted to his retreating back. From the corner of her eyes she saw James staring straight ahead.

"Your friend doesn't like to lose an argument, does he?" she asked.

"Arren can be stubborn," James agreed.

"So can I," she warned.

"I've noticed," James said tersely. Then he too urged his horse away, but in the opposite direction from Arren.

Alone, Ti balled her fist ineffectually. Then she laughed. No matter what Arren thought, she was going all the way to California!

The night had descended quickly, and with it had come the cold air of the higher mountains. Ti had realized, as the miles had passed beneath Samson's hooves, that they had been going steadily into higher ground.

But it felt good to breathe the cool crisp air. The men sat around the cooking fires, keeping warm and drinking coffee. The atmosphere was lighter than yesterday, and Ti felt at peace.

"Coffee?" Arren asked.

"Thank you," she replied with a soft smile. She

watched him rise gracefully and walk to the fire. Then, as he spoke to one of the men, Ti sensed another presence beside her. She looked up into young Billy Raferty's face.

A familiar warmth filled her and she smiled broadly. "Good evening," she said.

"'Evening, Miss Ti."

"Come sit with me, we haven't had a chance to talk yet," she offered.

Billy smiled shyly and joined her on the ground. "I sure am glad you're safe," he said.

"I am too, and I'm glad you weren't in the middle of the fighting."

"I woulda liked to be, but Mr. Barkley sent me after the cattle," he said. The disappointment filling his voice was clearly discernible to Ti, who forced herself not to smile.

"It was for the best," she said, trying to comfort his young and wounded ego.

"Still, I coulda helped," he whispered. Hard determination replaced the disappointment, catching Ti off guard with its fierceness.

"There'll be other times, other places," Ti told him wisely. "How do you like being on the trail?"

"Just fine," he said, nodding enthusiastically. "I like it just fine. Miss Ti?" he asked, his voice changing suddenly when he spoke her name.

"Yes?"

"Do you love your father?"

Again Ti was caught off guard. She studied Billy's face intently before answering. "Very much."

"I loved my father, too," he whispered. "General Sam said my father was a brave man. Even when he died, he said he died like a true soldier."

"I know," Ti whispered. "Your father was a true soldier, and more."

"I ju . . ." Billy started to say, but stopped as Arren returned. "'Evenin', Mr. Barkley," he said. "I think I'll go check the horses now."

"You don't have to run off," Arren said as Billy rose. "I know you haven't had a chance to talk to Ti yet."

"That's all right, I just wanted to say hello." With a wave, Billy left, and Ti watched until his back faded into the darkness.

"I didn't mean to chase him away, he's a good boy," Arren said.

"He is. I don't think you chased him. We were having a very strange talk. I think he said more than he expected to, and you saved him from himself."

"Oh?" Arren questioned.

"He was talking about his father. Billy's father was on my father's staff. He died last year."

Arren stared at her for endless moments until finally he handed her the cup of coffee. "Raferty? William Raferty?" he asked.

"Yes. We called him Sarge from the time we could speak. He was always with my father." But Ti's voice faded when she saw Arren's eyes close. She waited, the coffee held an inch from her lips, until his lids were raised and he spoke.

"What does Billy know about his father's death?" he asked in a tight voice.

"That his father died bravely in battle against the enemy," Ti whispered, aware that something was wrong, but unsure what.

"He died bravely, but not on the battlefield as

everyone was told. He was killed in Richmond," Arren whispered.

Ti thought she was going to be sick as Arren's words reverberated against the walls of her mind. She too had read the letter her father had sent, commending his old friend for bravely facing the enemy, and dying under their onslaught.

"No. . . ."

"Yes. He was in Richmond, masquerading as a mercenary gun trader. His job was to sell ten thousand rifles to Lee. It was a brilliant plan. The Confederate Army needed the weapons desperately. So much so that they were willing to part with some of their very low supply of gold. The deal was made, and the delivery date was set. The rifles were crated and looked as if they'd just come from the factory. But each one was useless. The barrels were scored beyond repair."

Arren paused for another tortured breath and held Ti's gaze evenly while he spoke again. "Steven and I, plus two others, were on the boat bringing the weapons in. Just before we docked, we heard several shots. Raferty was on the edge of the dock, signaling us away. We held back, hoping he would dive into the water and swim to us. Instead, he turned and fired at the oncoming men, sacrificing himself to make sure we got away. Will Raferty died like a hero!"

"I never imagined. . . ." Ti's eyes filled with tears at the memory of the gruff sergeant she'd known all her life, and had loved second only to her father. "Poor Billy."

"When we reported what happened to your father," Arren continued, grasping Ti's hand within his, "he . . . he said thank you to Steven and me and asked us to leave. He locked his door, and no one saw him until three days later. Ti, your father loved William Raferty."

"We all did. Why didn't he write Billy the truth? There was nothing wrong with what happened."

"All of us who work for your father agree about one thing. If we're caught and die in enemy hands, our families are only to be told we died honorably on the battlefield. It's a kindness," he whispered.

Ti nodded slowly. "Arren, I love you," she whispered.

They sat like that for a long while, until Arren left her to talk with Lieutenant Tremain and make sure the watch duties had been assigned. When he returned, he smiled and lifted her to her feet. "Time for sleep," he said.

Ti agreed, and they went to their sleeping rolls, set up side by side, and succumbed to the call of their dreams.

A lone man's eyes searched the area furtively, and only when he was satisfied that the camp was asleep did he slink forward toward the two men whose backs were facing him.

The night was quiet. The only sounds were those of the cattle. Two guards sat side by side, keeping each other awake as they watched over the sleeping forms of their prisoners.

They heard nothing behind them, and only when a hollow thud echoed, and the guard on the left fell, did the other guard try to lift his rifle. Before he could, cold metal pressed against his ear.

"Ssshhh," was the only sound he heard. Then the

pistol barrel slowly drew away, and as the soldier breathed a tense sigh, it returned and another hollow thump sounded.

Still moving with the utmost stealth, the lone man returned his Colt to its holster and slipped the strap across its bone-handled butt. Drawing his knife, he watched it glint dangerously in the night. Carefully, slowly, he crept to the prisoners. When he reached Maddox, he stopped. He nodded, and his hand flashed. The heavy rope securing Maddox to the other prisoners parted quickly.

With his hands free, Maddox pointed to the only other prisoner whose wounds would not prevent escape. The man with the knife freed the other prisoner, and the three walked quietly away.

When they reached the edge of the camp, they stopped. "You have to stay," Maddox whispered.

The man nodded his acceptance.

"I'll be back for you, and to finish our job," Maddox promised as his hands went to the other's shoulders. "Be ready," he whispered.

As silent as he'd been earlier, the man returned to the camp and to his bedroll. He glanced at the prisoners lined against the wagon and saw the guards had not yet recovered. *Good,* he thought. A smile curved his lips as he fell into a dreamless sleep.

Chapter Thirteen

TI SANK INTO THE UNACCUSTOMED LUXURY OF THE bath and willed her muscles to relax within the soothing warmth of the water. After nine hundred miles of mountain and desert, Albuquerque was a paradise on earth. And the small hotel was the gateway to heaven.

Although the room itself was not large, it was pleasantly appointed. Ti's eyes swept across the papered walls, enjoying the artwork of European heraldry. There were many coats of arms she recognized from her early studies, and many more she'd never seen. A large oak dresser stood against one wall, and a simple but well-made four-poster bed was across from it. An upholstered chair was centered between the windows of the third wall.

The two curtained windows faced the plaza, and when she'd entered the room and gazed through them, she'd seen the staunch power of San Felipe, the large and multitiered church that was the oldest building in the small city, the Spanish settlers' original defense against Indian attacks.

Sinking deeper into the hot water, Ti closed her eyes and leaned her head back. When she did, thoughts of the day that had just ended returned, and with them came the memory of her harsh awakening in the early-morning hours before the sun had risen.

Anxious shouts yanked Ti from the comfort of her dreams. She sat up quickly, blinking and looking around. She saw Arren already standing, his Colt drawn. Ti slipped her Colt from its holster near her head and rose beside Arren. When she did, one of Arren's men ran up to them to report, "Maddox and another prisoner are gone. The guards were knocked out, one's hurt bad," he said.

A chill raced through Ti's mind, and she involuntarily shuddered. She saw Arren's face go tight, and his strong jaw jutted out angrily.

"Have the injured man taken care of. I want to see the other one. Lieutenant Tremain!" Arren shouted. A moment later the young officer stood before him. "I want five men ready to ride. Full gear!" he commanded.

"Yes, sir!" Tremain replied.

Arren, with Ti at his side, walked quickly to the two injured guards. One was still unconscious; the other sat on the ground holding his head. Ti bent to the unconscious man, and her fingers probed along his scalp until they felt dampness. "Light," she called.

In a moment one of the men returned with a

lantern and held it over them. While Ti looked closely at the soldier's scalp, she heard the guard's reply to Arren's rapid questions.

"His head is cut. It must be cleaned and bandaged," she informed the man holding the lantern.

"Yes, ma'am, I'll see to it," he said. He set the lantern on the ground and called out for bandages before he took over from Ti.

Ti stood and went to Arren's side, just as the guard finished his story: "We were watching the prisoners carefully. They all seemed asleep. And I . . . That's the last thing I remember," he said.

"All right, Marlowe, get some rest," Arren said in a tense but not unkind voice. Spinning on his heels, he walked back to his equipment, just as the five men Tremain had picked came over to him, leading their mounts.

"You can't track him without light," Ti said, half-running in her effort to keep up with him and trying to judge the time but failing.

"I don't have any choice. Or do you think it's better to have Maddox haunting us for the next five weeks?" he asked harshly.

"Arren!" Ti snapped.

He shook his head slowly and put his hand on her shoulder. "Sorry. I prefer waking in a different way," he said. Ti saw his features loosen, and the handsome lines of his face soften. Shaking his head, he bent to his equipment and strapped on his Colt. He reached into his small bag and withdrew a shiny round object. He opened the cover and Ti realized it was a watch.

He held it close to his eyes and read the time. "Light in an hour," he whispered.

Before Arren could mount his horse, another rider came up to them. Ti breathed a sigh of relief when she saw James Strong Blade astride his pony.

"They left the camp from the east. Two men went in one direction, one returned to camp," he told Arren.

Ti watched Arren's face but was unable to read the expression. Then Arren turned back to Tremain. "You know what to do," Arren said.

"Yes, sir," Tremain replied.

"And, Lieutenant, if we're not back by sunup, start the drive, we'll catch up." With the reins of his horse in his hand, Arren came to Ti. "I'll be back soon," he told her.

"Be careful," she whispered. She wanted to say more, but held herself back. She watched the seven men ride out, until they disappeared within the darkness surrounding the camp. When they were gone, she turned, wondering what to do and hoping that Arren would find Maddox quickly.

Maddox scared her. But she knew it wasn't the man she feared; rather it was the insanity that held him in its grip. Ti also realized that Maddox's escape meant that there was yet another spy among the men from Texas.

"What happened?" came a husky, sleep-riddled voice.

Ti turned to see Billy walking toward her, rubbing his eyes. She told him and watched as he shook his head. "Do you think the man who stayed to guard you at their camp helped them escape?" he asked.

"I don't know," Ti replied. She'd forgotten about her own jailer. Perhaps it had been he, and not someone from the camp. When Arren had sent two men back after the battle, they reported the man Ti had left bound to be gone. James might have been mistaken. She hoped so. But still her nerves screamed a warning, and Maddox's fanatical eyes loomed within the dark recesses of her mind.

When the sun rose and Arren had not yet returned, Tremain began the drive. Once again Ti tasted the dust that thousands of hooves raised.

Two hours later, Arren and his men returned, but Ti saw that James was not with them. After speaking with Tremain, he rode to Ti's side.

"What happened?" she asked.

"We lost their trail in the rocks."

"James?"

"He's still trying to find them."

"Arren, I was talking to Billy after you left, and he said something that made sense. Could the man who escaped from Maddox's camp have been the one to free him?"

Arren looked at her for a moment, his face thoughtful. "It's possible, but my instincts tell me it was someone here," he said.

Ti was about to say something else, when he leaned across the space between them and brushed her lips with his. Ti almost gasped when he did, and she felt the blood rise to her face. "Arren!" she hissed. "The men."

"Rank has its privilege," he said with a chuckle.

They gazed at each other for a few silent moments. "I hope you'll like living in California," he said suddenly. Before Ti could unfreeze her tongue, he whirled his horse and rode away.

A smile played at the corners of her mouth, and her mind spun madly. "Yes," she whispered, "I hope so too."

It was midafternoon when Arren called the second stop of the day. While the men began to make camp, she gazed out at the landscape.

The highest mountain she'd seen thus far on the drive rose hazily in the northeast distance. Then she looked west, and gasped. A ridge of lower mountains stretched out, and Ti saw by their shape that there were at least five volcanic tops.

She looked ahead, and again her breath caught. Spread out before her, for as far as she could see, was a valley. It was an arroyo formed between the old volcanic mountains and the eastern range holding the large hazy mountain. Then she knew she was seeing the Sandia Mountains and that Albuquerque was no farther than two hours away.

"It is magnificent," Arren said, and Ti drew her eyes from the sight and looked at him.

"Yes," she sighed.

"We'll be leaving in a little while. Why don't you get the mare while I give Tremain his orders," Arren suggested.

Ti stiffened, but forced herself to relax. "I won't need all my things. You said we're going to be there for only a day or two," she reminded him.

"Bring them anyway," he said.

Ti held his stare, not allowing herself to be intimidated by him. Then she smiled. "All right." She saw him blink and chase away the expression that had raced across his face at this small victory.

Arren started to say something, but changed his mind and rode toward the men. Only when he'd reached the men and started to give Lieutenant Tremain his instructions did Ti let her smile free.

"It's too late to stop me now, Mr. Barkley," she whispered. "I'm going to California with you."

Ten minutes later, with Kay's mare tied to hers, she, Arren and five of his men started for Albuquerque. In their midst, within the confines of two wagons, were the injured Federal soldiers and the Confederate prisoners.

When Albuquerque loomed nearer, Ti turned to Arren. She had one question that was unresolved. "What if James finds them?"

"He'll track them until he knows where they're going and then join us," Arren informed her.

"I hope he'll be all right."

"He will. He knows we need him to finish our mission."

"Why are we coming to Albuquerque? Isn't it a waste of time? You could be hundreds of miles closer." She watched him for a moment, hoping his reason for coming here wasn't just to bring her to safety.

"Between the Comanche and the Cherokee, almost all the western posts are running out of supplies. The army has sent as many men as could be spared to help, but the supply trains are continually attacked. Your father instructed me to deliver half the herd here for distribution in the western territories. I'm also picking up another detachment of troops for California."

Then everything fell into place. Especially the reason for splitting the herd. Ti nodded slowly, and smiled as her own fear of being left behind diminished, but did not leave.

Further conversation ended as Albuquerque came into view. The first sights were of low scattered adobe and wood buildings. When they passed these structures, Ti gazed at Albuquerque for the first time.

It was not a large city, more the size of a small town, but Ti knew it was the largest settlement in New Mexico. Many small brownish adobe homes were scattered around the road leading to the larger homes and the center of town. Once they passed these, Ti could see the bell tower of a church rising into the air.

"San Felipe," Arren said to her. He told her of its history until they reached the plaza and stopped. Ti saw many buildings surrounding the squared center; among them were several businesses, shops, and a two-story hotel, all built from the same adobe clay. Across from where they stood, the Federal flag flew proudly in the wind; below it was the large low building of the Federal army post.

Arren gave the command, and the small band started toward the post. When they reached it, two sentries greeted them and Arren presented his papers. A moment later a blue-and-gold-uniformed colonel walked out to greet them.

From that point on, everything happened with fast military precision, and a half-hour later, Ti, escorted by both Arren and Colonel Barstow, the post's commander, went to the hotel, where they left her to refreshen and change. Dinner had been arranged for eight in the hotel's dining room.

A few minutes after Ti had reached her room, there was a knock on her door. She opened it and found two Indian women standing in the hall. They nodded and brought in the tub she had requested. They left, only to return with pitcher upon pitcher of water. When the tub was filled, but before Ti undressed, yet another knock sounded.

When she opened it, she saw the hotel owner's smiling face. "Excuse me, señora, the colonel sent this over for you," he said, handing her a parcel.

"Thank you," Ti replied. After she closed the door, she opened the package and smiled. In it was a simple cream-colored dress and petticoat. She spread the dress out on the bed, and with no further thoughts about anything other than the hot water awaiting her, she stepped into the tub.

A low knock on her door pulled her thoughts back, and she asked who it was. She didn't hear the words, but recognized the voice as a woman's.

She stood quickly in the now almost dark room and wrapped the waiting bath sheet around her. Going to the door, Ti opened it just enough to see an Indian maid holding a lighted taper. She opened the door, and the woman walked to the sconce on the near wall and lit the candle. She repeated that three more times, until the room glowed with soft, warm light. When the Indian left, Ti began to dress.

It was a simple enough dress, with a high bodice reaching to her neck, and close-fitting sleeves that buttoned at her wrists. The petticoat fit well, but the dress was too large around her waist, and the hem swept the floor.

Looking around, Ti tried to think of a way to fix it. Her eyes landed on her saddlebags, and she went to them and rummaged until she withdrew a wide belt. She lifted the waist of the dress until the hem was at the proper length, then tucked it under and pinched the extra material at the side of her waist, folding it back until the true narrowness of her waist showed.

She nodded to herself as she looked down, then paused, confused. Both hands were occupied with the material, and she had no way of putting on the belt.

"Damn!" she spat, unwilling to release the dress and start anew.

Again, there was yet another knock on the door. "Come in!" Ti shouted, anger filling her voice.

The door opened, and Arren entered with a puzzled look on his handsome face. "You look lovely," he said, gazing with approval at the dress's fit.

"And in order to stay looking nice, you'll have to feed me. Ohhh!" she spat. "Don't stand there gawking, help me."

"Yes, ma'am," Arren said with a smile. He walked to her and slowly lowered his lips on hers. He kissed her deeply, and drew her tight against him. The heat of her lips and the softness of her breasts on his chest sent sparks of desire shooting through him.

Ti tore her mouth from his forcefully. "Let me go!" she cried. Arren released her and she almost fell. "The belt!" she said.

Arren smiled at her again and took a step forward.

"Arren . . ." Ti warned, taking another step back.

His smile grew wider as he gazed at her. "Do you

know," he began, taking his time and watching her fidget before him, "this is the first time, since the moment I met you, that you're helpless?" Then he took one more threatening step forward.

"Not for long," she warned. She tried to move back farther, but the dresser blocked her retreat. Drawing her shoulders straighter, she defied him with her eyes.

"Do you know," he said again, "that you and your sisters share a common trait?"

"Really?"

"Really. You love to make threats!"

"Arren!"

"In a minute. Let me enjoy myself," he said as he crossed the last foot that separated them. Then he was against her.

Ti, still refusing to release the waist of her dress, tried to hold back, but when his lips gently kissed hers, her willpower fled and she moaned in defeat.

The kiss lasted forever, and her blood flowed heatedly. At last Arren drew away and walked to the bed. When he held the belt in his hand, he looked at her seriously. "You affect me strangely. You bring out the best in me, and the worst."

Before Ti had a chance to reply, Arren came back to her and slipped the belt around her waist. He buckled it, and as Ti released the material, slid the belt down.

"Thank you," she snapped.

"You're very welcome," he whispered.

"Well?"

"Well what?" he asked, puzzled.

"How do I look?" she said, emphasizing her

question with a downward swing of her hands along the dress.

"Shall I show you?" he asked as he started to embrace her.

Ti spun away, laughing as she neatly evaded his hands. "I'm pleased you like it. Shall we go?"

"Of course," Arren said. He took her arm in his, and together they left the room.

By the time they reached the dining room, Arren had told Ti that they would be eating with Colonel Barstow and another officer. Arren's tone when he mentioned the other man sounded off key to her attentive ears, but she withheld her questions.

The dining room was a nice size, with candles flickering along the walls, illuminating the room, and the people in it, with a soft glow. When they entered, Ti saw Colonel Barstow stand and wait for them. At his side, another officer rose.

Ti looked at the new face but did not recognize it. The officer had longer hair than was usual, and the lines of his face were severe.

At the table, before they sat, Colonel Barstow made the introductions. "Miss Bennett," he said with a smile, "Colonel Christopher Carson, commander of the First New Mexico Cavalry."

Ti extended her hand, and felt it grasped securely by the other. "A pleasure," she said.

Arren held Ti's chair, and when she was seated, he sat between her and Colonel Carson. After she sat, she thanked Colonel Barstow for the dress.

"I'm just glad you managed to make it look so lovely, Miss Bennett." Then Colonel Barstow lifted an unmarked bottle of wine from the table's center and filled each glass. Ti was suddenly conscious of a strange tension at the table. She saw Arren lift his glass and repeat the ritual he had performed at the ranch in Texas.

He sniffed the wine, and glanced at Barstow. Then he raised the glass another inch to take the barest of sips. He let the wine run across his tongue, holding it in his mouth for a moment before swallowing. When he put the glass down, he nodded to Barstow. "Bordeaux region, fifty-five or fifty-six," he said.

Ti blinked at his words and almost spoke, but Barstow's laugh stopped her. She looked at the officer and then at Arren and the smile covering his face.

"Fifty-five," Barstow said. "Kit, you owe me another five," he told Colonel Carson.

"Major Barkley, I hope it's at least five years before we see each other again," Carson said. Then he drew a gold coin from his pocket and handed it to Barstow.

"I'd think you would know better by now," Arren told Carson, but Ti sensed something deeper behind his words, more of a dislike of the man than his light tone showed.

Before anything else was said, an Indian woman came over to the table and began to put plates before them. "I hope you don't mind, but the menu is limited, so I took the liberty of ordering," Colonel Barstow explained to Ti.

The meal was good, if not elaborate; the conversation was about the war and its eventual outcome. Later, when coffee was served, the conversation veered, and Colonel Carson took the lead. He spoke about the visions of the future, when the war would be over, and the probable migration of thousands of people westward. He spoke eloquently, and Ti was drawn into the power of his feelings. But while he spoke on, she was aware of certain deviations within his words.

"But if, as you say, there will be thousands of people settling New Mexico and Arizona, what will happen to the Indian lands?" She asked the question directly and innocently, and was not prepared for either the vehemence of his words or Arren's quick kick to her shin under the table.

"Indian lands?" Carson asked. "What right do they have to lands? Every person who comes west, comes in fear of his life. We've tried to be reasonable with them, but for the most part, all we get for our efforts are more dead settlers. The Apache are bloodthirsty killers, and the rest of the Indian nations follow their lead. We have no choice but to fight them as mercilessly as they fight us!"

"Surely, Colonel Carson," Ti said when he'd finished his tirade, "there must be a way to solve the problems between the Indians and ourselves peacefully."

"I'm afraid not," Carson replied tersely.

"Kit," Barstow cut in as he glanced at Arren, "has just received orders from Washington. It seems that too many troops are being drawn from the war to help us out here. He has been ordered to subdue all hostile Indian nations."

"By force, I suppose?" Arren asked as he glared at Carson.

"If necessary. I'm awaiting the arrival of mountain howitzers. When they arrive, I have seven hundred men ready to ride. By the end of the year, New Mexico will be cleared of all hostile Indians!"

"Hostile Indians, or all Indians?"

"Barkley, everyone is familiar with your love for the red man. And especially for your *brother*. I think any further discussion between us would be pointless." Carson rose and bowed to Ti. "Miss Bennett, I'm sorry to have lost my temper. Please give my regards to your father. Good night," he said.

"Arren," Barstow said as he exhaled forcibly, "I thought you promised not to get into an argument with him?"

"Sorry, John," Arren replied while he shook his head. "I'm just tired of listening to his bigoted words. I imagine one day Kit Carson will be hailed as a great hero."

"Most likely. Arren, he's got a tough job. And yesterday, when the dispatches came in, he received orders to negotiate a treaty with the Navajo or chase them out. Washington wants their lands."

"They'll never get them. The Navajo won't leave their lands. And the Canyon de Chelly is almost impregnable."

"I know, that's why he's waiting for those howitzers."

"Damn!" Arren's open palm slapped the table angrily. "Can't we stop it somehow?"

"I wish we could, but try to tell that to the bureaucrats and politicians. All they want is fertile land to offer the settlers. No, we can't stop it from happening."

Throughout the conversation, Ti sat immobile,

watching Arren's anger grow and understanding perfectly what he was thinking.

"Arren, when are you planning on pulling out?" Barstow asked, deftly changing the subject.

"Tomorrow," he said. "The men are ready?"

"They're camped in the North Valley. Captain Stevenson is waiting at the post to speak with you."

When Arren had said "tomorrow," Ti caught her breath. He'd told her they would be staying for two days. Why had he changed his mind?

"Then I think we should go over there. Ti," Arren said, turning to her and smiling, "would you like to join us?"

Ti was momentarily taken aback by the offer. She had already started to think of a way to accompany him there tonight. She wanted to know every detail of what was happening. "Yes, thank you."

When they left the hotel, the church bells began to toll the hour, and Ti was surprised to find it was already eleven o'clock.

It was after midnight when Arren escorted Ti back to the hotel. She had sat silently while the officers spoke. She listened intently to the plans of the coming battle and its hoped-for effects on the Confederacy. Then, while Ti waited in the colonel's office, Arren and the other two men went to speak with the prisoners. When they returned, Ti and Arren said good night.

Ti stopped in front of the hotel and faced Arren. "Why are we leaving tomorrow? You told me we'd be here for two days," she challenged.

"*I*. Kit Carson changed my plans."

"*We*. How did he do that?"

"*I* am leaving tomorrow. *You* are staying. And Carson changed my plans by what he told us tonight."

"*We* are leaving together. About the Navajo?" Ti asked, realizing fully the extent of what Kit Carson had said. "James . . ." she whispered.

"Exactly."

"But what can we do?" she asked, suddenly very worried.

"I don't know yet, but James and I will work something out," he promised. Ti saw the determination in his eyes, and knew he would do whatever possible to help his friend.

"He was referring to James when he said your 'brother'?"

"Yes. James and I are blood brothers. We have been since we were sixteen. That's why I'm leaving tomorrow. It gives me another day's head start. Carson won't get his cannons for another month. I need that time."

"We," Ti repeated. "Arren, let's go upstairs."

"I," he reiterated quietly before taking her arm and leading her inside.

At the door to her room, she turned to face him. Gently she lifted herself onto her toes and kissed him.

"Ti," he whispered, pulling her close, "when this is over . . ."

"No more talk. Are you coming in?" she asked, her eyes locking with his. He gazed at her for several moments before he nodded.

Inside, only one candle still burned, casting subtle shadows over them as they kissed deeply. The room was quiet, and the only sounds were of their breathing and the rustle of clothing. At last they entered the bed, and in a gentle, wondrous moment out of time, joined together in love, until their mingled cries reached out to the night. A few minutes later, Ti and Arren fell asleep within the comfort and security of each other's arms.

Chapter Fourteen

TI WOKE WITHIN THE WARMTH OF ARREN'S EMBRACE. She stayed still, content and satisfied for this moment. But even while she lay there, his words of last night returned. He was no less adamant about her staying than she was about going. She knew it must be resolved this morning, one way or another.

She moved carefully, and as Arren sighed and turned onto his back, she shifted to rest her head on his chest. Listening to the strong, even sound of his heart, she tried to think of anything but the days ahead.

Then his hand moved and caressed her back. Ti kissed his chest lightly before lifting her head. "Good morning," she whispered. Even in the dull gray predawn light, she could see the sapphire glint in Arren's eyes.

"Good morning," he said with a smile. He kissed her gently and drew her tightly to him. The feel of her full naked breasts against his chest was comforting as well as exciting. But Arren held his desire in check, sending his passion away as he took his lips from hers. He didn't want to make love to her now, not before leaving. And after the perfection of last night, he wanted no hurried coupling to interfere with his memories.

What they'd shared last night was too important. He would wait until the time came when they would spend their lives together. "I will return to you," Arren said in a husky voice.

"No," Ti stated, shaking her head and pulling away from him. "I'm going with you!" She had not raised her voice, but the power within it echoed plainly in the room.

"Dammit, Ticonderoga Bennett, you're as stubborn as the fort you were named after. I will not have you exposed to more danger. I want you alive so that we can be married and live full lives!"

"And I feel the same!" she shot back. "Arren Campion Barkley, I am not going back east. And if you think so, you are badly mistaken!"

"No! I can't fight a battle and worry about whether you're safe or not at the same time. Ti, if I must have John throw you into the stockade, I will! You are not going to California!" he stated in a loud, harsh voice. Ti turned from him suddenly, her pain and hurt welling up uncontrollably. She stared at the wall, her naked back to him.

After a minute of deadly silence, she took a deep breath. "All right, Arren, if that's what you want," she whispered. Then his hands were on her shoulders, and she jumped from the bed. She walked five feet before turning back to face him. "I love you, and I will listen to you," she said.

Her voice was unemotional, almost sweet, and Arren felt a warning jar his mind. She had given in too easily. When he spoke, his voice was low and wary.

"Ti, the next stage of the journey is going to be hard. We have to go through Arizona, and then cross the Mojave. When we get there, we have to face the Confederate troops. It's no place for a woman."

"I said I won't argue with you. Besides being a woman, I'm a trained soldier. I can obey orders," she said in a level voice.

"Ti, what are you going to do?"

"Do?" she replied innocently. "What you asked. I will stay behind."

"Don't lie to me," he growled.

"Damn you, Arren," Ti spat angrily, "you just told me why you don't want me with you. I agreed. What more do you want?"

"Your promise."

"Arren," she said, drawing in a deep breath and crossing her arms over her bare breasts, "you gave me several valid reasons for not being with you. I won't argue with you, I said, even if I feel exactly the same way you do, even if it is I who have to worry whether you live or die."

Arren shook his head and left the bed. He stood next to Ti and his hands went to the satiny skin of her back, pulling her to him. When their bodies met, and her arms went around him, he spoke again. "I still want your promise."

Ignoring the fiery heat of their contact as it raced through her, Ti smiled at him and nodded. "I promise I won't go with you this morning."

Angrily he flung her from him. He glared at her silently for a moment before turning and going to the window.

She watched him stare out, but did not move. Then an unreasonable and savage anger gripped her and she stalked to him. He stood still, as if he'd not heard her move. "Arren!" she hissed.

Still he refused to move.

"Damn you! Turn around!" she yelled as her fists pummeled his back.

Still he refused to move.

"I won't have you killed on me! I won't!" she screamed. Then tears rose and spilled from her eyes. A wrenching sob tore from deep within her. Slowly, as her fists stopped their attack on his unprotected skin, she sank to the floor. "I promise," she whispered finally.

Arren withstood the punishment of her fists, holding himself in check, fighting the fierce emotions that assaulted his every sense. His love for her, and for her strength, was fast overwhelming him. Yet he knew he must wait silently until her rage burned out. But when she'd stopped, and he'd heard the heart-rending sob come from her throat, he could not stay immobile.

"No," he said, lifting her from the floor to hold her to him. "No, don't promise what you can't do. There will be no lies between us!" he told her in a barely audible, husky whisper.

Ti gazed at him while his words echoed in her

mind, and she realized what he'd said. Then, clearing the mists that veiled her eyes, she smiled. Then she gasped. Carefully, with her heart pounding, she kissed away the wet paths that streaked his cheeks.

"As much as you love me, I love you," she said.

"I know," he said. "That's why I can't fight you anymore."

"I must be with you," she said.

"I know." Arren took a deep breath and shook his head. "Your father will court-martial me and throw me in jail."

"He'll have to fight me first," Ti replied, half-seriously.

Arren's smile turned into a laugh that he had trouble containing. When he'd gotten himself under control, he stroked Ti's long blond waves. "That would be a fight I would love to see," he told her. "But if we don't get dressed, we're going to be in even more trouble."

"Yes, sir!" Ti said, stepping back and saluting smartly.

"Ti," Arren whispered, his mouth suddenly dry at the sight of her standing before him, her breasts bobbing gently and crying out to be kissed.

"I'm going," she cried. The change in his eyes hastened her move toward her clothing.

The day turned hotter as the long line of men crossed the Colorado River and entered California. At the head of the troops rode Arren Barkley, Ti Bennett and James Strong Blade.

It had been a grueling journey which had eaten away another three weeks, but because they had not been held back by a herd of cattle, they'd crossed the mountains in a direct line toward their destination. And because they were traveling faster, Arren had been able to warn James of Carson's plans and give him the opportunity to warn his people. Although he knew that in doing so he risked his life and his rank, there were certain things Arren would not sit idly by and let happen, especially to someone he loved.

He had been gone three days while the men and Ti rested at the outpost known as Fort Defiance. When they resumed the trail, James had returned. But Arren and Ti had seen in his face that his people would not leave their lands in order to save themselves. They would defend their land, and die if necessary.

From that point, James had become quieter than usual, and Ti's heart broke with the knowledge of what faced him.

But aside from that, and the company of almost a hundred and fifty men, Ti found each day to be more beautiful than the last, and with each beautiful day her love for Arren grew without restraint.

Although they could not share their bodies and express their love in that way, just being with him was all that mattered for now. There would be other times, in the years ahead, but at present all she wanted was to be within sight of him.

Ti twisted farther in her saddle and looked behind her. One man waved, and Ti waved back. She felt good, seeing Billy and fifteen of the original thirty ranch hands who had started the drive.

When they'd left Albuquerque and returned to

the herd, Arren had called all the cowhands together. He'd confirmed to them what they'd already surmised. Then he explained that for them the drive was over. They would be quartered at the army post and, at the proper time, sent back to Texas. He'd also told them that they would receive their full pay, as if they'd finished the trail drive in California. Then he'd thanked them.

When he'd finished, and the men had spoken together, half of them had come to him and, with Billy among them, volunteered to go to California with Arren and fight with him.

Ti had been surprised by this offer, but when she'd gazed at their faces, she'd seen the r pect they all held for Arren.

Arren had been moved by this unexpected offer, and had agreed to take them along. "I need every man I can get. If we win in California, the war will end much sooner," he'd told them. Later he'd told Ti that he trusted the men who were staying, especially since each of the hands had been working for the Bennett family since before the war. He had not thought any of them to be the spy who'd freed Maddox.

When Captain Stevenson and his hundred men arrived, the ranch hands who were not continuing on had been escorted by Federal troops to Albuquerque.

Then, when all was ready, Arren signaled the men on, and they'd begun their long trek.

"We should camp here," James said, drawing Ti from her thoughts.

"It's still early," Arren protested.

"We are only a short distance from the spot where

your other men are to meet us. I think it would be wise for us to ride alone and see them," James said pointedly.

Ti sensed something pass between the men a bare second before Arren nodded, and intuitively knew the plans had changed. Arren turned to the two officers who rode behind him, and signaled them forward.

"We'll make camp here," he told Stevenson and Tremain. "I'll be back shortly." They saluted smartly and wheeled their horses about. Then, as their orders sailed through the air, Arren turned to Ti, but her face stopped him from speaking.

"I'm going too," she stated, anticipating his words.

"Not this time," he whispered. "We need to be alone."

Ti stared at him for a moment before looking at James. Then she understood exactly what the change in plans would be. Nodding her head, she urged Samson next to James.

"Thank you," she whispered, fighting the moisture her emotions brought out.

"As Arren is my brother," he said in a low voice, "so too are you my sister."

"Be swift, be sure, be brave," Ti intoned, repeating to James the very words he'd spoken to her on the morning of Maddox's attack. "Good-bye, James Strong Blade. And may your gods stand behind you in your time of need."

Then they were gone. Ti watched until they were out of sight before riding back to where the troops were setting up camp.

*　*　*

A half-hour after leaving the bank of the Colorado River, Arren and James crested a small hill and looked down upon the second half of Sam Bennett's herd. Fifteen thousand head of cattle grazed on the last vegetation they would have for the next twelve days. General Bennett and he had estimated at least a third of the steers would die crossing the Mojave, but it was necessary and would be done.

Besides the thirty men who had started west with the steers in New Mexico, and the ten Indians who had guided them, another fifty Federal soldiers had joined them, bringing Arren's command to over two hundred men. When Arren reached San Marcos with the cattle, another hundred specially trained troops would be joining him. If, he reminded himself, everything went according to plan.

"Shall we?" Arren asked.

"No. It is time. Arren, I cannot delay longer. You know that," James said.

"Yes," he admitted. He looked deeply into his friend's eyes, imprinting every feature of his warrior's face within the sanctity of his mind. "James . . ."

"You have already lost much, but you have found much too. Your life will be full. Arren, do not become as the others," James whispered.

"I shall not."

"They come," James said, turning to watch the arrival of the Indian guides. Arren held back the words he wanted to say, as the mixed group of Apache and Navajo rode up and stopped in a semicircle around Arren and James.

One Apache brought his pony forward. Arren

recognized him as one of Cochise's subchiefs. He stopped his pony when he was three feet from Arren. When he spoke, it was in the Chiricahua dialect that Arren understood.

"Cochise has sent a message. It is for you to pass on," he said in a low voice. Arren saw the intensity in the warrior's eyes and in the tight set of his mouth. "Never again will the Apache help the white man. Never again will a white man pass safely through the lands of the Apache or their friends!"

Arren was startled, both by the man's words and by the hatred behind them. "Goyathlay, what has happened?"

"Never call me by the name I was given at my birth! Goyathlay is dead! Only *Geronimo* lives. You, your men and your cattle are alive today because Cochise gave his word to the Navajo. Mangas Color-adas has been taken by your soldiers under a flag of peace. We know he will never return alive. Only Black Kettle and the Cheyenne still believe they can trust the white man." With that, Geronimo whirled his pony and returned to the others.

Arren, fear coursing through his mind with this latest of follies by the army, turned back to James. "Will they help your people?" he asked.

"If there is time. Arren, I hope that one day we will ride together again."

"I will do what I can to stop this insanity."

"Nothing will stop it. I saw that when I lived with you. The whites want land, anyone's land. To them, we are inferior. Good-bye, my brother," James said, stretching out his arm and clasping his fingers around Arren's firm biceps.

Arren returned the farewell, and as he grasped

James's sinewy arm, he spoke in a low voice. "Be swift, be brave, be sure," he whispered.

"And you," James replied. Then their hands loosened, and James joined the other Indians. Together, with James and Geronimo leading the way, the Indians rode east.

Arren watched until he could no longer bear to think of his loss. With a heavy heart he rode toward the camp and the cattle.

Darkness came swiftly on the California desert, and Ti, sitting next to Arren, maintained her silence after Arren had told her of James's departure and Geronimo's chilling words.

A few minutes later, Ti took a deep, preparatory breath and spoke. "When your mission is over, we will go to my father. He will do something!"

"Not even you or your father can stop the future. There are too many people who want the land for themselves. There is nothing we can do."

"But—"

"No, Ti, listen to me. Remember James, and remember the strength of his people. We will honor his memory, not by begging, but by understanding."

Ti held Arren's hand within hers, lifted it and kissed it gently. "I will remember," she promised.

"How bad will the trip across the desert be?" she asked.

"Bad. We have a hundred-odd miles of waste to cross. We'll travel mostly at night, and let the cattle rest in the heat of the day. Our seven wagons of grain and the other wagons of water will help. I only hope they'll be enough."

"Arren, can we walk alone tonight?" she asked.

He studied her shadowed features and slowly nodded. They stood and walked along the bank of the Colorado River until they found a private place hidden from the eyes and ears of the troops, and came together, in love and need, until they were both spent and had eased their sadness and worries by sharing themselves and their love.

Chapter Fifteen

LUCK HAD BEEN WITH THEM, AND TEN DAYS AFTER entering the Mojave, they reached its western tip. Ten days of brutal heat they had forced themselves to sleep in. Ten nights of blackness in which they'd driven the cattle mercilessly, doing their best to keep the large herd together and pushing forward over the hard-baked land.

Arren's and General Bennett's estimate of losses was accurate, with almost five thousand head perishing in the waterless expanse. But they had been lucky. Eighty miles into the desert, they'd come across an abandoned Indian well that still contained water. They spent a sleepless day refilling their water barrels and skeins, as well as breaking down two wagons and keeping them filled with water so that as many head as could be reached were given the life-nurturing liquid.

But even though they traveled in the cool of the night, the day took its toll on everyone. Tempers were short, and except for the discipline of the professional soldiers, the desert crossing would have become a rolling disaster.

But they had survived, and lost not a single man, when the green California mountains finally beckoned to the ragged troop and their quarter-mile-wide herd.

It was dawn of the eleventh day when Ti saw the hazy edge of the mountains. At first she thought she was imagining them. But when Arren rode up to her, she saw the expression on his face and knew the end was within reach.

"Will we stop for the day?" she asked.

"No. That range is close. We can reach it by midday, and the lake at its base," he informed her. "You did well, Ti," he whispered gently.

"There are only two things I want right now," she replied, accepting the compliment gracefully. She waited for a moment, and spoke only after his eyebrows rose, commanding her to continue. "The first is a bath!"

"The second?"

Instead of replying, she lowered her head and looked at him through almost closed lids.

"I see," he replied, his voice turning husky. "You are insatiable, you know."

"In many things, Arren, in many things," she said with a smile.

Captain Stevenson rode up to them, drawing their attention from each other to the job at hand. "Sir?" he inquired.

"We'll go on. And, Alan, I want three men riding point. I don't want any surprises."

"Yes, sir!" he said. Stevenson wheeled his horse

about and called out three of his men. They came to him, listened to his orders, and a moment later rode toward the mountains.

Two hours later, one rider returned. He went directly to Arren and reported in. When he was finished, the three officers' faces were etched with relief. Everything was clear, and there were no signs of any large bands of men or horses.

By noon the herd was drinking from the crystal water of the lake and grazing along its pasturelike shore. The men had made camp, and once the noon meal had been cooked and eaten, the officers had assigned watch patrols, and the rest of the men crawled into their bedrolls for a much-needed sleep.

Ti watched it all while she drank a cup of coffee. When the officers finished their meeting, Arren came over to her and sat. "We'll stay here today and tonight, and tomorrow we'll push on for San Marcos. We should be there in three to four days."

"There will be men at the ranch?" she asked, thinking about the herd's final destination for the first time.

"Your father explained to me that it is already a working ranch. This herd will be added to the others."

"It seems so long ago that he bought the ranch, and at the time, I didn't care. I thought he was being foolish to have unsupervised property."

"Your father plans for the future with the same tenacity he uses to plan the strategies of a war. He's one of the few men whose intelligence I respect totally," Arren admitted. "But I still don't understand why he named you after a fort."

Ti laughed and shook her head quickly. "My

mother told me they fought for a month about my name, but he refused to give in. He is a scholar of the Revolution, and loved the forts of the time. He told my mother that Ticonderoga was the only fort with integrity, with an unyielding personality that survived all changes until victory came, and he expected his daughter to be the same."

"He wasn't wrong," Arren said in a deep, serious voice.

"But," Ti continued, "Mother refused to accept another fort in lieu of a daughter. Jenna and Kay escaped my fate."

"Do you mind?"

"Not now. When I was young and living in Philadelphia, I hated it. I was teased a lot, but now I like it."

"So do I." Then, without regard to the men surrounding them, he leaned forward and kissed her warmly. When he drew back, he smiled at the surprise and sudden flush that rose on her face.

"Do you still want that bath?" he asked. The brightness reflecting on her face was answer enough. "Sergeant Lowell and a few of the men are going to look around the area with me. If I can find a place that's private enough, I'll take you there when we get back. In the meantime, get some rest," he ordered gruffly.

"Yes, sir!" she replied. By the time Arren and his men rode out of camp, Ti had fallen asleep on top of her bedroll.

High above the lake, hidden within the cover of the trees, three men gazed down at Arren's camp and the men sleeping within it.

"We could raid them tonight," said one. "It would be easy."

"No. Not yet. We have to find out how much they know, and how many more troops will be joining them."

"Captain," protested the first man, "we can hurt them bad. It's too good an opportunity."

Joshua Maddox lowered his binoculars and turned his bloodshot eyes on the speaker, waiting until the man's gaze wavered. "I have been put in charge of this campaign, and I make all the decisions. Do you understand?"

"Yes, sir," he said, backing down and pulling his eyes from Maddox's.

"Very good. Ashford," he said, turning to the man on his left, "do you see him?"

"Yes, sir, he's riding on the far edge, keeping the cattle confined."

"Good, get down to him, unseen, and give him his orders. Tell him to do exactly as I've said."

"Yes, sir," replied Ashford. Maddox and the other officer watched the third man make his way down the wooded mountain and head toward the cowboy. A half-hour later they watched Ashford give the man his orders and then slip away as quietly as he'd come.

"Soon, Barkley," Maddox whispered. "Soon."

Ti was called up from the depths of sleep by gentle butterflies wandering along her face. She opened her eyes and saw Arren's face. Reaching up, she stroked his cheek tenderly, forgetting where they were and who was with them.

"I love you," she whispered.

"And I you," he replied in a low voice. "Come," he said.

The sun was dropping behind the mountaintops, painting the sky and the land with golden hues as Ti sat up. Most of the men were still sleeping, and the cooking fires were not yet replenished.

Standing, Ti stretched languidly, aware of Arren's eyes roaming freely along her body. It made her feel good, the way he looked at her, even if the clothing she wore was filthy and sweat-stained. "Did you find anything?" she asked. She saw his quick nod, and the slight frown on his tired but handsome face, and waited for him to speak.

"There have been others here recently, but nothing seems of any importance. Prospectors, I would imagine."

"And a place for me to bathe?"

"Yes. About a quarter of a mile west is where the lake is fed from the mountains. There's a small pool there."

"Good. I'll go now," she declared as she bent to her bags and searched for the soap and the one clean top she had left.

"I'll go with you," he told her. But Ti heard the depth of tiredness that filled his voice, and when she stood again, she challenged him in stance and words.

"No, sir, not this time, Major Barkley! You are going to lie down and get some sleep."

Arren stared at her for a moment, wanting to argue, but the very tiredness she'd seen in his face stopped him. He smiled gently at her. "Yes, ma'am," he replied. "But take someone to stand watch, I don't want you alone—there's still something not right, I feel it," he whispered fiercely.

Hearing the intensity of his words, Ti went to him and embraced him. "I'll take someone, but you sleep, you need the rest." She kissed him lightly and pointed to the bedroll she had spread out for him earlier.

Arren lay back and his eyes followed Ti. He saw her speak to Billy, and a moment later they rode out. Then he closed his eyes, trying to banish the feeling of wrongness hovering over him since he'd ridden out two hours ago.

Ti and Billy followed the edge of the lake until she found the off-branch going inland that Arren had told her of. Taking the lead, Ti guided Samson through the thickset trees until she reached the small pool. When she did, she sighed contentedly. Arren had found the perfect place. One side was a solid rock wall, its rough face glistening under the stream of water falling from its top, creating a small but lovely waterfall.

She looked around, trying to decide where Billy could stay while she bathed. But before she found a spot for him, Billy spoke.

"Miss Ti, why don't I go back a piece, near the lake. If'n you need me, I'll hear you," he assured her.

"All right, Billy. And, Billy," she said, smiling at the maturity that had grown on his face since they'd left the ranch, "thank you, I appreciate your being with me throughout the drive."

"Yes, ma'am, I'm real glad also. I think Pa would be pleased too," he said before leaving, and giving Ti privacy for her bath.

Undressing quickly, she placed her holster, with the Colt in it, on Samson's saddle. Then she entered the water, and exhaled with the deepest pleasure. A few moments later she washed ten days of Mojave dirt from her skin, and then did the same for her long blond mane.

Ti, her body slippery with soapy lather, walked to the small waterfall. Standing under its chilly water, she rinsed off the soap and let her mind free. She wished Arren was standing naked next to her under the cascading water, sharing this wonder as he held her and loved her. Willfully Ti shook her wanton thoughts away, and with goose bumps rising on her body, swam to the shore, dried herself and dressed, feeling better now that she was clean and wearing a fresh top.

As she reached for her holster, she heard a twig snap behind her. "Billy?"

"Why, Miss Bennett, what an unexpected pleasure," said Maddox in his slow Virginia drawl.

Ti froze for a second as a chill rushed through her. Then she moved quickly, reaching for the Colt. But before her hand touched its butt, she was grabbed from behind and thrown cruelly to the ground.

"Billy!" she shouted as she tried to gain her feet, but a large booted foot pushed her back. Ti looked up into the barrels of three guns and froze. "Billy!" she yelled again.

"Yes, ma'am?" Billy said as he stepped between two of the gunmen.

Ti stared at him until she realized that he was not there to help her. She turned to Maddox, whose insane eyes glittered wildly. "You bastard!" she spat.

"Such language," he said with a shake of his head. "Your lack of breeding is showing through, Miss Bennett. No gentle-born Southern woman would ever use such a word. Billy," Maddox said, looking up, "I don't know how you stood living at that Yankee ranch. All right, boys, let's take Miss Bennett to camp."

They hauled her roughly to her feet and held her arms tight. But all Ti could do was stare at Billy with a combination of question and disgust. "Why?" she whispered as she tried to pull her arms free.

The men held her firmly while Billy answered. "Because of my father," he said in a tight, pain-filled voice. "Because my father was a Confederate, and because Federal spies killed him!"

The shock of his words robbed Ti of her senses for a moment. Shaking her head, she stared at him in amazement. "It's a lie! Billy, it's a lie! Your father was not a Reb! He was a United States soldier, and proud of it!" she told him bluntly. "He died at the hands of the Confederate people!"

"It won't help to lie about it anymore, I know the whole story," Billy said. Then he turned from her to face Maddox.

When he did, the men holding her glanced at Maddox, and she moved quickly, yanking one arm free. The instant it was free, she balled her hand and swung at the second man.

The sound of her fist hitting his cheek was shot-like, and the man unwittingly loosened his hold on her arm. Everyone froze and stared at her in surprise. Moving quickly, Ti whirled and ran. "Get her!" Maddox shouted. Before the words died, Ti's feet were knocked from under her, and a heavy body landed on her back.

Her breath was crushed in her chest. She fought the pain and the whirlpool of darkness that was sucking her down. Hands roughly grabbed her and rolled her over. Still she couldn't move or catch her breath.

"Tie her up," Maddox ordered. A second later, her arms were jerked behind her, and one of the men tied her wrists together. "Her legs too."

Finally Ti was able to breathe, and as the men stood over her, she glared silently at Maddox. "Soon, Miss Bennett, I will have my satisfaction with you, and with Barkley!"

Ti ignored the chilling tone of his threats and drew her shoulders straighter. Then she smiled tauntingly. "You've made a big mistake."

"No, you made the mistake in New Mexico when you warned Barkley. You see, I've planned this very well. My superior officers know all about Barkley's mission here. I have been assigned the task, and honor, of stopping him and all the Federal troops. Nothing will stop me from carrying out my orders!"

"Arren will stop you," Ti stated calmly.

"No, thanks to you. When Barkley comes after you, we will destroy him, his men, and soon after that, the North."

"Arren will not come after me. He will not endanger his mission."

"Ordinarily, I would agree with you. And for now he will not, but when the time is right, he will, and when he does, he will leave *all* his troops at our mercy. Throw her across her horse and tie her there!" he snapped to the men holding her. Then he turned back to Billy. "Billy, we and the people of the South owe you a great debt."

"Can I come with you now?" Billy asked quietly.

"Not yet. We still need you to stay with Barkley."

"But he'll know I'm working with you after this."

"No he won't," Maddox said as he gazed at Billy and drew his gun. "I won't hurt you, but it has to look good," he whispered. "Turn around."

Ti closed her eyes and tried to shut out everything around her. But the hollow sound of Maddox's gun when it hit Billy's head threatened to make her sick.

"Tie him to a tree," Maddox ordered.

A moment later, with Ti strapped facedown across Samson, the small group began to move through the trees. *Arren,* she cried silently within her mind, *Arren, help me. . . . Arren, I'm sorry. . . .*

"No!" Arren yelled, sitting up suddenly and looking around. Breathing deeply, he tried to calm himself and find out what had happened. As he forced himself to relax, he realized he'd been sleeping. The sun was gone, and the sky was darkening. Then he knew! A premonition had filtered into his dreams, jarring him awake.

Standing quickly, Arren called Stevenson to him. "Did Ti get back yet?" he asked.

"No, sir, I haven't seen her."

With those words, fear raced through Arren's mind. "Get my horse saddled!" he ordered in a tight voice.

Without questioning his superior, Stevenson did as he was told. Arren, moving with speed and precision, strapped on his holster and checked its load. Turning, he walked toward his horse. When he reached it, the soldier had just finished saddling the gelding, and without a word, he mounted. Staring straight ahead, Arren pushed the gelding into a gallop.

Stevenson stared at his back, wondering what had happened and hoping that whoever was at the other end of Arren's eyes was ready for death. He'd seen the look on Arren's face before, on other men. It wasn't a pretty sight.

Arren forced his mind to become blank while he rode to the spot where he'd sent Ti. He knew something was wrong, deadly wrong, and he prayed he wasn't too late. At the edge of the trees he drew back the reins and slowed the horse to a walk. The light was fading fast, and as it did, his worry increased.

He heard the sound of the waterfall before he saw it. Entering the small clearing, he froze and searched with his eyes.

Samson was gone, and Billy's horse was nowhere in sight. Dismounting quickly, Arren looked at the ground. He read the earth, using all his experience, and learned the story of what had happened. He saw the marks of a fight, and followed it to where someone had fallen. He read the long furrows indicating someone had been dragged. By their size and depth, he knew it was Ti's boots that made the marks.

Holding back the rage that threatened to consume him, he continued his search of the ground. Then he saw another, larger double line. His breath hissed angrily when he'd found its source. Unconscious, tied to a tree, a dark narrow stain of blood trailing along one cheek, was Billy Raferty.

Silently Arren drew his knife and cut the bonds. Billy fell forward, and Arren grabbed him. He lifted him and brought him by the water. There he cleansed Billy's face and checked the wound. When he did, Billy began to stir and open his eyes.

"What happened?" Arren asked, controlling his voice and the anger within him.

"I'm sorry, Mr. Barkley—"

"What happened!" Arren demanded, cutting off the boy's apology.

"I . . . I heard Miss Ti scream and I came a-runnin', but before I reached her, two men jumped me. Mr. Barkley, it was the Reb who escaped from you in New Mexico."

"Maddox?" Arren whispered.

"Yes, sir," Billy said as he tried to sit up. A low groan issued from his mouth and he fell back.

"Easy," Arren said, steadying Billy. But his eyes no longer saw the young cowboy; they saw only the misty features of Ti Bennett. Suddenly there was a commotion behind him. Arren stood, drawing his Colt and spinning to face whoever was there.

"Major," called the first man through. Arren exhaled slowly and uncocked the gun as Sergeant Lowell stepped closer. "What happened?"

"Maddox! He took Ti. Sergeant, see to this man, he's been hurt," Arren ordered as several more men walked into the clearing.

While Lowell attended Billy, Arren went back to the tracks. The light was almost totally gone, and even while he studied the markings, darkness ended his search.

"Major, there's nothing you can do until morning," Lowell said.

Arren glanced at him, then nodded. "Get Billy back to camp. I'll be back in a little while."

"Sir?" Lowell said, about to argue with him.

"Do it, Sergeant. If you'll feel better, leave a man with my horse." When Arren stopped speaking, he walked toward the edge of the pool. Staring at it, he berated himself for his stupidity in letting Ti go off without him. They had crossed twelve hundred miles of mountains and deserts, and with only a hundred miles left, he'd become careless. He had lost her!

"Damn you, Maddox!" Arren shouted to the night. "Damn you! You won't take another person I love from me!" Then slowly Arren bent and picked up Ti's shirt and held it tightly clenched in his fist. "You won't," he whispered.

Arren sat on the edge of the pool for a long time, until slowly the wrongness he'd felt became a tangible thing. He stood, calling to the soldier who'd remained behind. He gave him an order and then waited.

Fifteen minutes later the soldier returned with a lantern. For another hour Arren inspected the ground until he was certain that he knew what had happened.

Why? he asked himself, unable to believe what his eyes had told him. *How could it be?* He knew now that he must be careful. He must plan properly, and not make a single mistake. If he did, there would not be another chance.

It was past midnight when Arren returned to the camp. He rode in silently, with the one soldier riding behind him. When he dismounted, he went over to Stevenson, Tremain and Sergeant Lowell.

"Sir, we're—"

Arren stopped Tremain with a wave of his hand as he looked at each officer separately. "This didn't happen by accident. Maddox didn't just happen to be here. It was planned. Now," he said, tempering the rage in his voice, "we're still one day ahead of schedule, but that's all the time we have. Tomorrow I want three search parties to go out. I want Maddox's camp found. But I don't want him to know. Is that understood?"

"Yes, sir," replied the three men.

Arren nodded and turned. He went to his bedroll, sat on it and stared up at the star-filled night sky. "I'll find you," he promised Ti. But all the same, he was afraid. Time had suddenly become his enemy.

Ti gritted her teeth against the pain of the ropes, and forced herself to move with Samson's powerful gait. After Maddox and his men had ridden away from the pool, they'd stopped and, on Maddox's orders, unstrapped Ti from the saddle to let her stand.

"We've a long ride ahead of us, Miss Bennett," Maddox had said. "I don't think you would survive lying on your stomach. I'm going to untie your legs, but your hands will remain bound. Please don't try to escape. I will not hesitate to shoot you!"

Ti glared at him silently as the men untied her legs and helped her back into the saddle, but her arms were still behind her, her wrists painfully secured.

"How far do we have to go?" she'd asked.

"Far enough," he'd replied. Then they'd started off again, and for endless hours they'd ridden along a dirt highway.

Ti judged it to be well past midnight when Maddox called another halt. They rode the horses off the road and into a thicket of low trees. There, two of the men forced Ti to sit with her back to a tree, and bound her to it.

She sat in silence, watching them while they unsaddled the horses and spread sleeping rolls out. After each one lay down in his blankets, Maddox walked over to her, a bulky object in his hands.

"As you can see, we're spending the rest of the night here."

"How far is it to your camp?" Ti asked, hoping that now he would tell her.

"We'll be there tomorrow afternoon." Then, with a gallant wave, he shook open the bundle and unfurled a blanket, which he covered her with. "It doesn't matter whether you're a Yankee whore or not, I was brought up as a gentleman, and I won't let this war interfere with my honor," he explained.

"Honor?" Ti questioned. Anger at his words filled her voice with venom and sarcasm, and by the expression on Maddox's face she saw she'd hit her mark. But his face changed once again, and he smiled.

"Yes, honor. I am a gentleman and an officer, Miss Bennett, unlike the men you are used to. And one night soon, you will see just how much of one I am. Good night," he said with a bow.

Ti shivered at the images his words conjured up. When he too was lying in his blankets, Ti began to work on her bonds, but their very tightness stopped her. She knew that for now she would be unable to free herself, but soon she would, she promised herself.

As tired as she was, sleep eluded her. The slowed circulation in her hands and arms bothered her and she made herself concentrate on other things. How did Maddox know Arren would come after him later, but not now? Why was he so sure of himself and his ability to defeat Arren and his men?

Did he already know where the others were who would be joining Arren once the cattle had been delivered? The only thing Ti knew with any degree of certainty was that Arren must be warned.

She thought of Billy suddenly, but angrily forced the thoughts away. She wouldn't, couldn't think of his treachery. Not now, not yet.

Then she thought about what Maddox had just said. They would arrive at the Confederate camp tomorrow afternoon. Gauging the distance they'd traveled tonight, and estimating the time tomorrow, Ti realized that Maddox's camp must be about forty miles from where Arren was now camped. Did that mean something? she wondered.

Chapter Sixteen

ARREN PACED AIMLESSLY WHILE THE SUN ROSE. THIRTY men were saddling their mounts, three groups of ten. But Arren knew the chances of finding Ti were slim. Why had he let her out of his sight? *Because I was tired,* he told himself. He knew the excuse was only words; the responsibility and the result were his to bear.

He'd not slept well when he'd returned to the camp last night, but he'd had the beginnings of a plan working. By the time he rose, he knew he'd find a way to be certain. Then he would do whatever he was forced to.

"Sir, may we speak with you?" Captain Stevenson asked. At his side was Lieutenant Tremain.

"What?" he replied tersely.

Stevenson and Tremain exchanged glances, and Arren knew they wanted privacy. "This way, gentlemen," he offered as he guided them away from the men. A short distance from the closest soldier, Arren turned to face them.

"Major, may I respectfully—"

"Enough!" Arren ordered. "Just say what's on your minds."

Stevenson held Arren's eyes for a moment. "All right, sir. I don't think we should wait here while the men are searching for Miss Bennett. I think we should start the herd."

"And you, Mr. Tremain?" Arren asked in an unemotional voice.

"I'm sorry, sir, but I agree," said the young lieutenant, obviously nervous about bucking his superior.

"There's no reason to be sorry. You're both right. Miss Bennett should not have been along, and because she was, she made *me* vulnerable. I know my duties and obligations."

"Sir, I respectfully request permission to accompany one of the search parties," Tremain said in a stronger voice.

"Permission denied, Lieutenant. As you have reminded me, I shall remind you. In four days we will join with the rest of our troops. Of the three hundred men, there will be only four officers. I cannot risk you, or you, Alan," Arren said as his eyes flicked to the other's face, stopping the protest that was on the man's lips.

"Sergeant Lowell will lead one party, Corporal Simmons another, and I'd like you to pick out the best tracker among your men to lead the third," he told Stevenson.

"Yes sir," Stevenson replied. Both officers left to issue the appropriate orders.

While they did that, Arren began to pack Ti's belongings. As he did, the private who was his orderly came over and told him the search parties were ready to leave. Leaving the soldier to finish packing, Arren went to the mounted parties.

He called the leaders to him and issued their orders, telling them that if they found nothing by midafternoon they were to find them on the trail. However, if there were traces of Maddox, two men were to return, while the rest trailed Maddox. Under no circumstances were they to be seen by or to engage the enemy, he directed.

A half-hour later, Arren was sipping coffee and still trying to think out last night's treachery. "Major, we're ready," his orderly informed him. Standing, Arren threw the remains of his coffee onto the ashes of the fire. Steam hissed upward as he turned to take the reins of his horse from the man and went to join Tremain and Stevenson in the lead.

Before they left, Arren issued one other order. There was to be one soldier assigned to each of the ranch hands, and under no circumstances were they to be let out of sight.

By noon they crossed a gentle sloping mountain and saw beneath them a rolling expanse of emerald green.

"Unbelievable," whispered Alan Stevenson.

Arren smiled at the look covering the captain's face, remembering the first time he had seen California. "Isn't it," he said, wishing Ti was here to see this sight with him.

A little while later Arren ordered a stop for the noon meal. While they ate, Arren continued to refine the plan he thought would work best. The black mood that had gripped him had not lessened, and although he accepted the blame for what had happened, he could not rid himself of the impotency of the situation.

"Mr. Barkley?" came a voice that drew him from his thoughts. Glancing up, he saw Billy. He forced himself to remain calm and keep his features unemotional.

"How's the head?" he asked, motioning Billy to sit next to him.

"It's fine now, Mr. Barkley. I just wanted you to know . . ."

"It's all right, Billy, it could have happened to anyone. Maddox is a madman, and you're lucky to be alive."

"Is he a madman because he's a Reb?" Billy asked.

Arren laughed bitterly and shook his head, trying to judge just how far he could push the boy. "No, he's a madman because he's insane. Billy, Joshua Maddox will use anybody or anything to get what he wants and to win the war so that his ideals will prevail over any other persons."

"I see," Billy said in a low voice.

Arren looked at the young cowboy, at the worried expression on his face. The resemblance between his father and himself could be seen in his eyes and his mouth, and Arren wondered if he had been wrong. Could Will Raferty's son be a traitor? He had to be! There was no other possibility.

"Don't worry about Ti, we'll get her out of his hands," Arren promised in a voice laced with fury. "Damn!" Arren spat. "I do wish Will was here."

"Will?" Billy asked, a puzzled look on his face.

"Your father," Arren explained, watching his reaction carefully.

"You knew my pa?" Billy asked, his eyes opening wide.

"Yes, I knew him well." Again a strange expression passed across Billy's features. Arren saw sadness and an indefinable something else. "He was a hell of a man, Billy. His loss was hard on us all."

Billy's face was immobile until he stood. "If you go looking for Miss Ti, would you take me with you?"

Arren stared into his eyes for a moment and then nodded. He watched Billy walk away, staring at his back for a long time, silently hating this war for what it did to the once innocent people who became its victims.

Shrugging, Arren stood just as Tremain came over to him. "We're ready to pull out, sir."

"Any signs of the search parties?"

"Not yet, sir."

"Very well, carry on, Lieutenant."

As the sun set, casting a serene beauty over the rolling hills, Ti stood under the shade of a tree, her wrists manacled and secured to its trunk. Yet, it was better than her hands being tied behind her, she thought.

She watched Maddox's men go about their duties and wondered how Arren was. For some reason, Ti was no longer afraid for herself. She'd gone beyond that, but she did fear for Arren, his men, and their safety.

Ti knew that he could not come after her. She was too knowledgeable in the stratagems of warfare, having had to listen to her father whenever he reminisced about his fighting, to expect Arren's succor. But at the same time, she knew his concentration might be endangered because of her, and that could spell disaster for him and his troops.

For that very reason, Ti had forced herself to pay attention to every last detail of what happened around her. From the moment they had started out this morning, she'd watched everything around her, paying special attention to whatever was said.

An hour ago they'd ridden into this encampment, and Ti saw, by its size, that it was not the main body of the Confederate troops Arren expected to meet.

There had been perhaps three score men awaiting Maddox's return. When she rode past them, she'd heard the murmured surprise they viewed her with. After dismounting, Maddox had called two men to him and ordered them to shadow the herd and report back when the men were on the move.

"I expect," he'd said to Ti, "that Barkley will spend the first day looking for you. Then he'll head out."

"And what will you do?" she'd asked.

"What I must. Because I have you, Barkley will head directly to where he is meeting the other Yankee troops, so he can turn over his command and search for you himself. But once all the Yanks are together, we'll crush them!"

Ti had watched his face when he spoke, and had seen the insanity return. His gaunt features hardened, and his eyes had glazed over. Then he'd ordered Ti manacled to the tree.

The sound of hoofbeats drew Ti's mind back to the camp. One of the men Maddox had sent out earlier had returned and gone directly toward the officer's tent, just as Maddox stepped out, resplendent in Confederate grays.

"They're on the move," the scout reported.

"Already?" Maddox questioned with lifted eyebrows. "Very well. Josephson is still watching them?" he asked.

"Yes, sir."

"All right, tell Massey and Stewart to ride out and relieve him. They're to stay until dark. I don't want Barkley out of our sight for a minute in the daylight. Damn!" he swore as he turned to stare at Ti.

He walked over to her, shaking his head slowly. "Your lover is in a hurry to die," he said.

"Then you should be smiling instead of angry," Ti said sweetly. "Or is Arren already upsetting your plans?"

Maddox's arm whipped up, and his hand struck her cheek. Ti's face stung from the blow, but she did not let the pain show.

"Yes, I see just how much of a gentleman you are," she whispered.

"Hold your tongue, woman!" Maddox snapped. Then he turned away from her and went back into his tent, calling out for Ashford to join him.

"Scum!" Ti hissed in a low voice as she tasted the blood from the inside of her cheek.

Twenty fires burned in the dark. Ten thousand head of cattle moved on a grassy plateau, grazing and sleeping under the watchful eyes of the Federal troops.

Around one fire were Arren, his two officers, and the three leaders of today's search parties. They had just finished eating and were discussing the results of the search. Stevenson's tracker was the only man who had seen any tangible evidence of Maddox's trail, and had followed it until it was lost on the main road west.

The herd was now parallel to that very road. But because of the road's hard-packed dirt surface, the traces of Maddox were hidden.

"Why did he take her at all?" Tremain asked.

"To use as a hostage against me," Arren stated honestly.

"It was a stupid move. He could have stayed hidden, attacking us whenever he wanted to. He lost his advantage."

"You have to realize we're dealing with a man who's insane. He wants me to know that he's out there somewhere."

"But it's still stupid," Tremain insisted.

"Really?" Arren said with a smile. "What have you been thinking about all day? Where is he? Are they watching us? When will they attack? In two more days you'll be so on edge that you'll jump at any shadow. No, he knows what he's doing."

"What do we do?" asked Sergeant Lowell.

"Wait," he said simply.

Everyone grew silent as Arren's word floated in the air. They saw the lines of his face grow taut and his eyes become distant.

"Casey," he said at last, calling to Stevenson's head tracker. "When you went over the ground by the pool, was there anything unusual about it?"

"No, sir," he said in his slow Indiana accent. "But then, there were a lot of our own boot tracks covering Maddox's."

In a voice that was a combination of anger and logic, Arren explained everything he'd seen and what he had really learned last night. Then he told them about Billy. When he'd finished, he sat up and looked at the men.

"Are you sure, Major?" Casey, the tracker, asked.

"I just don't see how, if Billy was fighting with them while they were fighting with Ti, there weren't more marks. No, it had to be Billy."

Standing slowly, Arren glanced around the camp until his eyes fell on the group of ranch hands. He shook his head sadly and started off to implement the next step of his plan. Before he took his second step, Tremain and Stevenson were at his side. "We'll go," they said as Stevenson put a restraining hand on Arren's shoulder.

"No. I know what I'm doing," he stated in a steel-tinged voice that brooked no argument. "Sergeant Lowell, follow me, but stay back. The rest of you, wait here," he ordered.

Arren walked through the camp, acting relaxed and greeting each of the men he knew by name. Reaching the group of ranch hands, he paused until he spotted Billy, sitting alone at the edge of a campfire. Going over to him, Arren tapped him on the shoulder. "Walk with me," he said.

A few minutes later, they had walked out of earshot of the men, and Arren turned to Billy. "How are you holding up?" he asked.

Although the night was dark, the moon lit the land around them, and Arren was able to see Billy's face clearly. On it he saw worry and tension. Billy was growing up fast, but he was still a boy.

"I'm doin' fine," he replied.

"I hope Ti is," Arren said. "I hope Maddox's only reason for taking her is to draw me out."

"Why else would he take her?" Billy asked, and again Arren saw concern flash across Billy's face.

"I told you, Maddox is a sick man. He might do anything to her," Arren said as he put his arm around Billy's shoulders in a friendly gesture. "You know, when we first started out, I didn't realize who you were, but Ti told me. Billy, I was with your father when he died."

Billy stiffened and pulled out from his grasp. "You were with him?" he asked in a low voice.

Arren nodded. "Your father didn't die the way the general wrote you. But he did die bravely, fighting for what he believed in." Then, scrutinizing Billy carefully, Arren told him the true story, the same story he'd told Ti. When he finished, he waited for Billy's response.

"Why'd you tell me that?" Billy demanded, his voice harsh with emotion.

"Because I thought it was time you knew the truth," Arren said. Then he took another deep breath, hating what he must now do, but knowing that he must get at the truth. "Why, Billy? Why did you join Maddox?"

The color drained from Billy's face, but Billy did not speak.

"Your father was a brave man, a loyal soldier. If he were alive today he—"

"Liar!" Billy shouted, the color returning to his face as he stared angrily at Arren. "You're lying. Pa was killed by Yanks! I know that for a fact!"

"That's not true, Billy. Your father was killed just the way I told you."

"No! He was killed trying to help the Confederacy!" he argued.

"Where is Ti? Where is Maddox?" Arren asked in a calm voice.

"Go to hell!" Billy spat as he went for his gun.

"I'm already there, Billy," Arren whispered coldly. His iron-strong fingers stopped Billy's hand before it reached the Colt's handle. "Sergeant!" he shouted. Out of the darkness, Lowell appeared, pistol in hand. "Keep him with you. Don't let him out of your sight, and while you're at it, try to talk some sense into his head." Without another word, Arren walked away.

Returning to the fire and the waiting men, Arren told them what he'd done. Then he explained his plan, detailing every step that would be followed.

During the long hours of the night, Arren sat by the fire lost in thought, praying that his idea would work. It must work! he told himself.

An hour after the sun had set, two men had come and freed Ti from her manacles. They escorted her to a densely wooded section, and after warning her that they had been ordered to shoot if she tried to escape, let her relieve herself privately.

She knew better than to try to escape now. She also realized that it would be easier if they thought she'd given up that hope. She went about her business, and when she returned to the men, she even smiled.

Instead of bringing her to the tree again, they took her to Maddox's tent, opened the flap and directed her in. When she entered, she saw Maddox standing at the far end, resplendent in his uniform, illuminated by a lantern hanging in the center of the tent.

"Good evening, Miss Bennett," he said with a smile. "I've decided that even a Yankee woman deserves more than being fed under a tree like a dog. Please, have a seat and join me." Ti saw a small table set with two places.

The tent itself was not overly large, but had enough room for Maddox's bedroll, the table and a trunk. Taking a deep breath, Ti nodded her head. This too would be part of her plan. She would go along with his whims, to a point.

"I hope this isn't representative of a prisoner's last meal?" she asked.

"My dear, no. It does get lonely eating with the men, and I do miss the company of the gentler sex," he told her. Then, with a gallant bow, he waved her to a seat.

Ti forced herself to smile, not to show the disgust his words brought out. When she sat, Maddox went to the door flap and called out to one of the men. When he returned, he sat across from her and smiled.

"I must apologize for the quality of the food and lack of proper spirits, but we are at war, and must make do." Then a soldier entered the tent, carrying two plates. Maddox stopped talking until the food had been served and the man had left.

They started to eat in silence, and Ti studied Maddox while she chewed the tasteless food.

"You know, Miss Bennett, you're a very attractive woman. I think you'd be even more beautiful if you would wear the proper clothing."

"I hardly think the trail is the place for a ball gown," Ti replied without thinking. A flash of anger raced across Maddox's face and she held her breath.

He stared at her for a moment, then blinked. "Nor is the trail a proper place for a woman." Maddox paused, then suddenly smiled. "It will be hard on you, when the war is over, to adjust to the ways that will be expected."

"Expected?"

Maddox nodded his head and began a monologue of what he envisioned the future to be, with men like himself running the government, controlling everything in a society based on slavery and his own peculiar sense of chivalry. When he finished, his eyes glowed with madness.

"And you, my dear, if you want to survive, will need a gentleman like myself as your benefactor."

"In hell!" Ti spat, again without thinking.

"Here, or in hell," Maddox said in a low voice, "I will have you!"

Ti shivered at both his voice and the look on his face, even as a molten rage built within her.

"I will not only have you, but I will destroy Arren Barkley as well," he added.

Ti rose slowly and stared at him for a moment. Then she turned to leave. "Where are you going?" Maddox asked.

"Outside. Back to the tree. I prefer being chained like a dog, to your company!" she hissed.

"Don't you take another step!" he ordered as he stood and went after her.

Grabbing her arm, he spun her around and glared hotly down at her. "You will not do anything unless I

tell you! I have gone out of my way to be nice to you.
I could have taken you and used you whenever I
wanted, but I have repeatedly told you I am a
gentleman. Don't make me lose my temper."

"You are a pig!" She threw the words at him
savagely as she tried to pull from his grip.

"Damn you!" he shouted. Then he pulled her to
him, and covered her mouth with his. Ti fought him,
hitting his chest with her fists, but his hands were
hard and cruel on her arms, and his mouth hot and
fetid.

She opened her mouth and, before he realized
what was happening, bit his lower lip. He threw Ti
violently down on the hard-packed earth. Maddox
stood above her, wiping his mouth and glaring at
her.

"That is the second time you've hurt me. There
will not be a third time. Get up!" he ordered
harshly.

Ti stayed where she was, and Maddox stepped to
her. He moved quickly, his arm shooting out to grab
a fistful of hair and pull her painfully to her feet.
"Bitch," he spat, ignoring her fists as he again pulled
her to him and cruelly ground his mouth on hers.

"Captain Maddox!" came a loud shout. Ti was
suddenly free as Maddox pushed her from him.
"Don't you move, I'm not finished with you yet," he
said before stepping out of the tent.

Sitting on the dirt, Ti heard Maddox and another
man talking. She looked around the tent, hoping to
find a weapon she could get. Her eyes fell on the
table, and she stood quickly.

There were no knives, only spoons and forks.

Making her decision, Ti took a fork and slipped it into the waist of her buckskins. She put the other utensils in the plate, and put the second plate on top of it. With luck, no one would notice the missing fork. She started toward the tent's flap, but Maddox stepped inside just then.

"I'm afraid we'll have to postpone our little . . . get-together," he told her. "Guard!" he called. A moment later the man appeared. "Take this Yankee bitch back to her tree. I want someone watching her at all times."

The guard took Ti's arm and escorted her out, and as he did, Ti breathed a sigh of relief. She had a weapon, and had been spared Maddox's advances. *For now,* she thought bitterly.

But what had happened to stop Maddox from trying to use her tonight?

Ti stared at Maddox's tent for a long time, watching the steady parade of men go in and out, until finally Maddox reappeared and went to his horse. She watched him ride off, still puzzled by the rapid change in events.

The sun dropped inexorably downward, and the western horizon was filled with a palette of colors. The herd was moving smoothly along, and Arren judged they'd made a remarkable twenty miles today.

But that wasn't enough for him. He wanted more. He wanted the herd delivered, and all the Federal troops joined. He wanted the coming battle to be over, and he wanted Ti to be safe.

"Major," came Sergeant Lowell's voice. Arren turned to look at the grizzled veteran. "I've picked the men and given them their instructions. I'm taking Casey, too."

"Very good, Sergeant. Remember, not a word to Tremain or Stevenson."

"Yes, sir." With his face reflecting the honor Arren gave him, Lowell returned to his position.

Arren signaled Stevenson to him and gave him new instructions. "We're not stopping until full dark. Tell the men I want another two miles," he ordered.

Stevenson was about to argue, but the determined lines of Arren's face stopped him. He saluted smartly and rode off. Then Arren spurred his horse to the head of the line and gazed down at the multicolored landscape.

"Where are you, Maddox?" he whispered. He closed his eyes for a moment and thought about the plan he and Lowell had worked out. Later tonight, the man watching Billy would fall asleep. They expected Billy to escape and go to Maddox. When he left, they would follow. It was simple, and it should work.

That, or the way he and the guards were working on Billy, repeatedly telling him that his father had been a loyal soldier. If he finally believed them, he would tell Arren what he knew. But Arren didn't think it would be that easy. That was why they'd worked out the other plan.

The darkness surrounding the camp was total. Only two fires remained burning, and almost every man, with the exception of the guards at the perimeter of the herd, was asleep.

Arren lay on his side, his eyes open and staring at

the spot where Billy lay. The only sounds in the air were the occasional bleating of steers and the crackling of the fires. He lay still and waited.

His body tensed when he saw Billy's silhouette move while the guard's did not.

Billy moved slowly. When he saw the even rise and fall of the guard's chest, he slipped from his blankets. Moving stealthily, he ran, bent low, toward the horses. There he whistled softly, and the gelding he had trained so well came to him. He picked a bridle from the pile and slipped it over the horse's head. Still moving silently, he led the gelding from the camp, ever cautious of the perimeter guards, and when he thought he was safe, he jumped onto the horse's bare back and rode off.

When Billy led his horse into the darkness, Arren slid from his blanket as quietly as had the young cowboy. His eyes scanned the darkness, and he saw Lowell and the four other men moving in the same direction as he. Two minutes later they were on the horses that had been waiting for them for the last two hours.

Without a word passing between them, they started off after Billy, riding slowly, keeping him just in view.

Ti's eyes were closing, and she couldn't stop them. The camp was quiet now, with only a few men awake, and those were guards posted out of sight.

It had been a long day, with little to do except watch and listen. She'd learned a great deal, and especially that Arren was making better time than Maddox had anticipated.

The Confederate madman had been angered by

that, which helped to buoy Ti's spirits. Then some
other news had come, but what it was, Ti didn't
know. A rider had entered camp before dusk and
had gone into Maddox's tent. When the night had
come, and her food was brought to her, she'd
breathed a silent thanks that whoever Maddox was
meeting with prevented a repeat of last night. But
while she ate, she watched the elongated figures
within the tent, silhouetted on the walls by the
lantern. She wished she was nearer so she could
overhear what was happening. Ti knew she would
find a way to escape, and whatever information she
could gain would be helpful to Arren.

Sounds of bootsteps reached her ears, and Ti
opened her eyes. Maddox and the other soldier were
outside now. The stranger mounted his horse and
rode away, and she tried to estimate the time, and
thought it to be around midnight. Shaking her head,
Ti closed her eyes again and dozed.

Without warning, her foot was prodded. Opening
her eyes, she saw Maddox standing above her.
"What do you want?" she asked, her words dripping
with hatred.

"You," he whispered. "Don't bother to fight,
there's no one here to help you. Stand up!" he
ordered.

Ti took a deep breath, trying to decide what to do.
Finally she exhaled and stood. She was still manacled to the tree, and until she was loose, there was
nothing she could do.

When she was on her feet, Maddox unlocked the
iron band and grasped her arm painfully. They
crossed the distance to his tent, and once inside, he
released her.

Spinning, she faced him with angry, flashing eyes. "Keep your filthy hands off me."

"You still haven't learned, have you?" he asked. "But you shall, my dear. Tonight you shall."

"I'll kill you," Ti threatened, stalling in her efforts to judge her chances of overpowering him.

"I doubt that," he said as his eyes roamed over her, stopping at the swell of her breasts. "Yes, I think it's time to find out what made you so appealing to Barkley."

"He'll make you pay for this."

As soon as she spoke, she saw Maddox stiffen. Anger suffused his face, turning the gaunt lines ugly. He shook his head violently before speaking. "No. He'll be dead. Damn him!" he yelled. "And when he dies, he'll know that you died first!"

Ti watched Maddox's eyes change, and held her breath. When he spoke again, his voice was calm. "You see, there's been a slight change in plans. I've been recalled to the coast. My orders have been changed, and I'll have to wait a few more days before I kill your lover!"

"Doesn't your commander think you can do your job any longer?" Ti asked, taunting him brashly in an effort to keep him talking, his attention focused anywhere but on her hands.

"Slut!" he spat, taking a step toward her. Ti stepped back under the fury of his face. "I am capable of my job. But I am needed at the coast. However," he said with a crooked leer, "you will not be joining us. In fact, you will be left on the trail for Barkley to find. Of course, you won't be alive to greet him."

"No!" she spat. Moving quickly, Ti drew the fork

from her waistband even as he reached for her. She jabbed upward, and the metal tines bit into his palm.

Maddox's arm froze when he saw the flash of metal, but he was too late. "Bitch," he yelled, holding his hand out before him.

Sidestepping, Ti tried to get by him, but Maddox recovered and grabbed her. She spun out of his grasp, only to fall against the table. She regained her feet just as Maddox caught her again.

"No!" she screamed, stabbing at his face. When the fork hit his cheek, she ripped it harshly downward. A cry of pain echoed loudly and his grip weakened on her shoulder. She spun again, trying to reach the entrance.

Just as she touched the canvas, the world exploded brightly in her eyes. She fell to the ground, barely able to see. She was dragged back and turned over. Maddox bent and viciously slapped her face until she opened her eyes.

She saw the blood running along the furrows of his cheek as his crazed eyes burrowed into hers. "Whore," he shouted, slapping her again.

Ti tasted her own blood, but refused to cry. She stared at him and then spat. Maddox jerked away, and then slowly wiped his face. Before Ti could react, he bent again and imprisoned her wrists in one hand. She fought, kicking upward, trying to hurt him in any way she could, but it was useless as he dropped his body across her thighs, straddling her and stopping any further resistance.

"Fool," he whispered. Suddenly Ti was aware of his hardness pressing against her leg, and realized that her fighting had only served to excite his lust more.

She went limp, staring at him with hatred and anger. Slowly, with his sour breath on her face, he grasped the material of her shirt and ripped it downward. The sound of tearing fabric echoed loudly in her ears, but still she did not take her eyes from his.

His eyes moved to feast on her exposed breasts. She did not move. She waited for the right moment.

Using his free hand, Maddox cupped one breast and smiled. Then he stroked it gently. Revulsion raced through Ti, and nausea built in her stomach.

Suddenly Maddox's fingers gripped a nipple, and he twisted it painfully. Ti gasped, but still she did not move.

Maddox lowered his head and shifted his body. The heavy weight left her legs for a moment, only to return lower, near her knees. Then his lips were on her breast, sucking and biting madly. Bile rose to the back of her throat. Rage, anger and hate grew until her mind was a black and seething whirlpool.

Closing her eyes tightly and arching her back suddenly, Ti jerked both hands into the air in an effort to break his hold. "No!" she screamed loudly. Then she heard a loud thud. Maddox stiffened on her. A second later, she was free.

Opening her eyes, she saw Billy Raferty, a thick branch in his hand, hate distorting his young face as he stared at Maddox, lying unconscious on the ground beside her.

Billy dropped his club and looked around. His face softened when he gazed at her. "Hurry, Miss Ti," he pleaded. Pushing her questions aside, Ti stood and tried to pull her shirt together. Then she saw the slice in the side of the tent and knew how Billy had gotten in.

She bent, holding her shirt with one hand and taking Maddox's gun with the other. Then she stood and faced Billy. "Why?" she whispered.

"Please, we have to get out of here." Ti stared at him for a brief second before making up her mind. Turning, she went to Maddox's trunk. "Watch him," she told Billy as she rummaged through the clothing until she found a shirt. Then, with her back to Billy, she took off her shirt and put on Maddox's.

"Let's go," she whispered. They left the tent and, running low, Ti followed Billy. Samson was next to a tree, his bridle on, but without a saddle. She saw Billy's horse there also.

They ran to the horses and jumped on their bare backs. With Ti in the lead, they galloped through the middle of the camp, uncaring of the sleeping men. But before they were clear, a shot rang out. Ti turned and fired the pistol, but even as she did, she saw Billy slump across his horse's neck.

She reined Samson in, fired again, and caught Billy's mount's reins. Before she could start off, a volley of rifle shots came from behind her.

"Arren!" she cried, urging both horses toward the sounds. Twenty feet later, riding low against Samson's neck, with Billy's reins secured in one hand, she reached them. Arren and the troops surrounded her while they fired again and again into the camp.

"Move out!" Arren shouted.

Five minutes later the small group stopped. Arren dismounted, and as he went to Billy, he spoke. "Sergeant, I want two men left here to watch

Maddox's camp. Send another back to ours. I want a platoon dispatched immediately to take Maddox! And I want him alive!" Before he finished, he had Billy on the ground, examining his wound in the darkness.

Ti joined him, and together they drew Billy's shirt down. The wound was bad, but not fatal. Ti was grateful that Billy was unconscious. She took his shirt, and forming a makeshift bandage, wrapped it around his back and chest while Arren held him.

When the bandage was secured, Sergeant Lowell was at their side, helping them lift Billy. "Put him with me," he said. Lowell mounted his horse, and Arren and Ti hoisted Billy up to the burly sergeant. Then Ti and Arren went to their horses.

Turning when she reached Samson, she stopped and gazed deeply into Arren's eyes. Before she could speak, his arms were around her, crushing her to him. His lips covered hers in a quick, burning kiss that exploded through her body. When he released her, she took a deep, shuddering breath.

No words were necessary to tell of their love. Then Arren smiled and he stepped back. Ti mounted Samson's bare back and waited for Arren. Together, with Lowell and Billy, they rode to their camp.

On the evening of the next day, Arren Barkley's men and the herd they had brought from Texas entered the low rolling hills of coastal California. By early tomorrow morning the herd would be at its destination, and Arren, with his men, would be preparing their battle plan.

Ti sighed as she looked at Arren. Since she'd

escaped Maddox last night, many things had happened. The platoon that had gone after Maddox had returned without firing a shot.

Tremain and the men had met one of the troops who'd been left to watch the Confederate camp. A half-hour before the platoon reached them, he'd gone back to report that Maddox and his troops were making a hasty evacuation. The other troop, Captain Stevenson's tracker, Casey, was trailing them. Wisely, Tremain had decided to return to the camp.

When Tremain had reported in, Ti had been surprised at Arren's lack of anger. "It's better this way. Casey will track them to the main headquarters of the Confederates. When he returns, we'll know where all the Rebels are," he'd said.

Ti had nodded, understanding the logic, even if she'd been disappointed that Maddox had not been caught. He was too dangerous, she thought, too dangerous and too fanatical.

After that, they'd checked on Billy, who was lying in one of the supply wagons. He'd regained consciousness, and when he'd seen Ti, he smiled, but when he'd looked into Arren's eyes, the smile had gone.

"I'm real sorry about what I did," he'd said.

"Then you believed me, and what I told you about your father?" Arren asked.

"No, sir, at least not at first," Billy had admitted. "But you made me think a lot about it. I wasn't real sure about anything anymore. You see . . ." Billy had then told about his recruitment by the Confederates and how they said the Yanks had killed his father when he'd warned them about a phony gun sale, and had told him that William Raferty had always been a loyal Southerner, and had never forgotten the birthright he'd grown up under in Georgia.

"Then why did you help me?" Ti had asked.

"Miss Ti, when Maddox told me to help him get you so that he could stop Mr. Barkley, he promised you wouldn't be harmed. When I escaped and came to tell him they knew about me, I sensed somethin' wrong. I snuck into camp and looked in his tent. I saw the two of you fightin' and I knew he'd lied. I got Samson and then I went back. He was goin' ta hurt you, I saw that. Then I knew Mr. Barkley had told me the truth. I'm real sorry, Miss Ti, I am . . ."

"But I'm safe now, and so are you. Everything will be all right," she'd assured him.

When they'd left him, she'd asked Arren what would happen to Billy. "I don't know. I'll see what I can do. He's too young to go to jail for a mistake, but I don't know." When he'd spoken, Ti had sensed that Arren would do whatever he could to help Billy, and she knew also that she would make sure her father did the same.

Then everything had been wiped from her mind as Arren took her hand in his and walked them away from the men. They'd walked for a long time, enjoying the silence and their closeness. When the sounds of the cattle faded and they'd entered a stand of tall trees, Arren had turned and swept her into his arms.

Their lips met, and all the bad flew away as Ti surrendered to Arren's power. Fire raced through her body, and she'd known it matched his. In a blending of love, need and relief at being reunited, Arren and Ti had sunk to the soft earth. At first their kisses had been gentle and caressing, but as the need within them had grown, so had their passions and desires. In a mutual abandoning of restraint, they'd undressed each other quickly. Ti's mouth had hungrily devoured every part of Arren, even as his did the same to her. But when his lips touched her breast, he'd drawn away and his breath had hissed angrily when he'd looked at the bruises on it.

Without a word, he'd kissed every part of her breast gently, healing it with the magic of his mouth and love. Finally, when neither could hold back any longer, their mouths had joined again, even as their bodies did.

But, protected within the California forest, and covered with a ceiling of sparkling stars, their desire and passion had not been the all-consuming thing of the past. Rather, their lovemaking had been a gentle, wonderful sharing of more than their bodies. When they had made love, they had moved slowly, each drawing everything from the other, while returning as much, and more, until they again rose, but this time to peacefully soar above the earth. They had shared a joining of their spirits that left them both shaken, and at the same time relieved that they were once again together.

"Rider coming!" shouted the man on point, jolting Ti from her reveries. She looked into the distance and saw a low dust cloud raised by horse's hooves. She glanced at Arren; he was staring hard ahead.

Arren raised his arm in command, and the troops behind him halted. Off to their left, the herd continued its slow pace forward.

Three minutes later, the lead soldier shouted again. "It's Casey."

Arren nodded, and spurred his gelding forward, even as Tremain and Stevenson followed. Ti held Samson back, knowing that she must wait to hear what the tracker had found.

A few minutes later, the four riders returned. All of them were smiling broadly. Ti, suddenly impatient, glared at Arren.

"We know where they're headquartered," he told her simply. Then he turned to Stevenson and Tremain. "Send two men ahead to San Marcos. Let them know we're not stopping tonight. I want all the hands and the troops at the ranch to meet us and escort us in."

"Yes, sir," the officers said, and wheeled their mounts around to do as Arren had bid. When they were alone again, Arren reached across and grasped Ti's hand.

"It's almost over," he whispered.

Chapter Seventeen

Ti ROSE THROUGH MISTY LAYERS OF SLEEP AND reached out to touch Arren. But her hand found only the material of the bed covering, and she opened her eyes quickly. He was gone.

Standing, Ti glanced around the strange bedroom. It was large, with the mighty four-poster dominating the room. Dark wood beams ran in straight lines across the ceiling and rose evenly along the walls. The gleaming wood floor winked back at her, and Ti breathed deeply of the fresh scent of the California morning.

They had arrived late, and after everything had been seen to and greetings exchanged, the foreman of her father's ranch had escorted Ti to her room. In it, one of the servants had already set a steaming tub. Gratefully Ti had sunk into it and a moment later had fallen asleep.

She'd been woken by Arren, who had also bathed and changed. He'd taken her from the tub, dried her

tenderly, and then carried her to the bed. But Ti had
been awake, and demanding suddenly of his comfort. Without argument, Arren had undressed and
joined her in the bed.

They'd kissed gently, but before Ti's passions
rose, she'd again fallen asleep, this time within
Arren's strong arms.

"Where is he?" she wondered aloud. A low knock
sounded at the door, and Ti quickly returned to the
bed, drawing the covers over her nakedness.

"Yes?" she called.

One of the servants, a young raven-haired
woman, entered and placed a tray on the bed.

"Thank you," Ti said, "but what I really need are
my clothes."

"I will bring them in moment, señora," the young
woman replied in a light Spanish accent. "They are
being dried now." Smiling again, the woman bowed
her head slightly and left.

Shrugging, Ti ate a biscuit and drank the dark,
strong coffee. By the time she finished, the young
woman had returned with her buckskin pants and a
cotton shirt.

"Thank you," Ti said. "What is your name?"

"I am called Angelita," the girl replied.

"Angelita. . . . Have you been here a long time?"

"Sí. My father is . . . how you say? Front man?"

"Foreman?"

"Sí, foreman."

Ti nodded and left the bed, drawing on her
clothing quickly while the young woman watched.

"Do you always wear the pants, señora?" she
asked, her eyes appraising Ti critically.

Ti laughed as she buttoned the shirt and tucked it

into her waistband. "No, Angelita, and it is 'señorita.' No, I don't always wear pants." Then Ti saw the younger woman blush, and realized that she had taken it for granted that she and Arren were married. Ti shrugged, not knowing what to say, and smiled again at Angelita. "Where are the men?" she asked.

"Everywhere," Angelita replied shaking her head.

Again Ti laughed. "No, I mean the officers."

"On the patio," she replied.

Then, following Angelita, Ti went to the patio. She saw Arren, Alan Stevenson and Peter Tremain, with two other officers and one civilian, deep in discussion. Instead of interrupting them, Ti stood where she was and listened to Arren detailing the battle plans and explaining his strategy. Ti was fascinated, caught up in the way he spoke and the meticulous thinking he displayed.

Arren paused for a moment as a prickling sensation spread along the nape of his neck. He turned quickly and from the corner of his eyes saw Ti standing near the double doors. He flashed her a smile before returning his attention to the men and the business at hand.

"According to your reports," he said to the civilian, "two ships dropped anchor late yesterday. One longboat came ashore and was met by three men—is that correct?"

"Yes, sir."

"Would you tell the others exactly what you told me earlier," he ordered.

The man nodded and began to speak. "I stayed out of sight until the men were mounted on horses and riding with the others. I followed them to the mission San Luis Rey. I wasn't able to get close enough to hear, but later, when I did, I overheard some of the men talking about unloading the ships tomorrow."

"Yes," Arren said with a nod, cutting the man off, "and based on that information, I have drawn our plans.

"Gentlemen, we are outnumbered two to one, but we have one advantage. We know where they are. What I've planned is simple, but should prove effective. We will wait until all the weapons are unloaded from the ships, and when the Rebs are almost finished loading them on their wagons, I, with a hundred men, will attack them." Arren paused as his eyes swept the group.

"You," he said, pointing to Tremain and Stevenson, "will be waiting in the hills overlooking the beach. When we have all their men attacking us, you and your men will attack their flanks from two directions.

"They will be fighting us and not expecting a second attack. If everything goes well, we will win the day!"

"Sir," Stevenson called quickly, "how can we get to the hills without being seen? They're bound to post sentries."

"Naturally. That's why each of you, with your hundred men, will get into position tonight, after dark. Then you will each appoint ten men to wear Confederate uniforms over their own. When the Reb sentries arrive, take them and replace them with your own men."

"Yes, sir," Stevenson and Tremain said in unison.

"All right, then, I want you to gather your men and prepare them to face the enemy. Dismissed!" he said.

All the men stood and left, and only then did Arren turn to Ti. He smiled, feeling the now familiar spread of warmth through him as he walked to her.

"Did you enjoy your first night in your new home?" he asked.

"I slept well," she replied. "But this is not my new home."

Arren gazed into her eyes and then leaned forward to graze her lips with his. He understood instantly what she'd meant. "Soon," he whispered.

"Steven?" she asked.

"No word. I can only hope he succeeded in his mission. If he did, it won't matter whether we win or not tomorrow."

"Only one thing matters," Ti whispered, her voice husky and low. "That you live."

"I will," Arren said fiercely. "For you."

"Arren . . ." Ti cried softly as her hands reached up to cup his face.

"Hush, we must believe in ourselves. Now," he said in a louder voice, "would you like to see your father's ranch?"

"Yes," she said, blinking away the tears that threatened to spoil her vision and hide the perfection of her man's face.

Together they left the main house and went to the corral. There she again said hello to the foreman, Jorge Mendoza, and mounted Samson, while Arren mounted his horse and Jorge prepared to join them on their tour.

The ranch was set within a small valley. The

rolling green hills surrounding it, and the blue sky above, told Ti that this was the most perfect of places. It was fertile and lush, with water in abundance and ranges that cried out to be filled with cattle. The warm breeze washing over her was a soft caress against her cheeks, and the salty scent in the air proclaimed the ocean to be near.

By the time they returned to the ranch, Ti was in love with this place. But as they approached the house, she again felt awe at the sight of it. The main house was large, two stories high, and of Spanish design. The red tile roof and white stucco walls shone softly in the sun's light. The house itself was larger than the Bennetts' abode in Texas, and Ti knew her sisters would also love this place the moment they saw it.

But marring the perfection of the ranch, off to one side, were the three hundred soldiers dressed in their blue uniforms. The officers and sergeants were going from man to man, checking over the troops and their equipment.

Glancing at Ti, Arren saw the sudden tension on her face. He stopped their horses and took her hand in his. "I will come back to you," he said.

Ti gazed into the sapphire depths of his eyes, and this time did not stop the tears from coming. But even as they fell, she slowly nodded her head. "And I will wait for you," she whispered, knowing that to say anything else would only cause apprehension and worry to shadow him when he fought.

"Thank you," he said.

"When do you leave?"

"At sundown."

Ti took a deep breath and looked at the turquoise sky. There were still several hours before then; she would make the most of them.

"What did you give Steven for me?" she asked, forcing away the sadness, cocking her head to one side and raising her eyebrows at the same time.

"You'll find out tomorrow," he said, laughing suddenly, releasing her hand and wheeling his horse around.

"Damn you, Arren!" she yelled, her laugh joining his and rising toward the bright sun above as she urged Samson after his retreating back.

Ti sat on the silent patio, trying to ease her worried mind. Arren and his men had left two hours ago, and their parting had been heart-tearing.

She felt helpless. She wanted to be with him, but knew he would not want it. He was facing great odds, and she prayed that he would be victorious.

But how can I wait here alone? Suddenly a smile rose on her lips. She fought it, but lost. Rising from her chair slowly, she left the patio and went to the long, low bunkhouse that some of Arren's men had used last night. There she went directly to the only occupied bed and stood over the silent form on it.

"How are you feeling, Billy?" she asked.

"Better, thank you, ma'am," he said.

"Billy, where's you father's Colt?"

Billy smiled. "Sergeant Lowell gave it back to me, said he thought he could trust me after what happened. He was right," Billy told her with a look of fierce determination on his face. "I know I did wrong, and I'll accept any punishment I have to."

"Billy, everyone's entitled to a mistake. I'm sure Arren feels you've already been punished enough. Can I borrow the Colt?"

"Sure, but why do you need it?" he asked, puzzled.

"I think it best if I don't tell you," she said, smiling at him while she waited.

"You're not going to fight, are you?" he asked, his voice edged with concern.

"Billy, can I borrow the Colt?" she asked again, forcing the irritation from her voice. Their eyes locked and held for a long moment before he finally nodded.

"Be careful, Miss Ti, please."

"I will, Billy, but I can't sit here and wait."

With Billy's holster in her hand, she returned to her room. She took off the long Spanish skirt and the low-cut blouse that Angelita had lent her, that she'd worn to say good-bye to Arren and the men.

Then, standing naked in the room, she glanced at the rest of the clothing that had been cleaned for her. Nodding, she began to dress. When her buckskin pants were on, she took the chemise she'd worn under the cotton shirts when they were on the trail and ripped it in half lengthwise. Wrapping it around her chest, she pressed her breasts flat, binding them effectively.

If she were to fight, and ride hard, she did not want any of the pain that accompanied the actions when her breasts were free.

She put on her buckskin top, lacing it tightly at the base of her throat. She buckled on the leather belt, and adjusted the knife and sheath to sit on her left hip. Next were her boots, and last she strapped on Billy's holster. She drew the bone-handled Colt and carefully loaded the chambers with bullets. Then she filled a small leather pouch with extra rounds and attached that, too, to the holster.

With a deep breath, she left the room. The house was silent except for the chiming of a clock. Midnight.

Once outside, Ti went to the small stable near the main house. She took her saddle, gratefully recovered from the camp Maddox had fled, and went to the corral to saddle Samson.

When he was saddled and she led him out, she found her way blocked by Jorge Mendoza and four other men.

"Miss Bennett, it is too late to be riding," he said in a cordial tone.

"Mr. Mendoza," Ti replied with a sweet smile covering her shock at seeing them, and what they represented. Arren had warned them. Arren knew that no matter how much she'd promised, she would still follow him. "Please get out of my way."

"I'm sorry, señorita, but I cannot do that."

When he spoke, Ti saw the concern in his face, and knew he himself was wondering if he dared to really stop his patron's daughter.

"Señor Mendoza, I am leaving. Please step aside."

Mendoza smiled nervously, then shook his head. "Señor Barkley told me it was your father's orders that you stay here."

Ti let her shoulders sag, and watched the men as she did. The moment their faces relaxed with the victory, she moved, jumping onto Samson's back and drawing her Colt the moment she was firmly in the saddle.

With the pistol pointing at the men, she spoke. "Señor Mendoza, I will tell my father that you did your best to stop me. Now, please, walk to the house."

When they were near the house, Ti looked at the foreman. "Please accept my apologies, but I cannot stay here, and no man alive can make me. I will see you tomorrow, with luck."

Wheeling Samson around, Ti urged the large gelding into a full gallop. Behind her, a rapid dialogue in Spanish flew. When it was over, the men walked from the house shaking their heads. Their male pride was wounded, yet their very wonder about a woman who handled herself so well helped to ease their loss.

The sun had risen, waking Ti from her light sleep beneath a majestic tall tree. She had stopped last night when she'd thought she was near enough to the sea. Then she'd waited patiently, ignoring her hunger. On the ride, she had tried to plan her actions, but knew that she would have to wait. When the fighting started, she would then go forward.

Suddenly she heard the echos of hooves, and rose quickly to her feet. She walked Samson deeper into the stand of trees and, stroking his muzzle gently, watched hundreds of men ride along the main road. In their midst were three dozen wagons, all empty. Then she saw one of the Confederate officers, and her breath caught.

Maddox! She wanted to draw the Colt and shoot him, but she knew better. Ti waited patiently until the sound of their passage faded, and then mounted Samson and began to follow them.

Forcing calm on her nerves, she rode smoothly until the sound of the ocean drifted to her ears. Then she stopped and guided Samson from the road, to sit and wait.

In front of her were low-rising hills, with grass and trees growing on them, but near their tops she saw the grass thin and knew that the other side would be barren.

Unable to wait any longer, Ti walked Samson up the hill, and when she was near the crest, stopped. Slowly, with Samson's reins dragging the ground, she left the horse and crawled to the top.

Below her, a magnificent panorama unfolded, but she did not see it as her eyes took in everything that was happening. Two large ships sat at anchor only a few hundred feet out. Fifteen longboats were in the water, some coming to shore, others returning to the ships.

On the beach, in the middle of a widespread circle of men whose rifles pointed outward in every direction, were fifty soldiers loading wagons. Ti stared at the armed circle and knew that Arren's plan was doomed to failure. He would never be able to charge the phalanx and draw the men after him. But as she waited for long unendurable seconds, she prayed for a miracle to happen.

Still, she forced herself to wait. A moment later she saw a smaller boat push off from the far side of the second ship. It was too far out to see its occupants, but she did notice it held only two people. Then she drew her eyes from the boat and looked back at the men on the beach.

Arren watched the scene on the beach and drew in a deep breath. He glanced at his watch and shook his head. Something had happened to Steven. He'd been watching the ships since four that morning and had not seen the prearranged signal they'd agreed upon in Washington.

Knowing now that the odds of victory were even slimmer than before, Arren said a silent prayer in memory of his brave friend, and called Sergeant Lowell to him.

"We can't wait any longer. We have to go in now."

Lowell stared at Arren for several seconds before nodding his head slowly. "Yes, sir," he said in a level voice. "Major, thank you for choosing me to come with you."

"How about thanking me afterward," Arren replied with a forced smile. "Let's go, Sergeant," he said in a firm voice.

Together they went to the men and their horses. Silently, using hand signals, they ordered the men to mount and prepare their weapons.

When they were ready, Arren lifted his hand and Lowell did the same. Dropping his hand suddenly, Arren spurred his horse's flanks and led the charge around the small hill, directly at the Confederates.

Ti gasped when she saw the blue-uniformed horsemen charge from cover and head for the circle of Confederates. Before the first shot was fired, a loud, rocking explosion shattered the morning. Suddenly everyone's eyes went to the ocean and watched as the second ship blew apart.

And then Arren's men were on the Confederates, joining with them in deadly combat. Ti stood quickly and mounted Samson. She drew her Colt and also the Henry rifle. But she stayed where she was, waiting to see what would happen.

She watched Arren's men charge through the circle of guards, and only then did she see what she had missed before. There were not as many men as there should have been.

"Dear God!" she cried. Turning Samson, she raced along the crest of the hill toward the concealment she knew either Tremain or Stevenson was waiting behind. But even as she rode, the sound of fighting and the thunder of mounted men reached her ears. Two hundred yards away, a wall of gray-coated men rose from the spot where Arren's men should have been. Maddox had guessed Arren's battle plan.

Again Ti whirled Samson and headed toward the fighting, parallel to Maddox's men, her fear being chased by the knowledge of what was to come.

Arren felt the explosion before he saw it. When he was a hundred yards from the first Confederates, he saw them turn to stare at the fiery ball that had been one of their ships.

Steven! he thought. *He'd made it!* Then everything was forced from his mind as he fired point-blank at the first of the Rebel soldiers.

A moment later he was in the thick of the fight. Battling furiously, he rode his horse until the poor animal was shot from under him. He fell, rolling smoothly and regaining his feet, his Colt held before him. Firing at the gray uniforms who charged him, Arren ducked as a bullet whined past his head.

The man charging him fell, and Arren whirled to face his next attacker. He shot him and turned again. His Colt was empty and he dived to the ground, prying a Henry rifle from the lifeless hand of the man he'd just shot.

With the weapon in his hand, Arren rolled on the ground and rose to his feet. He fired at three men charging forward, and as the three dropped to the ground, he saw a troop of cavalry charge over the ridge of a hill.

Before he could feel relief, he saw the uniforms were gray, not the blue of Tremain's troop. Something had happened.

Glancing over his shoulder as he fired, he saw Stevenson's men charge down the opposite hill, heading toward the Rebel cavalry.

"Lowell!" he shouted. "Form the men around me!" He fired again and again, as each of his men retreated from the onslaught of the Confederates. Finally they were grouped in a circle, three men on the inside reloading the rifles as the others fired.

Arren knew the end was near, as the bodies of his men began to litter the beach, but his rage grew with it, as he fired at the enemy.

Then they were out of ammunition, and Arren drew the sword of his rank and prepared for hand-to-hand fighting. Lowell and the other survivors held their bayonet-tipped weapons, preparing for the same.

The Confederate soldiers paused when they faced the wall of steel before them. Most had also run out of ammunition, and they too raised their own gleaming steel blades.

A hundred yards away, the two troops of cavalry met in a bloody confrontation of bullets and steel that echoed loudly in the air. Slowly the Confederate troops came toward Arren.

Ti saw everything unfold before her eyes as she charged madly toward Arren. Pushing aside her fear, she turned in the saddle and, using the Henry, fired at the advancing Rebel cavalry. Her shots hit their marks, and bodies fell, but nothing she did stopped the charge.

She saw the Federal troops riding toward them, yelling their charges and firing into Maddox's men. They met in a loud clash, and Ti swerved Samson away. From the corner of her eye she saw a clipper come into view and heard the echo of its cannon fire, but could not wait to see if it hit the surviving ship.

She drew Samson to a jarring halt. Her breath escaped in a hiss when she saw Arren and what remained of his men, with only bayonets and sabers, facing fifty Confederate soldiers.

Everything seemed to be happening in slow motion around her as she saw the small boat from the second ship come onto the beach. But she tore her eyes from it and hefted the Henry in one hand, while holding the Colt in the other. Dropping Samson's reins, she kicked his flanks hard, and the horse charged forward as he had been trained to, four years earlier.

Ti screamed and fired at the charging Rebels a bare second before they engaged Arren and his men. Red rage covered her eyes and freed her of any fear other than Arren's death.

Then an iron fist slammed into her chest, and she was thrown from Samson's back. As she struggled to her feet, she was grabbed from behind, her head yanked harshly back. She saw a dagger flash in the air, and fought to escape the descending blade. Then whoever was holding her froze, and the dagger fell from lifeless fingers. Suddenly Ti was free, and she turned to face her rescuer.

"Kay!" she screamed, unable to really believe it was her sister, dressed in seaman's clothes. Smiles flashed brightly as they looked at each other for a split second; then Ti bent and retrieved her Colt. When she did, she saw the man that Kay had saved her from.

Anger and rage sped through her mind for a moment. But Joshua Maddox would never haunt her or Arren again. "How?" she began to say, but Kay shook her head quickly. "You wouldn't believe it," she shouted as she handed Ti one of three extra Colts stuck in her waistband.

Then there was no time for anything as Ti again raced forward, her sister at her side, both their hands now holding Colts. They fired at the backs of the Confederate soldiers and jumped across the bodies until at last they reached Arren and his small band.

With her heart pounding madly, she saw he was unhurt. She threw him a pistol just as he withdrew his sword from the arm of a Reb soldier. He caught it, his eyes widening at the sight of his savior, before he fired at another Reb.

A moment later, with Ti on one side of Arren and Kay on the other, the fighting around them ended.

Ti let go a long-held breath and tried to stop her

muscles from trembling, but even as she did, she heard loud screams behind her, and another volley of shots began.

Turning, they saw two people surrounded by a small group of gray uniforms. Ti's face drained of blood when she recognized them, and even as she stepped forward, she heard Kay's scream reach out.

Ti fired her Colt, but it was empty. Throwing it to the ground, she drew her knife and started to run. At her side, Kay did the same.

But Arren passed them both, his sword flashing in the sun, and a Confederate soldier cried out. Ti leaped forward, arching smoothly in the air; at her side, flying above the ground, was Kay. They landed simultaneously on two soldiers' backs, their knives hitting the mark, and as the men fell, the women rolled free.

The rest of the Rebs turned and, seeing themselves attacked from the rear, ran.

When Ti and Kay regained their feet, they stared at the two people before them, standing back to back, swords in their hands.

"It took you long enough," Steven shouted. Dropping his sword, he covered a slashed shoulder with his hand.

Ti jumped forward and grabbed Jenna to her, even as Kay and Arren caught Steven before he fell to the sandy beach.

Tears flowed from the three sisters' eyes as they embraced each other. Then, before they could speak, the sounds of a trumpet echoed loudly, and a platoon of cavalry charged down the hill, routing whatever Confederate resistance remained.

But suddenly nothing else mattered at Ti looked at

Arren. They rose together, and met, embracing and kissing tenderly.

"Jamie!" screamed Kay, forcing Ti and Arren to turn. Yet another small boat had beached behind them, and five men, all carrying sabers, jumped onto the beach. Kay ran to the leader and threw herself into his arms. Arren, Ti, Jenna, and even Steven, resting against Jenna's breasts, stared openly at the sight before them.

A million questions flowed through Ti's mind now that the battle was over. How had her sisters come to be here? How?

Then a lone horseman rode to them, and everyone turned to face him. Ti's jaw dropped, Jenna stifled a scream and Kay stumbled as shock filled her face. Steven fought off Jenna's arms and forced himself to stand.

Silently everyone stared at the man, until at last he spoke.

"Major Barkley! Captain Markham! Captain Beaulais! Just what in the hell is the meaning of this!"

Arren glanced up at the mounted man and then looked around at the others. Suddenly he shrugged and smiled.

"Well, General Bennett, I'm afraid its going to be a very long story, and," he said as his smile grew wider and his eyes flickered over the faces of the other two men, "I can only tell you a third of it."

"Daddy!" Ti said in a loud, authoritative voice. "Get off that horse and come over here."

Samual Bennett looked at his daughter, then at his other two, and a slow smile spread across his face, softening the steel in his features. He dismounted slowly, and once he was on the ground, the three sisters raced to him, and he opened his arms and took them all to him.

Then he looked at the men. "I will expect a full report later," he commanded as he released his daughters and stared at the men.

Epilogue: Ti's Story

Napa, California, May 1866

A SMALL CARRIAGE CRESTED THE HILL AND STOPPED IN the middle of the wide dirt road. Its occupants looked down upon the lush valley spread out for miles before them.

"There," Arren said as his hand waved toward one specific spot within the valley.

"Yes," Ti agreed. Her hand reached out and covered his. Sun glinted from the narrow gold band on her ring finger while they stared at the beauty beneath them.

Then Arren glanced at Ti's stomach, and a slow smile spread across his face while he gazed at the full swell of the material.

"Soon," she whispered.

Arren lifted the reins and gently urged the two horses forward. As they descended into the valley, Ti closed her eyes and thought back to what had brought them here.

* * *

After the battle that had become known as the Battle of San Luis Rey, General Bennett, along with his hand-chosen officers, Steven, Jamie and Arren, had returned to Washington to continue with his obligations to the country. Ti, Jenna and Kay had remained in California to do exactly what they had done in Texas—run the new ranch.

But this time each of the sisters waited patiently for the war's end and the return of her man. For Ti, the time was excruciatingly slow. It seemed that life was playing a trick on her, a cruel trick; because for the first time in her life she had indeed fallen in love. And she knew her father had been right when he had told her many years ago that when she fell in love with a man, it would be a strong love, a deep love that would leave her shaken to the core. Through all the miles she had traveled, both following and riding with Arren, she knew she had indeed found that love. Her love for Arren Barkley was something that sustained Ti and gave her life a new and powerful purpose.

While Arren was gone, fighting in the remaining days of the war, Ti did the only thing she could. She ran the ranch, waking early and driving herself to her very limits in an effort to make the days pass swiftly. And never once did she doubt that Arren would return to her. Never once did she even question the love that continued to spring anew with each sunrise.

The war ended, even as her father had prophesied, not long after the Battle of San Luis Rey. And for Ti and her sisters the days turned even longer as they awaited the coming of their men. For Ti, there was no moment in the day that she did not gaze toward the entrance of the ranch, longing to see the light blue eyes and dark hair of her lover.

Then one early spring day Ti was out on the south range checking on some cattle when she saw dust floating upward. Spurring her horse into a lope, Ti rode toward the small road that cut through the property. She reined Samson in and squinted against the glare of the sun. Her breath caught in her throat as she recognized the lone figure. Even at this distance she saw the gleaming dark hair and the large muscular shoulders of Arren Barkley.

A smile split her face, and she dug her heels into the horse's flanks. Two minutes later she was almost abreast of him. Sitting back in the saddle, she drew the reins hard, and Samson stopped next to Arren.

Without a word, he lifted her from the saddle and drew her across to him, his mouth hungrily devouring hers, as their arms embraced each other tightly.

When the kiss ended, Ti drank in his every feature, and did not try to stop the tears that welled in her eyes from spilling over. She sniffed happily when Arren wiped them with his fingers before he kissed her again.

His kiss was slow and gentle this time, and Ti's breathing deepened in response. Finally they drew apart again. "I thought this day would never come," she whispered.

"It had to. I lived only to return to you and begin our new life together," he replied in a husky, emotional voice.

Ti looked over his shoulder but saw nothing. Yet

she knew Arren had read her thoughts even as he spoke. "Your father will be here in two days. Steven will be a little longer, and Jamie is coming by way of San Francisco."

"I had hoped everyone would come home together," she replied.

"They all have family to see, and to talk with, Ti," Arren said in a low voice, his eyes growing intense. "You are my family."

"I love you," she whispered, and covered his mouth with hers.

Twenty minutes later they were at the ranch house, and Arren was surrounded by all the Bennett women, welcoming him and asking about their men. When Arren explained about each of them, Jenna and Kay said they understood, hiding their disappointment well as they ushered Arren inside.

That night, Ti and Arren shared a bed for the first time in almost a year. When they came together, it was in a tender renewal. They did not rush, but explored each other, reacquainting themselves totally. Ti's lips caressed every inch of Arren's lean body, kissing his broad and muscular chest, stroking his powerful thighs even as his did the same to hers. But the passions and overwhelming desires which had always marked their lovemaking claimed them at last, and they joined together in an explosive consummation of their love. When dawn came, it found Ti and Arren still in each other's arms, their bodies joined tightly together.

In the time they had before Samuel Bennett arrived home, Ti and Arren had discussed, decided on, and refined their plans for the future. When her father arrived and she'd given him a few hours to relax, she and Arren came to him and together told him of their future plans.

At first Ti thought her father would object, but instead he hugged both her and Arren, and as a solitary teardrop cascaded along his leathery cheek, he gave them both his blessing.

A week later, Ti Bennett and Arren Barkley were married in a simple ceremony with only General Bennett, Jenna and Kay in attendance. But Ti knew it was yet another day she would never forget. She wore the ivory wedding dress that her mother had worn when she'd wed Samuel Bennett, with its full lace sleeves and dipping low bodice. Arren wore his full dress uniform complete with his formal sword. The golden cluster of his rank shone brilliantly in the small church as he knelt with Ti's lace-covered hand enfolded in his.

With the church bells pealing their tidings, Ti and Arren, escorted by the general and his other two daughters, rode to the ship that awaited them.

Their wedding trip would live on in Ti's memory also, for it was more than just a mere wedding trip, it was the very beginning of what they both hoped would be a long life. They had gone to France to walk on the lands that Arren's family had lived on for hundreds of years, and to purchase and bring back with them the vines that Arren needed to begin the vineyard which had always been his dream and to carry on the work of his grandfather and his ancestors.

Yet even this special time had to end, Ti knew, and when she watched the ship they would be returning home on, being loaded with what she and Arren prayed would be their future, her heart skipped a beat. In a few months they would be home again, living in a new house and starting a new way of life. And, she added as she stroked her abdomen lightly, bringing new life into the world also.

"Ti?" Arren called as he stopped the wagon.

Ti opened her eyes and gazed at him, still feeling the warmth of her memories.

"We're here." She looked around and gasped as her eyes went upward and read the inscription on the carved wooden sign above their heads:

THE BARKLEY VINEYARDS
ESTABLISHED 1866
ARREN AND TI BARKLEY

Suddenly her eyes were awash as she gazed into the deep blue eyes of her husband. All the love she possessed reached out to him, and they embraced, kissing deeply and silently pledging their love anew.

Author's Note

In 1864, Colonel Christopher "Kit" Carson, with a troop of six hundred and fifty men and two mountain howitzer cannon, laid siege to James Strong Blade's people, the Navajo nation, in the Canyon de Chelly.

In the bloody fighting that ensued, the Navajo refused to give in, until at last, starving and dying, they were forced to surrender.

Thus, the infamous long march was written into the annals of history, as Federal troops force-marched the eight thousand survivors across five hundred miles of mountain and desert to the place the government had decided would best suit their needs.

As Geronimo prophesied, Mangas Coloradas never saw his freedom. Captured as he parleyed under a flag of truce, he was forced to sit with other Indian prisoners until the officer in charge directed a soldier to heat a bayonet and then press it into the chief's thigh. When Mangas Coloradas jumped up, he was shot "trying to escape."

Sadly for Black Kettle of the Cheyenne, one of the few Indian leaders to actively seek peace with the whites, even more treachery was brought to bear. While an American flag flew over the main camp of the Cheyenne, Colonel John Chivington attacked them mercilessly, with rifle fire and artillery, killing three hundred Cheyenne, mostly women and children. The Federal soldiers scalped one hundred braves.

As for Geronimo, that story is well known.

If you've enjoyed the love, passion and adventure of this Tapestry™ historical romance...be sure to enjoy them all, FREE for 15 days with convenient home delivery!

Now that you've read a Tapestry™ historical romance, we're sure you'll want to enjoy more of them. Because in each book you'll find love, intrigue and historical touches that really make the stories come alive!

You'll meet brave Guyon d'Arcy, a Norman knight ... handsome Comte Andre de Crillon, a Huguenot royalist ... rugged Branch Taggart, a feuding American rancher ... and more. And on each journey back in time, you'll experience tender romance and searing passion... and learn about the way people lived and loved in earlier times.

Now that you're acquainted with Tapestry romances, you won't want to miss a single one! We'd like to send you 2 books each month, as soon as they are published, through our Tapestry Home Subscription Service.℠ Look them over for 15 days, free. If not delighted, simply return them and owe nothing. But if you enjoy them as much as we think you will, pay the invoice enclosed.

There's never any additional charge for this convenient service— we pay all postage and handling costs.

To begin your subscription to Tapestry historical romances, fill out the coupon below and mail it to us today. You're on your way to all the love, passion and adventure of times gone by!

HISTORICAL *Tapestry* ROMANCES

Tapestry™ is a trademark of Simon & Schuster.

_____DEFIANT LOVE
Maura Seger
45963/$2.50

_____MARIELLE
Ena Halliday
45962/$2.50

_____FLAMES OF PASSION
Sheryl Flournoy
46195/$2.50

_____THE BLACK EARL
Sharon Stephens
46194/$2.50

_____HIGH
COUNTRY PRIDE
Lynn Erickson
46137/$2.50

_____KINDRED SPIRITS
DeAnn Patrick
46186/$2.50

_____CLOAK OF FATE
Eleanor Howard
46163/$2.50

_____FORTUNE'S BRIDE
Joy Gardner
46053/$2.50

_____LIBERTINE LADY
Janet Joyce
46292/$2.50

_____LOVE CHASE
Theresa Conway
46054/$2.50

_____IRON LACE
Lorena Dureau
46052/$2.50

_____REBELLIOUS LOVE
Maura Seger
46379/$2.50

_____LYSETTE
Ena Halliday
46165/$2.50

_____EMBRACE THE STORM
Lynda Trent
46957/$2.50

_____SWEETBRIAR
Jude Deveraux
45035/$2.50

_____EMERALD
AND SAPPHIRE
Laura Parker
46415/$2.50

_____EMBRACE THE WIND
Lynda Trent
49305/$2.50

_____MONTANA BRIDES
DeAnn Patrick
46685/$2.50

_____DELPHINE
Ena Halliday
46166/$2.75

_____FORBIDDEN LOVE
Maura Seger
46970/$2.75

_____SNOW PRINCESS
Victoria Foote
49333/$2.75

_____FLETCHER'S WOMAN
Linda Lael Miller
47936/$2.75

_____GENTLE FURY
Monica Barrie
49426/$2.95

_____FLAME ON THE SUN
Maura Seger
49395/$2.95

Tapestry

Pocket Books, Department TAP
1230 Avenue of the Americas, New York, New York 10020

Please send me the books I have checked above. I am enclosing
$_____ (please add 75¢ to cover postage and handling. NYS and NYC
residents please add appropriate sales tax. Send check or money order—no
cash, stamps, or CODs please. Allow six weeks for delivery). For purchases over
$10.00, you may use VISA: card number, expiration date and customer signature
must be included.

Name _____

Address _____

City _____ State/Zip _____

671

Enjoy your own special time with Silhouette Romances

Take 4 books FREE!

Silhouette Romance novels take you into a special world of thrilling drama, tender passion, and romantic love. These are enthralling stories from your favorite romance authors—tales of fascinating men and women, set in exotic locations.

We think you'll want to receive Silhouette Romance regularly. We'll send you six new romances every month to look over for 15 days. If not delighted, return them and owe nothing. There's never a charge for postage or handling, and no obligation to buy anything at any time. **Start with your free books.** Mail the coupon today.

Silhouette Romance